DEATH BY DECIBELS

The door to the anechoic chamber was open and light spilled from it to just over the doorjamb. Another step.

"Tierneigh? Susan?" No answer. "Hello?" She raised her voice slightly as she approached the chamber.

Then she saw it. An upended speaker lay on its side on the mesh flooring.

"Hello?" she whispered, then froze as her eyes locked on a pair of red pumps, speaker cords wrapped around the legs above them.

She followed the legs to a second speaker that lay across Tierneigh's prone body. Her head was turned toward Elise, and something red pooled beneath it.

Her scream fell dead against the walls.

Death by Decibels
A Dr. Elise Harte Mystery

C.T. Merritt

DEATH BY DECIBELS
A Dr. Elise Harte Mystery
Book 1

MagPopAuD 

ISBN: 979-8-9897837-1-7

Printed in the United States of America

Death by Decibels

Characters in Alphabetical Order by Last Name

Susan Andres: Research audiologist responsible for testing and reporting benefits of the new hearing aid chip.

Bob Bell: Accountant at E. S. Hearing Labs, who thinks he found evidence of sabotage regarding the new hearing aid chip.

Maryelle Brown: Tierneigh Brown's sister, who lives in Mt. Harmony.

Tierneigh Brown: Doctor of Audiology and outside sales rep for E. S. Hearing Labs.

Jake Cagney: Audiology student in the last year of his doctorate program.

Nicole Cooper: Audiology student in the last year of her doctorate program.

Rick Dayton: Acoustical engineer responsible for the acoustics of the test rooms and anechoic chamber at E. S. Hearing Labs.

Helen Dean: Septuagenarian and longtime resident of Mt. Harmony, who, with her sister, Anne Thompson, founded Mt. Harmony's popular jacks team, Jacks of All Trades.

Laura Hanson: Owner of The Vibe, Mt. Harmony's local coffee shop and hangout.

Elise Harte: Doctor of Audiology and co-owner of Mt. Harmony Hearing and Balance, who moved from her home city of San Francisco to settle in Mt. Harmony, Illinois, with her husband, Cole, and twins, Becky and Jon.

Cole Harte: Elise's husband and boyhood resident of Mt. Harmony, Illinois.

Catherine Harte: Elise Harte's mother-in-law, who is celebrating her eightieth birthday with her much-loved, younger sister, Ida—she hopes.

Amy MacNeal: Doctor of Audiology and co-owner of Mt. Harmony Hearing and Balance. She and her husband Troy live on a farm on the outskirts of Mt. Harmony.

Deborah Miller: Catherine Harte's neighbor, looking forward to the annual Pumpkin Fair held at their farm.

Marcie Miller: Deborah Miller's daughter, who used to work at E. S. Hearing Labs, but who now works for their competitor, Lewelling Labs.

David Nubrey: Business student at the local university, who volunteered to be part of the study with E. S. Hearing Labs and its new hearing aid chip.

Noah Reed: Mt. Harmony Sheriff and avid rugby player.

Lucy Shambo: Office manager for Mt. Harmony Hearing and Balance Center.

Gloria Strauber: Manager for inside and outside reps at E. S. Hearing Labs.

Anne Thompson: Septuagenarian and longtime resident of Mt. Harmony, who, with her sister, Helen Dean, created Mt. Harmony's popular jacks team, The Jacks of All Trades.

"Cookie" Wallis: Baker and owner of the Sweet Spot Bakery.

Grady Weber: Young reporter for the *Mt. Harmony Herald*, owned by his Uncle Mike.

Theo Wrightman: CEO for E. S. Hearing Labs in Bluestem, Illinois.

Acknowledgement

As this is my first book, I have many people to thank—so many have helped me on this long-desired journey. To my family, to friends and colleagues, to those in the community, who were so forthcoming with their time and information—and of course, anyone who would listen! Thank you!

Special thanks go to my editor, Sue Toth and editor and proof-reader, Shannon Cave, for their input and polishing of this manuscript. Their work is greatly appreciated in how they made the story so much better.

A very special thank you with great appreciation to Alex Ortega, Senior Business Consultant, at https://www.creativesolutionss.com/, who created my website and helped with the business side of getting this out to the public. He has been a life-saver!

Special thanks also, to Police Dispatcher Annie Prater and local Fire Department #4490, with community information help. To Suzanna Jones and Alanna Sablotny at the Chatham Library, especially for their computer help, and to Taylor Roberts with even more computer help!

To those responsible for letting me ride in a real combine during the harvesting season—you know who you are—thank you! It was an experience I will never forget. More special thanks go to beta readers, Tina Schoorl, Sally Cadagin and Linda McCall. The importance of your input cannot be understated. I've learned so much, thanks to you. And a large thank you to Libby Kolaz for your constant support!

Thank you to my support-coffee group including Laurie Haxel and audiologists Kathleen Faloon and Cassandra Maillet. The support and ability to "confirm or deny" information I might use, and reap the benefits of your knowledge and experiences, was immeasurable. A special thank you, as well, to audiologist Mary Neill for years of help in my different audiology venues, from diagnostics to writing. Thank you to attorney, Marty Haxel, for information on being arrested—oh, not him—for my fictional character, of course!

A big, big thank you to my friend and colleague, audiologist Diane Leeworthy, from our time in private practice and everything that involved—from providing audiological services to hospitals, acute care rehabs, skilled nursing facilities, fighting for newborn hearing screenings, then seeing it become a reality, and so much more…the memories! I am eternally grateful. Thank you!

Of course, a profound thank you to Dr. Marion Downs and the legacy she left the world.

Thank you so much to my family—the good San Francisco memories with my parents George and Catherine—to my brothers, Ted and Bill, our daughter Jennifer and husband Chris, and their daughters Kaitlin and Nicole. Also to our son Paul, his wife Kari, and their daughters, Hailey and Payton—thank you so much for your support!

And a special, special thank you to my husband, Rick, who sat for hours and listened to me talk out scenes. He really was listening—even with his eyes closed—they'd pop open just as he thought of another twist or some detail that could be used. You know how much I love and appreciate you.

To all who have been involved in my endeavor - your input and support has been invaluable. Thank you!

Chapter One

— 1 —

E. S. Hearing Labs
Bluestem, Illinois
Wednesday, Early Evening

Dr. Susan Andres ran a hand down her arm, as if brushing off a spider that decided to use it as a slide. If it was a real spider, though, she knew darn well she wouldn't still be sitting there in her darkened office glued to her computer screen. And obviously, she couldn't see through the sleeve of her white lab coat, but glanced at it anyway, just as an icy chill shot up her back. Was this what a spy felt like when they broke into some bad guy's office looking for evidence? Except that this was her office, and it was her computer, and what stared her in the face threatened her very livelihood.

She allowed herself a moment of frustration and slammed her fist hard against the metal desk, then just as quickly regretted it. She clutched the throbbing hand tight against her stomach, wincing at the reverberant clangor that cut through the room, and she suspected, other offices down the hall. Her body froze as she listened.

Susan yanked out the middle desk drawer and rooted through it. One lone pen still shivered in the back corner. She grabbed it, pushed the drawer shut, and turned her attention to the wrinkled paper that, surprisingly, still rested on her keyboard. She slid it under the yellow-white light of the gooseneck lamp and, for the tenth time that evening, compared the raw data and her red-marked notes about inconsistencies with the official data on her computer screen. Both sets of data matched two weeks ago, as they should, but clearly did not match now.

"Dr. Andres!"

Her body jerked, and the last red pen escaped her grip, this time just missing the sharp-mouthed nubby little head of Bob Bell, the accounting manager. His elongated shadow lay on the floor, light from the hall exaggerating his height…just the way he liked it.

He trained his beady eyes on her, hands on the hips of his beige pressed khaki slacks.

Susan's eyes slid sideways toward him. "Just what I need," she mumbled. She lifted the sheet of paper closer to her chest. Her fatigued, carob eyes continued to dart between the computer screen and the accountant, as she used her free hand to pull ebony hair off her pallid face. "I thought you were long gone," she said between clenched teeth. "It's late."

"Yeah, no thanks to you," said Bob, his lips pressed together in a tight, thin line. "I've been waiting for your timeline report. You've pushed this way past the deadline, ya know." He clapped his hands like he was calling his dog. "Come on, let's go. I need it…now."

Her glare could've ignited what strands of red hair he had left on his shiny little head. "And I've told you, it's got to wait."

"Excuse me," a soft voice interrupted from the hallway. "Dr. Andres?" A troubled-looking woman in her midtwenties rocked from one side to the other behind Bob like a wobbling toy. The long red top over her black leggings swayed with her. "The reporter from the Mt. Harmony Herald's out front.

He knows it's past normal hours, but he said…that you said…he could drop by any time."

"Not now, Tessa." Dr. Andres pushed her roller chair away from the desk and stood, trying to make her five-foot-five height seem taller than it was. "Tell him to come back tomorrow."

She strode past the receptionist as Tessa said again, her voice quivering, "But you told him—"

Susan hissed, "Not…now."

The intruders stared open-mouthed at the back of Dr. Andres's white lab coat, and only when they heard the echoing click of the stairwell door did their eyes slowly meet.

E. S. Hearing Labs
Thursday, Early Morning

The E. S. Hearing Labs manufacturing building stretched its rectangle structure on five acres of land surrounded on its north, south, and east sides by picturesque golden cornfields. The town of Bluestem spread out on its west side and was about a half-hour drive, give or take, from Mt. Harmony. Of course, driving time could be affected during the planting and harvesting seasons, when farm equipment took over the fields and back roads, but the town of Bluestem welcomed the boost the lab gave to its economy for the last twenty-plus years and was more ecstatic than ever about its new technology. And one E. S. Hearing Labs employee decided to get a jump on it.

Dr. Tierneigh Brown ("Tear-nee," she'd say, to spare people who squinted at her name tag the embarrassment of their own interpretation) yawned as she flipped on the yellow recessed lights over the mounted white board at the end of the E. S. Hearing Labs' second-floor conference room. It was early, and it seemed she was the first person in the building, as eerie as that could be. Training rooms and the audiology department were on the first floor below her, and the majority of management on the third floor above her. Everyone else got an office on the second floor, which also included a generous conference room. An elevator split each floor into north and south wings, with a stairway at each end.

Tierneigh hoped she could have some uninterrupted time to get ready for the day ahead. But try as she might, she couldn't stop thinking of her dad and what happened the last time she saw him.

Her dad worked on a Midwest farm all his life, growing corn and soybeans, and the noise, mainly from heavy equipment, was finally doing a job on his hearing.

Tierneigh had taken him to lunch that day, and just as they were leaving the restaurant, a distinguished-looking man in his sixties stopped them and asked her dad if he was Evan Brown. Tierneigh's dad had nodded slowly, his permanently ruddy face from working so many years in the sun, completely still. His eyes regarded the man with a moderate amount of suspicion. The man continued to introduce himself as George Smith and said he worked with Evan's wife, Grace, for a short time at the local university's library.

Evan squinted. "What'd ya say your name was?"

The man repeated his name and said he recognized Evan from when he came into the university's library once in a while to meet his wife for lunch.

But Evan just continued to stare. "Well, sir," her dad finally bellowed. "I don't think my Grace ever worked with a commodore before."

"Dad…"

George leaned forward, slightly flustered. "Oh, no…not Commodore Smith. I said my name was Smith…just common ol' Smith."

Heads turned as they shuffled by the trio, the glass front doors constantly opening and closing with a sporadic stream of patrons.

Evan steadied his eyes on the man in front of him, straightened his back and tugged on the bottom of his favorite wool vest.

As an audiologist, Tierneigh knew the chatter from people around them, combined with background music from an overhead speaker, could make understanding speech more difficult…especially for those with hearing loss. Her auburn hair had brushed the back of his better-hearing ear as she had leaned toward him and repeated what Mr. Smith said.

Evan had just hissed, "Then why didn't he just say so?"

Tierneigh squeezed her eyes tight and brought herself back to the present. "You're going to like what we have here, Dad," she whispered to herself, and opened her eyes to survey the conference room, at the same time dropping her purse on a nearby metal chair. Next, she propped the door to the hallway open with her beige overstuffed work bag then turned to face the room.

Some things never changed. Just the people. They came and went before you had a chance to remember their names. She glanced at the sporadic notices push-pinned into the walls, informing employees of the latest company policies, industry trends and updates, and the always-present "Happy Birthday" list for the month. She stopped to take a closer look at the birthdays, wondering if there were any new names since she was last in. Being an outside rep for E. S. Hearing Labs and traveling so much had its advantages, but she'd really like to try coming to the same place every day sometime. No more rental cars, hotels, or trying to find clients' offices with bad GPS information.

Tierneigh didn't hold back the next loud yawn and tried again to brush away thoughts of keeling over after a night of tossing and turning. She had finally decided she might as well get up and come into work to make sure everything was ready…at least for her part in tonight's training for the company's new hearing aid chip. She didn't even put on her own hearing aids. Just put them in the case and threw them in her purse. She was glad she'd done something about her hearing and smiled, knowing her dad will be happy when he tried these new hearing devices, too.

Tierneigh kept the main lights off in the conference room on purpose. She didn't want to advertise the fact she was in yet, in case someone was around and interrupted her, as well as because people could see the conference room windows from the front parking lot outside.

The sky started to lighten as she inventoried the table in front of her, tapping her finger in the air at each item. Training materials lined up next to teetering piles of E. S. Hearing Labs' product manuals, brochures, and research reports on the latest hearing devices. She nodded her approval at the materials describing custom ear plugs and products to help hearing on the phone, with the TV, in public venues and more. Tierneigh's attention then turned to the red and pink gift bags filled with marketing ploys of small bouncy balls, pens, notepaper, and the like. She reached for one, when a sound like mumbling voices made her stop mid-reach. She grabbed her purse, rifled through it, and found her hearing aids. She quickly fingered them into each ear and paused.

A male voice snarled, "So what exactly are you saying?"

The voice came from the left of the conference room door and became louder as footsteps approached the room where Tierneigh stood frozen.

A second voice whimpered in reply. "I'm saying it's the cost over-run on this project. It's out of whack. I reevaluated the current sprints and timelines and made adjustments."

The voices receded as they passed the conference room

and down the darkened linoleum hallway to the right, lit only by sporadic nightlights placed close to the ceiling.

Tierneigh leaned against the side wall of the conference room just outside the yellow glow of the lights behind her. She pulled her cell phone from her purse, opened the red and pink hearing aid app, and increased the volume, constantly appreciating each advancement in hearing aid technology that made wearing them so easy.

Her eyes darted to the windows. A light breeze pattered red maple leaves against them. She focused back toward the door to the hallway, still propped open with her work bag. Hopefully, whoever was out there was too busy to notice it.

Tierneigh tilted an ear toward the door. Her nose wrinkled at a box of stale day-old donuts left on the conference room table.

"Yeah...yeah," snarled the gruff one. Footsteps tapped on an office's linoleum floor. At the same time, she heard a clicking sound near the stairway door at the end of the hall. Were they coming or going?

"I'm worried," the other voice whimpered. "I need you to explain this!"

A paper crinkled. Silence. Then, "What?" bellowed the gruff guy, with a sudden smack of a hand on a hard surface.

Tierneigh jumped. She could tell they were in the spare office at the end of the hall, near the stairs. She tapped open the hearing aid app on her cell phone again.

"Where'd you get this?" said the first voice, back to a snarling whisper.

"It was attached to the timeline report from audiology. Must've been a mistake or something. And...there's more...there's talk."

Clicking sounds of a computer keyboard caught her attention. Tierneigh cocked her head a little more.

"What talk? Spit it out, would ya?"

"There's talk…that the chip…doesn't work." The clicking stopped. "And that Dr. Andres knows about it."

Tierneigh drew in a sharp breath and clapped her hand over her mouth. Dr. Susan Andres? The research audiologist responsible for conducting testing and reporting for the new chip? Faster clicks on a keyboard.

"Rick…look at this," the voice whimpered again. "Hope you already sold your stock."

Tierneigh's brow wrinkled. Rick Dayton, the acoustical engineer, and Bob Bell, the head accountant? Why aren't they in their own offices on the third floor?

"This better not be happening," snarled Rick, "or we're going to be in it, deep. Does anyone else know about this?"

"I…I don't know, Rick. I don't think so."

Tierneigh dipped her head and fought the very real feeling that she had just been hit in the face with a brick. She tiptoed in her new red pumps past the end of the conference room table, when one pump met with a piece of waxed paper from the donut box. Her foot slid forward in slow motion along the linoleum floor, potentially forcing her into a long, slow, split position. Ugh! She held her breath and grabbed backward, toward the side of the table, to stop the forward momentum. Feeling somewhat stabilized, she slowly stood, let out a breath, and listened. She inched toward the door again.

Tierneigh heard the shwoomp of an elevator door opening and murmurs of conversation drifting down the hall toward the conference room she currently occupied. Office lights clicked on as the sounds came closer. Feet shuffled in the spare office, and both men stepped into the now-lit hallway, just in time to see a beige, overstuffed bag, with pink and red E. S. Hearing Labs lettering, slide slowly backward into the conference room.

"Who's there?" Rick bellowed, his eyes squinting under

thick black eyebrows.

The bag stopped. Tierneigh's pulse kicked up a notch. They were too close, and there was nowhere for her to hide. She picked up her work bag and stepped into the hallway.

A flush rose from her neck to her cheeks, and her mouth stretched into an awkward grin. "Oh, morning, Bob, Rick. You made me jump!" She giggled and flipped her hair back over one shoulder. "I didn't think anyone else was in yet. Came in to check on the handouts for the training tonight. It's going to be great, right?" She widened her eyes. "I'm so excited! We're supposed to have a great turnout. Don't the gift bags look great?"

Leaning backward into the room, she reached with a shaking hand for one of the gift bags, but her fingers slid awkwardly against it, causing the bag to fall and hit the stack of materials next to them, which then slid off the table, and in seconds, created a cascading mess. Laminated bookmarks, carabiners, bouncy balls, thumb drives, and red and blue pens topped with artistically shaped plastic ears tumbled and slid like kids learning to ice skate, out the door and into the hallway. Brochures and research papers on the new hearing aid chip teetered on the edge of the table, then gave way and joined the mess.

Tierneigh's shoulders slumped. Sure. Why not. She looked from the floor to the men and her grin melted. Forget it.

She grabbed one of the clear play balls from the floor and bounced it twice, causing an explosion of brilliant red, blue, and yellow colors. The third bounce hit the side of her foot and rolled down the hall, stopping at Rick's brown leather work boot. Tierneigh's eyes met his glare for a split second before she blinked and stared at a black scuff mark on the floor.

"Yeah...yeah, about the training," Rick said.

"It's gonna be awesome," Bob mumbled. The men turned and walked through the door behind them marked EXIT to the stairs, and she presumed, to their third-floor offices.

Tierneigh grabbed one hand with the other to try to stop them from shaking, then focused on the mess around her. She dropped to the floor to gather up the strewn items, her mind a mess of shock and confusion.

"Hey, who hit the piñata?" a young male voice laughed from the doorway. He swung his arms in the air like he was swinging a baseball bat, then turned to enter the office across the hall next to hers.

Steadying herself with one hand on the table, she stood and mumbled, "Ha…ha…ha," at her chuckling coworker's back.

Nate called over his shoulder, "I'll be right back to help."

In my dreams, thought Tierneigh, brushing dust off her black pants and adjusting the red jacket she'd bought just for that night's training. With a still-shaking hand, she dropped a pod into the coffee maker…just what she needed…and wondered if it was too early to add a shot of rum from that bottle everyone knew was stashed in the desk in the spare office.

The second floor at E. S. Hearing Labs grew into full swing in a matter of minutes. The conference room table was back to its pre-disaster state, and Tierneigh ignored the growing commotion and excitement that always seemed to flirt with chaos just before big events like this one. And this one was big. A ground-breaking new chip, that would help people hear significantly better in noisy situations than anything on the market to date.

She dropped her bags on her office floor with one hand, causing coffee to slosh over the sides of her "I Love Audiology" mug in her other hand, when a yellow sticky note in the middle of her computer monitor stopped her cold. Written in bold print was "CALL ME - ASAP!" It was signed "S.A." The landline phone buzzed, and a lighted button told her it was the receptionist downstairs.

"Morning, Tessa," she murmured, blowing bangs off her eyebrows and staring again at the yellow note from Dr. Andres, stuck to her now steady fingertips. "What's up?"

"Hi, Dr. Brown," said Tessa, muffling a yawn. "The TV news people are here for your interview."

Tierneigh squeezed her eyes shut. "Be right there." She clumped the handset into its cradle, stood up and straightened her jacket, but wanted to do something else first. She walked the few doors down the hallway toward the spare office. A memory of fourth grade popped into her mind, when she and her friend, Kaitlin, snuck into the nuns' quarters at school. They'd heard that nuns only ate bread and water, and they just had to see if it was true. They didn't find out, but they didn't get caught, either. That was the encouraging part…not getting caught. And yes, nuns ate more than bread and water, or so Kaitlin's older brother swore to, when he helped in their kitchen once.

Tierneigh's eyelids flickered at something out of the corner of her eye, and she sent a paranoid glance to the window in the stairway door. Must just be nerves. She tiptoed into the empty room. Ahead of her, stacks of paperwork and other office cast-offs crammed the desktop and littered the floor. Her eyes homed in on a single bright green folder resting on the computer keyboard. Everything to do with the company was red and pink. Maybe more like strawberries and bubblegum, she thought, wondering at her current level of sanity.

Her eyes darted around the room as she inched toward it. She held her breath and touched the lower edges of the green folder where a paper was barely peeking out, then extended her fingers to nudge the paper. Her hand brushed the keyboard and caused the monitor to explode into light.

She jumped and knocked the folder off the desk, the paper now skidding across the linoleum floor.

Tierneigh froze. She waited for alarms to blare, but nothing. Her eyes darted around the room and out into the hallway. She listened for any out-of-the-normal activity, then relaxed ever so slightly and picked up the wrinkled paper, obviously a copy of a data page marked with scattered red circles. She tilted it to try and read the scribbles in the margins, but the writing was small.

Her eyes narrowed and then grew wide, jerking back and forth between the monitor and the spreadsheet she was holding. Rows of dates were displayed with patients' initials and what looked like the results of hearing tests. "Test Subject JL…Test subject DN"…followed by dates and numerical test results. She squinted. Maybe the same data, but not quite. Something was different, but she couldn't figure it out right now. Is this what Rick and Bob were talking about? Bob's remark about the research audiologist, Dr. Susan Andres, "knowing about this" troubled her. Is that what Susan wanted to talk to her about? She needed more time to compare the data sheet with the information on the screen. The result would decide the next step. She hoped Elise Harte, her colleague and best friend, was still coming to the training tonight. She needed to talk to someone she could trust.

Tierneigh's eyebrows rose as an idea made her stop and listen. She leaned out the office doorway, glanced down the now-empty hall, and tiptoed to the conference room. She grabbed one of the thumbdrives on the table, slipped back into the spare office and tried to concentrate on what she wanted to do. What seemed like an hour was only seconds. Hands shaking, she copied the computer data onto the thumb drive, then stuffed it and the red-marked data page from the green file into her jacket pocket.

She stepped with weak knees out into the hallway, where a few coworkers now stood, deep in conversation. They stopped talking and turned to look at her. The toy ball that had bounced off Rick's foot earlier sat against the door-jamb near Tierneigh's left shoe.

She eyed it, grabbed it, and bounced it back to them. "We ready for tonight, ladies and gents?"

The bright kaleidoscope of colors brought cheers and whoop calls. Tierneigh's eyebrows lowered, and her head jerked as what looked like a shadow in the stairway door window moved sideways out of sight.

Fatigue taking over, she shook her head and could only think of one thing. Coffee.

Chapter Two

══ I ══

Mt. Harmony
Thursday Morning

Dr. Elise Harte, audiologist and co-owner of the Mt. Harmony Hearing and Balance office, closed her eyes and almost purred in response to the sweet aroma of her pumpkin spice latte...her usual morning order before heading out to work. Her hands gently cupped the off-white ceramic mug decorated with "Good Vibrations Café and Coffee Shop" written in royal blue script on its front. Just below the script was a simple outline of a bell with a squiggly line on each side, insinuating vibrations. A local farmer once called the café "The Vibe" for short, which eventually stuck for those "in the know."

Early morning sunlight crept across the sporadically cracked sidewalk and drifted over a long window box filled with yellow and orange mums. It glimmered through the café's oversized windows and brightened its pale yellow walls, mounted knickknacks on long white shelves, and arrays of ever-changing art work, courtesy of the local schools' art classes. A colorful mural filled the farthest wall to the right of the front door. It depicted Mt. Harmony residents immersed in various activities, such as a children's dance recital in the gazebo, two senior citizens talking on a park bench, the Fourth of July parade down Main Street, featuring the town's antique fire engine, and of course, patrons of The Vibe itself, reading alone at a table or in conversation with a group. It was the constant source of intrigue and polite disagreement, as patrons attempted to identify the characters, sure that Mable Peebles, the retired high school art teacher, had painted each one of them personally for the posterity of Mt. Harmony. Unfortunately, Mable had passed away, and the blank space at one end of the mural was used for patrons to write memories of their beloved teacher.

Elise opened her dark hazel eyes, her vision a slight blur from the relaxed state she'd begrudgingly pulled herself from. She needed to check the day's work schedule on her iPad but put it off for a few seconds more to gently reposition a single orange mum in the cut-glass vase just in front of her. The day was going to be busy, but manageable.

She started to smooth the orange and white checked oilcloth that covered the table, but then froze mid-brush.

"You can't move him if he's dead!" barked a deep male voice over the normal din of the café. "I was in the business of law longer than you've been in insurance, young man. You have to leave him on the grass and call for an ambulance. I can prove insanity. Rugby's a young man's game."

Elise jerked her head in the direction of the voices and stared with wide eyes. The movement made a wisp of chestnut brown hair fall across one eye, and she brushed it back.

"No way!" insisted a younger-sounding male. "She has to take him home, clean him up, and put him in bed, then call the ambulance. That's the only way Dr. Harte can get her husband's life insurance!"

The noise from the café's steaming machine stopped, allowing patrons of The Vibe to hear the diabolical scheme taking place right in front of them!

Keith Waters, the local, semi-retired attorney and Tim

Swanning, a newly licensed life insurance agent, leaned closer and closer toward one another over the table they currently occupied. Elise's jaw dropped as the men wagged their hands in each other's reddening faces.

Keith straightened his back and brushed thin salt and pepper hair off his forehead when he caught Elise staring at them. He winked, and with a devilish grin, said, "Guess you heard that, huh, Doc?"

"Oops! Morning, Dr. Harte," mouthed Tim, also turning to look at Elise, his blue eyes bright and blond hair slicked with hair product.

Elise opened her mouth to speak, but the café's owner, Laura Hanson, beat her to it. "You're awful," Laura chided with a mischievous smile, "talking about Dr. Harte's husband that way." Her pleasant face was slightly flushed as she made her way around the tables, tendrils of ash blond hair dangling loose from her low ponytail. She stopped at the men's table and lifted their stacked pastry plates with one hand while refilling their coffee cups from the pot she held in the other one. "You've scared poor Dr. Harte. Look at her face."

Patrons' heads swiveled to stare deadpan at Elise. She felt heat in her cheeks but then the pieces fell into place.

"You're talking about my husband's rugby game last weekend, right?" She took a sip of her latte and grinned. "He survived, but I'm not sure I'm looking to either one of you for good advice in the future!"

Eyes rolled as the patrons turned back to their own coffees and sweet treats, some with hints of smiles.

"You know she'll call me for the real info, though, right?" Keith needled, eyes narrowed at Tim.

"We'll see about ..." Tim started, but was interrupted by breaking news on the wall-mounted TV behind the café's glass counter and antique cash register.

Keith looked at Laura and boomed, "Can ya turn that up?"

She nodded, grabbed a remote off the counter, and pointed it at the screen.

The camera zoomed in on a news anchor's open hand and revealed what looked like two small hearing devices, then slowly panned back to include a woman in a white lab coat standing at his side.

The newsman smiled, flashing perfect white teeth, and spoke into the microphone. "Dr. Tierneigh Brown, is it true what we're hearing about this latest development? Will people be able to hear significantly better with your company's devices, as compared to the choices available now?"

Elise's eyes lit up when she saw her friend on TV and announced with pride, "That's Tierneigh! She's my manufacturer's sales rep!" Sometimes Elise forgot this was a small town, and everyone knew she and Tierneigh had been friends since they met at an audiology seminar soon after Elise moved to Mt. Harmony. Tierneigh's thick, auburn hair was tousled by a sudden breeze, and her long lashes squinted slightly over caramel-colored eyes. Elise definitely had to tell Tierneigh how photogenic she was!

"Yes, the extraordinary chip developed by E. S. Hearing Labs for this hearing device will revolutionize the industry," said Tierneigh, who then covered her mouth to stifle a small cough as her eyes jerked to one side then back to the camera.

Elise tilted her head slightly, eyes focused a little more intently on her friend, who normally was very comfortable speaking in public. Was it just her imagination or did she seem a little distracted?

Tierneigh continued. "Many people have hearing difficulties that affect their daily lives, their family relationships, and not least of all, their self-esteem. It's been known that background noise can make these situations worse. People may eventually withdraw from their family and friends, which can lead to feelings of isolation and depression."

"About how many people are we talking about, Dr. Brown?"

"According to the Centers for Disease Control, over twenty-eight million adults in the United States have hearing loss that can be helped with hearing aids."

Elise pulled her eyes from her friend and glanced at the percolating coffee pot clock mounted next to the TV. At the same time, her cell phone buzzed a preset alarm.

"I need to get going!" she announced, basically to herself as she stood, grabbed her black all-weather jacket from the back of the chair and flung it over one arm.

Eyes and ears in the café were still on the TV, except for the attorney's, who turned toward Elise, one elbow slung over the top of the chair.

He waved a hand at her. "What about that hearing device, Dr. Harte?" Keith nodded toward the TV. "I wouldn't mind trying that out."

Elise pulled her purse strap up on her shoulder. "I'm going to the final training tonight at E. S. Hearing Labs, and Tierneigh will be at my office tomorrow for our open house. I'll have Lucy give you a call and get you in for an appointment, okay?"

Keith gave her a thumbs up and a wide smile.

Out on the sidewalk, Elise stopped to take a slow, deep breath of cool air, lost in the soft breeze and the sight of sunlight twinkling through red and yellow maple leaves. So beautiful...until an ear-splitting woooo-woooo pierced the air, followed by what seemed like a never-ending, high-pitched screech of brakes announcing the arrival of a passenger train into the Mt. Harmony train station, just a half mile from the square. She winced, even more annoyed that she didn't cover her ears in time, then unclenched her jaw when the train finally stopped.

She clicked the remote of her forest green SUV, pulled open the back door, and threw her jacket on the seat.

A man's gravelly voice yelled from the park's gazebo across the street. "Dr. Harte!"

She followed the sound to a group of sixty-something-year-old men, some in jeans and pullover sweatshirts or mustard-colored overalls, sitting in a circle on their metal folding chairs. They smiled and raised their thermoses or to-go cups in salute.

"Good morning, everyone!" Elise yelled back, enjoying the scene.

The men would be there every morning, taking a quick break from work on their farms, until the first frost, when they'd be forced to move inside the café. She paused when she caught sight of a deep red cardinal flitting through a nearby tree. So beautiful.

Smiling, Elise opened the driver's side door, settled behind the wheel and tapped a preset number on her cell phone. A clear and professional young woman's voice spoke through the car's speaker.

"Mt. Harmony Hearing and Balance Center. How may I help you?"

"Hi, Lucy. It's me. I'm on my way."

"Oh, Dr. Harte. That's good. Ahhh…"

"Yeah?"

"Umm…"

"Lucy? You still there?" Elise eyed a half-dried, red maple leaf on the floor of the car.

"Oh…uh, yeah. Just needed to tell you." Her voice dropped to a whisper. "Your mother-in-law just called."

Elise heard the maple leaf crunch under her shoe.

Chapter Three

═══ | ═══

Mt. Harmony
Thursday Morning

"Yeah…" Lucy continued cautiously. "She wanted to know if you checked on the cake and the music for her birthday party and have you heard from her sister, Ida, yet?"

Elise let out the breath she hadn't realized she was holding. Keith exited The Vibe and waved at her. She smiled and spoke through it like a ventriloquist. "I completely forgot, with the open house and everything. I'll give her a call right now."

She watched Keith climb into his truck, then closed her eyes, breathed in through her nose, and savored the thought of warm apple pie…with, of course, a slice of cheddar cheese on top.

When she felt ready, she tapped the button on her cell phone under the picture of her smiling, gray-haired mother-in-law, Catherine Harte.

Elise raised her voice in response to a somewhat frantic, "Elise?"

"Hi, Catherine."

"You don't have to yell, honey. I'm using that volume thing on my phone." She blew out a breath and tsked. "I'm getting too many RSVPs for my birthday party, and I don't know what to do!"

"Oh." Elise lowered her voice. "That's good, isn't it?"

"Well, first of all, are you sure the Lake 'n' Bacon'll hold everybody? And secondly, I ran into Cookie, and she said you haven't been into the Sweet Spot Bakery, yet. You told me you were gonna to do that yesterday."

Oh-oh… Elise's head started to feel like one of those monstrous harvesting combines was rumbling through it. "We'll definitely have room for everyone," she said, in a reassuring tone, while at the same time hoping it was true. "Cole's putting together a playlist of the songs you gave us, and he's sure we'll find that special one you've been talking about." The problem was, she wasn't sure her husband was actually putting in the effort needed to find it. She'd have to ask him about it…again.

Catherine squealed. "Oh, that's wonderful!"

"I'll give Cookie a call as soon as I get to the office. Please don't worry. Talk to you later, okay?" Elise raised her finger to tap the screen and disconnect the call, but stopped midstream.

"Elise. Wait!"

"Yes?"

Catherine sniffed, and her voice dropped. "What…what about my sister?"

Elise closed her eyes and tried to sound encouraging. "We'll track her down. We've got a couple leads that your grandson's following up on. Please don't worry."

"Okay, honey. I know you're trying," said Catherine, not fully convinced.

"So how many RSVPs did you get, anyway?" Elise hoped to change the subject.

"About sixty-three…so far."

Her eyes widened, and she tried to resist the rising panic in her stomach. For Pete's sake, did Catherine invite the whole town?

"Oh, my goodness, you're popular!" She felt another weight added to each shoulder. "But eighty's a big birthday. Don't worry, Catherine, okay?"

"Okay, honey. Love you."

"Love you, too."

Elise dropped the cell phone into her purse, cracked the window open, and breathed in cool air while she started the car. She punched the symphony station on the radio, her go-to, to help herself relax.

Elise loved most all forms of music, but symphonies calmed her, taking her back to rows of metal chairs in San Francisco's Golden Gate Park, and the outdoor Sunday concerts on that beautiful white stage with the Italian Renaissance-styled bandshell and ionic Greek columns...her parents sitting on either side of her.

Elise chose the scenic route to work, meaning the road that took her to the outskirts of town in a half circle to her office. She could've gone through town, but once in a while liked to take the few extra minutes to enjoy the fall scenery while she could. Sometimes, someone would commiserate about what was coming next, meaning the dreaded winter. But as one wise woman reminded patrons at The Vibe, "You're saying you won't eat the apple 'cause ya don't like the core?" That put the kibosh on that.

Elise drove past huge combines that dotted the cornfields in their signature fire engine red or grass green colors. There were times when farmers would maneuver their heavy equipment through town, causing traffic to slow to a crawl. But instead of annoyance, the community became invigorated. Crisp mornings meant an abundance of fall festivals and good moods.

In a matter of minutes, Elise pulled into the parking lot of a one-story, red brick medical building, situated within walking distance of the Mt. Harmony Community Hospital. She turned off the engine and once again tapped a number on her cell phone.

"Sweet Spot Bakery, how can we sweeten your day?" asked Cookie Wallis, the midfifties owner and baker.

Elise chuckled and pictured the baker's jovial face, her gray-streaked black hair in a bun at the nape of her neck. She knew that Cookie's given name was Ruth but didn't really know how long it had been since people started calling her "Cookie." She wasn't sure that anyone knew.

"Cookie, hi, it's Elise Harte. You can tell me that you can make a larger cake for my mom-in-law's birthday party, a week from Saturday."

"Oh, no problem, honey. You wanted the yellow cake with butter cream frosting, right? And it's her eightieth birthday, right? A week from this Saturday? Gotcha covered."

"Thank you so much…you've saved the day!"

They both laughed, then said their goodbyes. Elise dropped her phone into her purse and mentally ticked that "to-do" off her list. She grabbed her computer bag, stepped out of the car, and focused on the workday ahead.

The Mt. Harmony Hearing and Balance office could be entered by one of three doors. The front door faced an open courtyard, where seven other medical and professional offices, two on each side of the square, could be accessed by a cement walkway that surrounded a landscaped area in the center. The courtyard could be accessed by either of two iron-gated entrances, one from the employee parking lot near Elise's office and one on the opposite corner of the courtyard near patient parking.

Elise loved the courtyard's native prairie grasses and flowers, arranged in a natural, but perfectly positioned way, to show off each plant. Red-purple leaves of a multi-trunked dogwood tree created a stunning effect in the center of the landscaped area.

The second door to Elise's office was located on the side of the building that faced the employee parking lot, and a third door on the back of the building provided access to the audiologists' personal offices.

It was the front door Elise decided to use this morning. She wanted to take one more look at what patients would see tomorrow for the open house, when the office introduced E. S. Hearing Labs' revolutionary new hearing aid chip.

Black lettering on the glass door announced "Mt. Harmony Hearing and Balance Center" with the names of the audiologists, Elise Harte, AuD and co-owner Amy MacNeal, AuD, both Doctors of Audiology. Narrow windows on each side of the door allowed natural light into the office, and exposed—disaster!

Elise opened the front door and stared in frozen horror. The banner she'd ordered from Precise Signs & Banners for their open house and "October is National Audiology Awareness Month," was not so precise! The colors were perfect, representing the fall season with reds, yellows, and oranges. The lettering was just as she ordered, but...

"November is National Audiology Awareness Month?" she announced, as she stepped into the waiting room. "Lucy, what happened?"

The late twenties office manager stared at her boss, unconsciously smoothed the front of her white blouse, and opened her mouth to speak, but instead, let loose an impressive squeak of a hiccup. She clapped a hand with melon green fingernails over her mouth, her honey brown eyes frozen wide.

"Why does it say November? It should say October! Didn't anyone notice?"

"Oh…oh." Jake Cagney, a thin audiology doctoral student from the local university, poked his head out of the first patient room at the beginning of the hallway just past Lucy's desk. His wide eyes blinked at Elise as he unconsciously rubbed his slightly deformed right ear, the result of a dog bite as a child. In his midtwenties, his baby blue polo shirt highlighted his equally baby blue eyes, which helped take the attention away from a few stains scattered across the front.

"Jake, did you pick this up? Didn't you look at it first?"

"Sorry, Dr. Harte. It was rolled up when I got it, and I guess I didn't notice when I hung it up this morning."

"On it," said Lucy, reaching for the landline phone. "I'm calling Tom right now. We'll get it fixed ASAP!"

Jake yanked up his beige khakis with one hand, while he grabbed a stepstool with the other and placed it on the slate gray vinyl tile flooring at one end of the banner. Elise took in the rest of the room, hoping that would be the only problem. Black faux leather chairs were clean and neat against the off-white walls. A display table featured a handful of different hearing aid manufacturers' products, including red and pink E. S. Hearing Labs brochures that announced their new hearing aid chip. An Assistive Listening Device (ALD, for short) table displayed items to help people hear better in specific situations. A TV monitor was positioned on the wall above the table, near the reception window, where Lucy Shambo sat to welcome patients. The opposite side of the room held brochures on a wall display, describing audiological services, such as tests for dizziness, ringing in the ears, children's hearing problems, and many other issues.

Lucy used both hands to brush light brunette bangs off her forehead. "Dr. Harte, your first patient'll be here in ten minutes."

"Thank you, Lucy," said Elise. "By the way, your nails look great."

Lucy held one hand up and turned it from side to side, admiring her newly manicured nails.

Calmer now, Elise started down the hall toward her office, but paused to perform her daily mantra. Each day, after she and Amy opened their business, she'd stop and lightly touch a finger to one of her most prized possessions...the oak-framed picture of herself; co-owner, Dr. Amy MacNeal; and their professional hero, Dr. Marion Downs.

Dr. Downs was the dynamic leader of newborn hearing screening programs, fighting for infants and their rights to hearing care for decades, among numerous other powerful, achievements. She was as much a hero to Elise as Giants baseball legend Willie Mays was to her mother in San Francisco. She'd bet Dr. Downs could hit a home run, too, if she wanted to. She could do anything she—

Bang! The door to one of the hearing test rooms at the end of the hall flew open, and what looked like a three-foot bat flew out, wings flapping, with a squeaking sound coming from what looked like its head!

Elise flattened herself against the wall, arms splayed to protect the Dr. Downs picture, when Amy stepped into the hallway accompanied by a slightly frazzled, taller woman beside her.

"Hello, Dr. Harte," said Amy. She slid her gold, wire-framed glasses into her white lab coat pocket and shook her light brown "bixie"-cut hair away from her face. Amy had had to explain to Elise once that a bixie cut was a combination pixie and bob. Elise agreed it was very attractive on Amy's oval face. "I see you've met Benjamin the Bat!"

Elise stepped away from the wall. "Yes, I think I did!"

"Benjamin!" shouted his mother.

The boy froze, wings wide, just before jumping at the back of an unsuspecting Lucy.

"Dr. Harte, this is Benjamin's mother, Joan. Ben is just

getting over ear infections, and his hearing has really improved."

Elise turned toward Ben's mom and smiled. "It's nice to meet you…and that's great news!"

Joan smiled back. "Ben was so excited that he was feeling better, I told him he could show Dr. MacNeal his Halloween costume."

Ben, the bat, ran toward Lucy again, who, this time, saw him coming and cowered, pretending to be afraid of him while he squeaked and laughed in delight.

A couple minutes later, the audiologists watched Mom and her skipping bat exit the front door, as Amy said, "He did so well with his hearing test."

Elise chuckled. "Always good to hear…no pun intended."

They walked to their respective offices.

Elise had met Amy when she first moved to the town of Mt. Harmony, a little more than twenty years earlier. Amy owned the business but had made the difficult decision to sell when it became too hard to maintain along with the family's farm. Elise and Amy hit it off from the minute they met and eventually made a deal to co-own the business, allowing Amy the freedom to spend time on the farm when needed and relieve Elise as she needed. The arrangement served them, and their patients, well.

Elise plopped her purse and work bag on her antique oak desk, switched her jacket with the white lab coat hanging on the back of the office door, and took a seat on her matching oak roller chair. The desk was something she fell in love with the minute she and her husband found it at an estate sale, in a town not far from Mt. Harmony. She was ecstatic when they were able to get it for such a good price, and even more ecstatic when Cole's refinishing job revealed even more beauty.

Elise smoothed her fingers across the top of the desk as she thought of that day, then turned her computer on just as Lucy appeared at the door.

"First patient's here, Dr. Harte."

The morning flew by, and the next thing Elise knew, her business partner was leaning around the jamb of her office door. "I'm walking over to the hospital cafeteria to get lunch now. Want anything?"

"No thanks," said Elise, rummaging through her desk drawers. "I've got some snacks in here somewhere. Hey, how 'bout the training tonight…need a ride? I didn't see your car in the parking lot."

"Yeah, thanks. Troy had to take my car to work…his truck is in the shop," said Amy, referring to her husband.

"Good…not about Troy's truck, but it'll be more fun this way."

The front office phone rang, and Elise heard Lucy announce, "Mt. Harmony Hearing and Balance Center. How may I help you?" After a brief pause, she continued, "Certainly. Please hold."

A red interoffice button lit up on Elise's office phone. She grabbed the handset. "Hi, Lucy."

"Dr. Harte, Dr. Tierneigh Brown's on the phone for you."

"Thanks." She punched the flashing button for the outside line and pulled a chocolate and almond snack bar from one of the side drawers. Underneath the snack bar was a picture of Elise, Tierneigh, and Amy, smiles big and arms around each other's backs. Elise was wearing her navy and light blue UC San Francisco sweatshirt, and Tierneigh and Amy were on either side of her, wearing their navy blue and orange University of Illinois sweatshirts.

"Hi, Tierneigh!" said Elise, resting back in her chair, smiling at the picture. "I'm so excited about tonight!"

"Oh, good. You're still coming," said Tierneigh in a tense whisper. "I wanted to make sure. Amy's coming, too, right?"

"Absolutely. We're completely booked for the open house tomorrow. Saw you on the news this morning. You looked great!"

"Oh…thanks. This place has been crazy. Any chance you can come a little earlier? I need to talk to you before it all starts."

"Sure. You okay?"

"Yeah, yeah, I'm okay. Gotta make some more calls to confirm people. Yeah, it's going to be great. Can't wait to see you."

Elise heard a click, and the line went dead. "Whoa," she murmured out loud. "She needs to relax a little when this is all over."

The afternoon flew by as quickly as the morning, until Lucy announced, "Patients all confirmed for tomorrow." She plunked the handset of her office phone into its cradle. "And Jake said he and Nicole will see you at the training," referring to the other audiology student, who also worked occasionally at the office.

"Good," Elise called over her shoulder from the waiting room, where she made one last walkthrough, smiling at the new, "October is National Audiology Awareness Month" sign. She stood now at the patient window just in front of Lucy. "By the way, did Noah Reed from the sheriff's department come by this afternoon?"

Lucy raised her head. "Yeah. He came in to get his custom ear plugs, and yes, even though he's had these before and knows how to use them, I had him put them in before he left. I told him you wanted to make sure about the fit. He said they felt great right now but would call if any sore spots or anything developed that might bother him." She pointed to the next day's schedule on her monitor. "Also, I squeezed Keith from the coffee shop in for you tomorrow afternoon. You're booked solid."

Elise turned to lock the office's front door then took the few steps back into the hallway and nodded. "Thanks, Lucy. Good on both accounts. That reminds me…" She looked in the direction of Amy's office. "I need Amy to make impressions of my ears for me. I can't find the custom hearing protectors I use as demos."

"I'll remind you." Lucy chuckled. "You all have fun at the training," she said as she patted the top of a weather radio on the counter. "We might be getting a storm later, so be careful."

"We will. Goodnight, Lucy."

Elise locked the side door behind Lucy, then headed back down the hall. She stopped at Amy's office door, but she wasn't there.

Thump…thump…thump…

Hmm? The noise sounded like it was coming from the hearing test room across the hall from her office.

"Amy?" Elise walked down the rest of the hallway and stepped into the test room.

Brightly colored paintings of sunflowers decorated the wall opposite the testing booth. No Amy. She glanced at the two-room, sound-treated booth that filled the far wall. Both the audiologist and patient doors were closed. She walked up a short ramp to the audiologist side of the booth and pulled on the chrome vertical handle that opened a weighted door and saw an empty desk. Test booths needed to be raised off the floor to minimize and control sound vibrations that could interfere with testing.

The lights and equipment were turned off. No Amy. From this side, the audiologist could see the other side of the test booth through a window in the adjoining wall. Elise looked but didn't see anyone. She noticed the button for two-way communication between the two sides was also turned off, so stepped back down the ramp.

Thump…thump…thump. Her eyes darted to the second door. She took one long stride, then up that ramp, and quickly yanked on the chrome handle of the weighted patient door. Two feet fell out with cords wrapped around the ankles! Half sitting and half lying on the floor was Amy, cords in each hand, trying to untangle herself.

Elise screeched, "Are you hurt?"

"Noooo." Amy winced. "I was cleaning up in here and tried to untangle the cords from the headphones, the response button, the bone vibrator, the ear inserts…and didn't realize they were wrapping around me…until I tried to move!"

Elise pressed her lips together, trying to hide her amusement, now that she saw Amy was okay.

"I thought you were done for the day," Elise said. "I didn't know you were…tied up."

"Ha…ha…" Amy smirked as she pulled the last cord off.

Elise, standing on the ramp, leaned forward to help Amy to her feet. "Hey, have you talked to Tierneigh lately?" Elise asked, as they closed the booth door and finished checking the rest of the room.

"No. Why?"

"She called at lunchtime. Something seemed off."

"Off? Probably the stress from the training and all."

"I thought about that, but she said she wanted us to come early so she could talk to us. She didn't sound like herself."

Both paused, jerked their eyes to the ear-shaped wall clock and shrieked, "The training!" They grabbed their purses, turned out the last few lights, locked the back door, and ran like crazy for Elise's car.

★★★

E. S. Hearing Labs, located on the east side of the town of Bluestem, had just celebrated their twentieth year of manufacturing custom ear products, such as ear plugs for work, swimming, music, or sleeping, as well as a line of hearing devices, which turned out to be very successful for the company, especially with the rapid and ever-changing field of digital technology.

It was about a thirty-five-minute interstate drive from Mt. Harmony if one drove directly north to Springfield, then west to Bluestem, or about a twenty- to twenty-five-minute drive diagonally on back roads from Mt. Harmony straight to Bluestem. The back route was quicker if one did not come upon farm equipment that could slow traffic down, and tonight that was the chance Elise and Amy decided to take.

They headed west right into the sun's last rays glowing underneath a smattering of gray storm clouds. Amy shielded her eyes with her hand, and Elise squinted as the light was just at the right angle where the car's visors didn't help. Luckily, no farm equipment was on the road itself, but red and green combines, depending upon one's preference for manufacturers, were still in the fields, headlights highlighting their progression down rows of corn.

"Too bad someone can't get a picture of that," said Elise, nodding her head toward a bright red combine as it crashed through rows of twelve-foot-tall yellow-brown cornstalks in the setting sun's orange light. "It'd definitely win first place at the state fair next year."

"I know. I love to watch those combines," said Amy. "It's amazing how the whole harvesting process is computerized down to each kernel of corn."

"Does your family use those on your farm?" asked Elise, keeping her eyes on the road as more dark clouds gathered.

Amy and her husband took over Amy's family farm so her parents could enjoy their hard-earned retirement and occasional travel.

"Nothing that size," she said, referring to a combine that looked bigger than her house. "That one out there's probably 400-500 horsepower and can harvest twelve rows of corn at a time. The front of the combine has these humongous cones sticking out—we call them snoots—that separate the rows to be harvested."

"They look pretty scary!" Elise had learned quite a bit about corn and soybeans since moving to Mt. Harmony and was always amazed at the process. She slowed down at a four-way stop, then proceeded cautiously through a fortress of cornstalks on all sides. "Can't wait until this section's done. The corn's so high, I can't see if any cross traffic's coming. How're we doing on time?"

Amy pointed to the sky. "We're good…should be at the lab before those storm clouds hit."

But as soon as they pulled into the E. S. Hearing Labs parking lot and rolled slowly into a spot, a boom of thunder made them jump, and rain pattered the windshield.

Amy grabbed her hair against a gust of wind as she exited the car. "So glad I just combed my hair," she said with a wry smile. "We don't get many thunderstorms this time of year…but ya never know."

The women pulled their jacket hoods up and scurried to the front doors, soon dropping to a shuffle as they joined a crowd of attendees under a long, stone portico leading to the front doors.

When they finally made it through the ten-foot glass double doors, their jaws dropped.

Chapter Four

E. S. Hearing Labs Manufacturing
Thursday Evening

"Whoa," whispered a wide-eyed Amy, as she scanned the spacious, white-walled lobby before her.

Curly white ribbons dropped from multitudes of pink, red, and silver balloons that swayed to their own rhythm like wheat in a soft breeze. A massive banner in similar colors hung from an open section of the second floor above a reception desk, promoting E. S. Hearing Labs and the newly developed hearing aid chip.

Elise and Amy smiled, dodging women and men in white jackets as they held silver trays full of half-filled crystal glasses.

Amy leaned toward Elise with her head down. "Did we just get on a cruise ship by mistake?"

A young man offered Elise and Amy glasses of champagne or ginger ale, then pointed them in the direction of the check-in table. Nodding their thanks for the ginger ales, the two shuffled into a line that led toward a white cloth-draped table to check in and claim their name tags.

"Elise! Amy!" The familiar voices of Todd Wilson and Kristin Miller, both audiologists and previous college friends of Amy's, brought immediate smiles to their faces.

Todd's hazel eyes laughed with excitement. Kristen smiled and patted the golden brown braid that circled her head like a crown.

"The wind out there is crazy!"

"I love your braid," said Amy. "And it looks like Todd even broke down and got a haircut for the occasion."

"Looks like he got 'em all cut," said Kristen, and they laughed at the bad joke as Todd lifted his chin, patted the top of his dark brown, buzz-cut hair with half-closed eyes, then fiddled with the collar of his forest green polo shirt.

Pfft…pfft…pfft.

Heads jerked toward the offending amplified sound to see a young man dressed in black pants and a white long-sleeved shirt tapping his finger on the top of a handheld microphone.

"Good evening, everyone, and welcome to E. S. Hearing Labs! At this time, I'd like you to please follow me down the south hall here." He turned and waved his right arm toward the hallway behind him. "We're headed to the main training room area. There you will find a few culinary treats that have been prepared by chefs in the Bluestem area just for you!"

Attendees fell in behind him, following their noses, already teased with savory smells of meats, vegetables, fresh fruits, and casseroles. White tablecloth-covered buffet tables topped with silver chafing dishes awaited them at the end of the hallway in an area just outside two sets of closed doors, which presumably led to where the training would take place.

"I'm starving," said Todd, as he tried to break through the line, eyes popping at the food table.

Kristin grabbed the back of his shirt, which stretched and stopped him mid-stride, one foot frozen in the air. "Hold on, big guy! You never did have much patience."

The women laughed, then gave in and swept their arms forward in tandem, inviting Todd to go first.

"Just like school," Amy tsked. She surveyed the area and spied a table with a tray of empty, obviously used glasses, and added hers to the group.

Elise placed her empty glass on the tray, as well, as they shuffled forward in line. "Hey, have any of you seen Tierneigh?"

"I saw her in Dr. Andres's office a bit ago," said Kristin, nodding her head toward the north hallway. "I heard her ask if anyone had seen you yet."

Elise glanced toward the hallway. "Okay. I'm gonna see if I can find her." She assessed the long line of people getting food. "I'll get something to eat when I get back."

Todd and Kristin looked at her with questioning faces, as Amy said, "Sure…no problem. I'll save you a place."

Elise nodded and set out in a half-jog down the hallway, back toward the reception area, weaving around late-arriving attendees. She reached the other side of the reception area and jogged down the north hallway toward the office of Dr. Susan Andres. She also wanted to see the anechoic test chamber where Susan worked. She knew from her Latin class in high school that "anechoic" meant "no echo," and was that right! She laughed to herself that Latin came in handy when she least expected it.

As a child, she'd always wanted to be a nurse, and when she was told that medical terms were based in Latin, she signed up for a class as soon as she got into high school. Not that the class changed her mind about nursing, she always told herself. What changed her mind was the first audiology class she ever took. She loved it, and the Latin helped!

Elise found the gray-painted door marked "Research Audiology" with "Susan Andres, PhD" below it. The office was on her right, almost to the end of the hallway. Two other doors lay just beyond it—one marked for a stairwell and the other an exit that led to an outside parking lot.

Elise tapped lightly on the door, paused, then slowly opened it. "Dr. Andres?"

"Hello! We're in here."

Elise stepped over the threshold, keeping the door open to allow light from the hallway in, and followed the voice to her left, just beyond Dr. Andres's darkened office. The only immediate light emanated from a silver gooseneck lamp on her desk.

She passed the desk, which was stacked with manuals, papers, old journals, and files, then surveyed the walls around it. Mesh cubbies stood in the shadows against the far wall to her right and held assorted test equipment accessories and toys to use when testing children, while the wall on her left was filled with a multitude of hooks holding cords of different lengths and colors. Elise had a similar wall in her office, though a third the amount Susan had, for cords used to hardwire hearing aids to computers that could not be programmed wirelessly.

She took a few steps past Dr. Andres's desk and couldn't help but feel awed at the anechoic chamber in front of her. Its open heavy door rested against the wall to the right, allowing more light to permeate Susan's office. To the left of the doorway were built-in shelves jam-packed with old hearing test equipment that Dr. Andres had collected over the years. Elise had a hard time pulling her eyes from the shelves. She loved vintage equipment and was dying to look at the different pieces and see how they worked.

"Elise, come in!" said Susan, practically whispering but clearly heard.

"Hi, Dr. Andres!" Elise decided to address Susan more formally since others were with her. She took a tentative step toward her but stopped at the chamber's threshold. Five students stood in an arc in front of the research audiologist, their heads rotating to take everything in.

"What do you all think?" Susan spoke softly, waving her arm around the room, which seemed larger than Elise and Cole's bedroom. A yellow-white overhead light gave an eerie effect to the area, as well as to the large gray-brown foam wedges that protruded from the walls and ceiling. More wedges could be seen below them, through a metal mesh floor.

Susan continued. "I was just explaining how the foam wedges break up sound waves and absorb them, therefore the immense silence. It's the ideal environment in which to evaluate our hearing aid products."

"Well," said one student, a stocky young man who pressed his hand to his chest. "It's so quiet in here…my heart feels like it's gonna pound out of my chest!"

"Yeah," whispered another student, who cupped the palms of her hands over her ears. "I didn't think I had ringing in my ears, but the quiet in here's making 'em ring like crazy!"

"The absence of sound in this test chamber is an experience people don't usually expect," said Susan. "Come back later and I'll show you how we test our new hearing devices with the chip we've developed."

The stocky man pointed to a chair surrounded by six speakers mounted on stands. "Is that why the KEMAR guy's in the chair?"

Giggles erupted at the sight of a dark gray, molded male torso, dressed like a scarecrow and positioned on the chair's seat.

"Yes," said Susan. "For those who don't know, KEMAR stands for Knowles Electronic Manikin for Acoustic Research. Basically, we can put hearing devices on his very calibrated head—"

The students snickered at that.

"—and vary the speakers for different test protocols used in our research. We usually do that before we test with live people."

The young man continued, "And he's dressed like a scarecrow because…?"

Elise stifled her own giggle now, while Dr. Andres answered. "We're not all stuffy research people, you know. We like to have some fun once in a while and thought it was only fair to enjoy the fall season here, too."

A tall young man, who Elise thought must play basketball, dressed in a pale blue shirt and darker blue tie, held his cell phone in front of him. "Can I use my phone in here?"

Susan shook her head. "We don't get reception in this end of the building…have to use landlines." She paused for a moment. "If there are no more questions, I think we should head back to the training room. Thank you all for coming."

"Thank you, Dr. Andres," murmured the students, still conscious of the effects of the room.

Elise's eyes followed the students as they left, reminding her of her days at UC San Francisco and how she couldn't wait to start work in her chosen profession. Her stomach growled as she turned to face the research audiologist, both now stepping onto the gray and white linoleum floor of Susan's personal office area.

"Susan, it's so good to see you! It's been a while, but I know you've been busy." They hugged, and Elise added, "I wanted to see you, but I was also looking for Tierneigh. Have you seen her?"

Susan turned her back on Elise, yanked open her top desk drawer without answering, and grabbed a handle attached to an oval mirror. She pulled a tube of lip gloss out of her white lab coat pocket and ran it over her lips.

Elise watched Susan's reflection in the mirror. Was she hesitating? Elise continued. "Tierneigh called me at my office this afternoon. Maybe it was my imagination, with everything that's been going on, but she sounded a little distracted. Maybe even upset. Do you know if she's okay?"

"I know she's tired," said Susan, turning to face Elise. "Everyone's put in tons of overtime lately, but…"

"But, what?"

"Well, we've had some issues here lately." Susan paused, as if deciding what she wanted to say. "A funny thing happened earlier."

"What do you mean, 'funny'?"

Susan pulled a comb out of the same desk drawer and lifted the mirror again, but this time faced Elise. She spoke as she ran the comb through her thick, dark hair. "I left a message in Tierneigh's office that I wanted to talk to her. She came down and was standing over there." She flicked the tip of her comb toward the doorway. "I guess it was a couple hours ago. She didn't look too good, but I thought she was probably just tired. Before she could say anything, Rick…you know him, right?"

"I think so. The acoustical engineer?"

"Yes. Well, he came up behind Tierneigh and looked at me over her shoulder. Tierneigh saw him and jumped about a mile, and then took off. I meant to look for her, but one thing after another's come up and…"

"She never said what she wanted?"

Susan opened her mouth to speak when a woman's voice called from down the hallway.

"Dr. Andres, they need you in the training room ASAP!"

Susan's eyes steadied on nothing in particular. She dropped her comb in the metal drawer and pushed it shut. "No, not really." She smoothed her white lab coat and smiled. "It's good to see you, but I really need to go. Can we talk later?"

Before Elise could answer, Susan darted down the hallway, leaving Elise by herself and slightly taken aback. She started to follow but hesitated, giving in to the urge to take a quick look again at Susan's collection of old test equipment.

"Oh, my goodness," she mumbled to herself, lightly touching the audiometers and tympanometers from the 1950s and beyond. She pulled her cell phone out of her purse and tapped the flashlight to see better. Large knobs, basic functions, and heavy, compared to today's equipment, which could test basic hearing levels and middle ear function, easily held in one hand. She stopped at one piece that looked like the bottom half of an old wooden box, with a section toward the front where headphones were stored. The back half of the box had a metal facing that held two big black knobs used to adjust the test tones and loudness.

"Oh, my goodness," she said again when she saw what was sitting next to it.

A brown rectangle metal piece of equipment that had silver hinges on one end of a flip top and a silver latch on the other end to lock it closed. She recognized it as a tympanometer that tested middle ear pressure. She smiled. A friend of hers in San Francisco used to have one just like it many years ago.

Elise peered once more inside the anechoic chamber. It was an amazing technological means for controlling sound…loudness, frequency, source of sound, and other parameters for specific testing. She figured she could take one more minute and placed a hand on the door frame to steady herself against the almost suctioning effect she felt on her body. She took one step over the threshold, then one more into the chamber, and actually started to feel a little dizzy, when all of a sudden, a blaring Gonk! Gonk! Gonk! shot through the air.

Her hands flew to her heart, then to her ears. Her stomach roiled, and she jumped for the doorway, letting out a yelp when her head knocked against the side door frame.

A male robot-type voice announced, "This is a weather alert for the counties of ..."

A weather radio! Elise followed the horrible noise to a small black and yellow weather radio, its volume turned all the way up, buried under a stack of audiology journals on Susan's desk. She slammed the palm of her hand against the radio's off button, causing some of the journals to fall to the floor.

Elise slowly inhaled warm, stuffy air and tried to calm herself, then found a pad of yellow sticky notes. She scribbled a note for Susan, saying she needed to turn the radio back on, since Elise didn't want that to happen again...so much for weather alerts...and put the fallen journals back onto Susan's desk.

But her heart did yet another flip when she stepped into the hallway and a deep voice came through a loudspeaker. "The training will start in approx-i-mate-ly five minutes."

Elise dashed down the empty hallway, through the reception area, and down the south hallway, calming only when she neared the training room and heard the murmur of voices and other familiar sounds of normalcy. She eyed an open seat next to Amy at one of the fifteen-foot, white tablecloth-draped tables. Her stomach growled as she sat. Computers were provided at every other seat to share during the training, along with pitchers of iced water and cut-glass bowls of hard candies.

"I missed the food!" Elise whispered to Amy, as she reached for the candy dish.

Amy whispered, "To the rescue..." She passed a small napkin-covered plate toward her.

Elise lifted the napkin. Her eyes floated over slices of triple chocolate cake, raspberry cheesecake, and apple pie. She closed them and reveled in the distinct smells of each treat. "You are the best."

Amy stifled a giggle.

Todd, who sat at the table just in front of them, turned bug-eyed and mouthed, "For me?"

"No!" Elise mouthed back, as she hovered her fork over one dessert then the other.

"Hello and good evening, everyone!"

Heads jerked to the front of the room. A somewhat short man in his midfifties, slightly stout, in a navy blue sports jacket and red-and-pink striped tie, spoke into a handheld microphone at the front of the room. He had a round face with coarse-looking salt and pepper hair. His eyebrows were dark from the inside to the middle, then turned gray on the outside, so from a distance, looked like he had a constant scowl.

"Welcome to E. S. Hearing Labs! We are extremely excited and pleased to have you here to help us celebrate this momentous occasion! My name is Theo Wrightman, CEO of E. S. Hearing Labs. I've been proud to be associated with this company for the last four years."

Kristin whispered to her friends, "Four years already? I remember him from his last three jobs in manufacturing. Wasn't something funny going on with him?"

A few people turned and glared.

Pressing her lips together, she turned her attention back to the CEO.

"As you all know by now, E. S. Hearing Labs developed a digital chip that we believe will take on the hearing aid industry as the most advanced and consequential product to date. It's been the proverbial 'long, hard, road,' and literally, couldn't have been done without the outstanding and dedicated staff represented by the people standing next to me." Turning to the line of people assembled next to him, he continued. "To my left, your right, I'd like to introduce Dr. Susan Andres, Head Research Audiologist, instrumental in the research, development, and testing of the chip." Dr. Andres stepped forward with her lips pressed together, nodded, and stepped back in line.

"Next to Dr. Andres is Mr. Rick Dayton, Acoustical Engineer, who, with his staff, works with Dr. Andres in creating the most conducive test situations for the chip and our human subjects."

Elise noticed his impatience, possibly with the attention he was getting, as he lifted one hand in the air. He looked to be in his later forties and had a slight but athletic build. Not rugby…she wasn't quite sure. His black, slicked-back hair shone in the overhead lighting.

"Next to Rick is Mr. Bob Bell, Head of Accounting, whose personal mantra is… 'Be audit you can be.'" Theo grinned, and his eyebrows wiggled, as a low rumble of groans could be heard around the room.

A tidy-looking man in his midforties, wearing tan khakis and a white long-sleeved shirt, stepped forward with an exaggerated grimace. His thin reddish-blond hair seemed to stick straight up. Elise thought there was a lot of hair gel floating around this place as he adjusted his tie with one hand and waved with the other.

"Then Ms. Gloria Strauber, head of inside and outside reps…" Theo paused as a woman in her late fifties, wearing a peacock blue crocheted scarf around her neck and cardinal red glasses, stepped forward. She wore a loose black skirt that fell below her knees and a black long-sleeved top. Her short curly chestnut brown hair had spots of gray.

Theo continued with a hand extended toward a slim

middle-aged woman wearing a dark red suit. Her blond hair was straight and fashionably cut to her jawline. "And…Ms. Dorothea Johnson, Head of Marketing and Advertising."

Dorothea flashed a smile of perfect teeth encircled in red lipstick. She mimicked a regal wave to the left of her, to the center, then to the right.

Theo grinned and paused through giggles and mild applause, then said, "Along the wall to your right are more of our indispensable staff, starting with Dr. Tierneigh Brown, outside rep and PR star…I know you all saw her on the local news this morning!"

Tierneigh scanned the room with a fixed smile on her face, her eyes taking stock of each row.

The CEO continued to introduce other reps, then came to the lab technicians. "Our lab techs…our 'hands-on' pros…are truly some of the best in the business. They'll be available at the break to give you a tour of the lab, where the custom products are made. Dr. Andres will be available after the training for those of you who would like to see the anechoic chamber, where tests are conducted with the new chip. If you're interested, please raise your hands, and Jake and Nicole here, our volunteer audiology students, will take your names and tell you where to meet. Let's take a quick break before we get started with the training. Please be back here in ten minutes."

Amy nodded toward the students as she stood. "I hope Nicole's not spreading herself too thin. She's going to be helping us with the open house tomorrow, on top of all this."

As if on cue, Nicole caught their eyes and gave a good attempt at a smile. Her caramel-colored hair hung in disheveled waves just below her shoulders. The shine of a dark plastic headband could be seen over the crown of her head and disappearing behind her ears. Her eyes seemed heavy under straight eyebrows.

Elise said, "I know what you mean. Jake's not looking too perky tonight either, and they've got finals coming up."

Todd stood, stretched with a loud yawn, and turned toward Elise, Amy, and Kristen. "Our office is looking forward to this new technology, but we might take it easy for a little bit to see what everyone else's experience is with it first." He was referring to the medical office where his audiology services were based in a city about two hours away.

Kristin nodded. "Might be a good plan. I like to know what's going on, in case an infant with hearing loss needs to be referred for more follow-up." Kristin referred to her job in a hospital's newborn nursery, where she administered hearing screenings and further diagnostic hearing tests if a baby needed more specific testing.

Amy turned to Elise. "I'm going to make a restroom stop."

"And there's Tierneigh." Elise lifted her chin toward the front of the room and locked eyes with her elusive friend. "I'll be with her."

Tierneigh waved at Elise, just as a slightly built man in his midtwenties, with black hair and wearing a slate blue suit stepped in front of her friend, hands waving. A close-cut beard hugged his jawline.

Tierneigh raised an index finger toward Elise in a "hold on a minute" signal, as the crowd pushed Elise toward the back door. Elise pointed toward the hallway and Tierneigh responded with a thumbs up.

After ten minutes of waiting, Elise was forced to give in to one of the lab's staff herding everyone back into the training room. She'd have to try to find Tierneigh later.

Back in the training room, Elise eyed Kristin and Todd standing with their backs to the front of the room, talking to a seated Amy, her table between them. Light laughter erupted from the three, and Elise found herself frowning at the dichotomy of their obvious enjoyment with her own worry about what might be going on with her other friend.

"Well, there she is!" said Todd, as Elise approached the table. "We've been waiting for you."

At that moment, the lights lowered and "E. S. Hearing Labs Presents" appeared on a large screen at the front of the room.

Kristin hit Todd playfully on his arm. "Come on and sit down. They're going to start."

Amy raised her eyes to Elise. "Did you see Tierneigh?"

"No," Elise mumbled, scanning the training room again, just in case. "If nothing else, we know she'll be at the office tomorrow morning."

"Yeah, it'll be okay. Come on…it's starting again."

A little over two hours later, after intense programming practice and troubleshooting of the new hearing aid chip, Theo Wrightman bid his farewell to all with deepest appreciation for the successful turnout and dedication by attendees to their profession.

The jovial atmosphere earlier had now changed to muted mumblings of goodbyes and shuffling feet.

Kristin stood and stretched her back. "Wow, am I stiff!"

Some around her turned and nodded in agreement, then all were startled to see gloved cleaning crews descending on the area with vacuums, floor buffers, spray bottles, and towels. The attendees gathered what energy they had left and quickly headed down the hall toward the front of the building.

Weary-eyed staff passed out gift bags, nodding their goodbyes and thanks, and it was at that moment Elise saw Tierneigh, gift bags hanging from her arm, striding determinately through the lethargic crowd straight for her.

Elise laughed. "Tierneigh…finally!"

"I'm so glad to see you," whispered Tierneigh, glancing

over each shoulder. Elise's eyebrows lowered at her de-meanor, as Tierneigh continued. "Can we talk somewhere?"

"Sure," said Elise. She turned toward her group. "Bye, everyone! Nicole, you'll be at the office tomorrow morning for the open house, right?"

"Bright and early," said Nicole, who then turned to di-rect a few audiologists to the anechoic chamber for the last tour of the night.

Tierneigh hissed, "Elise, I have so much to tell you. I don't know what to do!"

"What do you mean? Are you talking about the guy that cornered you at the break?"

She stared at Elise for a second, then shook her head. "Oh, no. That was David Nubrey. He's one of the volunteer students...one of our test subjects."

"He's an audiology student? Don't think I've seen him before."

"No...business," said Tierneigh, rushing her words. "He's getting his MBA. We have a few people from that de-partment. No, I needed to tell you about this morning. I came in early to check on things—" Tierneigh suddenly clamped her lips together, and her body stiffened.

Elise followed her eyes to a few feet away, where Rick Dayton was staring daggers at her friend. Tierneigh saw him and stunned Elise by breaking into a wide smile. Elise gawked at her.

"So, Elise...did you get a gift bag? You did? Well, you can always use another one, right? Give this one to Lucy, and here's an extra. One can never have too many thumb drives, right?"

"Okay...thanks. But..." started Elise, dumbfounded.

"I'll be at your office first thing in the morning, okay?"

Still stunned, Elise watched as Tierneigh turned on her heel and again disappeared into the crowd. Her eyes darted back to Rick Dayton, but he was nowhere to be seen.

Amy finished her goodbyes and came to stand in front of Elise. "Hey, ready to go?" She frowned at the look on Elise's face and waved a flat hand two inches from her friend's nose. "Whoo-hoo…Elise!"

"Oh, yeah, let's go."

Lightning jagged in the distance behind them as they lowered their heads against a gust of wind and ran across the wet, dark parking lot, rain spattering their faces. Elise silently counted. One thousand one, one thousand two… She made it to eight by the time she heard the rumble of thunder. Eight divided by five…maybe a mile and a half away. Not far enough away for her, but it did seem to be skirting the area.

Settled safely in the car, buckled in and doors locked, Amy leaned her head against the headrest, her chin up. "Home, please," she said, as she closed her eyes.

Elise giggled, pushed the heater button, and placed her cell phone on the center console tray. She liked knowing she could get to it fast in case of an emergency. "Your wish is my command."

An uneventful thirty minutes later, Elise flicked her headlights in response to Amy's goodbye wave, and watched her close the door to her two-story, red brick home. Her family's farmland sprawled in the darkness behind it.

The rain didn't amount to much of anything, which suited Elise fine. She checked the road and pulled away from the curb but jumped when the light from her cell phone burst into the darkness, followed immediately by an intrusive buzzing. Tierneigh's smiling face filled the screen.

Elise pulled the car to the side of the road and tapped the phone on. "Hey, Tierneigh…what's going on? You okay?"

"Quick…I can't talk…."

"What?"

"I need to see you. Tonight. It's important."

"You okay? You sound—"

"Elise, I really need to see you…now!"

"Okay, calm down, sweetie. I just dropped Amy off. I can meet you somewhere."

"Here, at the lab. I'll meet you at the main door. It'll probably be locked."

"Okay. I'm leaving now."

Elise left a short message on her husband's phone about what she was doing, then drove off, scanning the roads for sheriffs as she pushed past the speed limit. Eventually, she saw dots of light in the distance that she recognized were the lamp posts in the E. S. Hearing Labs parking lot. She glanced at the time on the dash display. Twenty minutes since Tierneigh called. Not bad.

She drove into the parking lot, now with just a few scattered cars in it, and pulled as close to the front doors as she could. She dropped her phone in her purse and ran, dodging scattered rain puddles, toward the cold, glaring light over the front doors that made her eyes squint. She grabbed the chrome handle, but the door just rattled. Locked. Just like Tierneigh said it might be.

She put her face to the window, cupping her hands around her eyes. Someone was coming at a pretty good pace. Good. Must be Tierneigh. The door pushed open, and she jerked to one side before it smacked her in the face.

"Oh," she said to one of the lab techs she recognized from the training. "I was looking for Tierneigh…Brown. I…ah…forgot something and need to find her."

"Oh, sorry. I didn't hit you, did I?" Her face was flushed. "Haven't seen her. Maybe in her office?"

"I'm alright, thanks. And yes, I'll check."

The lab tech nodded. "Goodnight."

Elise slipped in the door and jogged straight for the elevator. After a tension-ridden minute of wishing she'd taken the stairs, she exited the elevator and glanced down the darkened, second-floor hallway, illuminated only by scattered night lights. Except for one.

Light spilled into the hallway from an office she thought had to be Tierneigh's. It had been awhile since the last time she was there, since Tierneigh traveled so much, but she knew Tierneigh's office was across from a conference room, and this one was. She stopped at the doorway, but the office was empty. Maybe Susan was still here and she'd know where Tierneigh was.

She realized now that she was closer to the stairway, so jogged to the door marked EXIT, pulled it open, and slid her hand down the metal banister, as she clomped down the dimly lit stairs to the main floor and Susan's office.

The quiet is so creepy. She tried not to think of scenes from a horror movie she and Cole watched last Saturday, which had kept her awake most of the night. Not her cup of tea, but…she was now at Susan's door. It was slightly ajar, so she rapped lightly, just in case, then pushed the door open. The gooseneck lamp cast a pale yellow spot on Susan's desk.

"Susan?" Elise stepped into the office.

The door to the anechoic chamber was open and light spilled from it to just over the doorjamb. Another step.

"Tierneigh? Susan?" No answer. "Hello?" She raised her voice slightly as she approached the chamber.

Then she saw it. An upended speaker lay on its side on the mesh flooring.

"Hello?" she whispered, then froze as her eyes locked on a pair of red pumps, speaker cords wrapped around the legs above them.

She followed the legs to a second speaker that lay across Tierneigh's prone body. Her head was turned toward Elise, and something red pooled beneath it.

Her scream fell dead against the walls.

Chapter Five

Thursday Evening

"Tierneigh," Elise barely whispered now as she dropped to her knees and rested her hand lightly on Tierneigh's back. "It's me, sweetie, Elise." Elise thought she saw her mouth move but wasn't sure. "I'm calling for help. It'll be okay."

She bolted to Dr. Andres's desk and scattered the mess on top until she found the desk phone. She grabbed the handset and pressed it to her ear, but her hand shook, and she had to press hard to the point of hurting her ear so she wouldn't drop it. Then she froze. What's the number to 911? Oh. She punched the buttons.

A calm female voice answered. "911, what's your emergency?"

Elise responded to the questions put to her and remained on the line until she eyed a button marked "Security." After telling the operator what she was going to do, she punched the hold button, then hit Security.

"I'll let the EMTs in and bring 'em to the test room ASAP, Dr. Harte," said a gruff voice in response to Elise's call.

She punched the button back to the 911 operator and tried, unsuccessfully, to take a deep breath, stretching the cord as far as she could to keep an eye on her friend, while she waited for the emergency team.

Uniformed EMTs arrived in minutes, led by the lab's security guard, and efficiently assessed the scene, as well as their patient. A gurney had been wheeled into Susan's office but could not be maneuvered through the anechoic chamber door, so an EMT quickly pulled off the separate backboard that lay on top of it and placed it on the floor next to Tierneigh.

"What are these cords around her legs?" The EMT named Chris, according to his name tag, spoke in measured tones as he carefully unwound them from Tierneigh's legs. The other EMT prepared to roll her on her back.

Elise leaned over, her hands on her knees and her chest bursting, but immediately straightened and pointed. "Those go with the test equipment." She took a step forward. "It's easy to get tangled up in them," she rambled on, "but I don't know what she was doing or why she was in here by herself."

The second EMT mumbled something under his breath and looked at Chris, who nodded. They transferred Tierneigh to the backboard, stabilized her head with foam blocks, and attached the straps.

"What? What is...?" Elise felt her throat close. She wanted to know what the EMT said but at the same time was afraid to hear it.

Chris, still on one knee with eyes focused on his patient, said, "Where does she live, ma'am? Where's her family?"

"Mt. Harmony." Elise watched as he and the other EMT stood, lifted the backboard over the chamber threshold and placed it on the gurney.

"Good. We're taking her to the hospital there, ma'am. Who'll be meeting us?"

They pulled more straps across Tierneigh and secured them. The whole procedure took a little more than a minute but felt like a year.

"I'll call her sister, Maryelle. She lives there."

"You a relation?"

"No...no...a...a good fri—" She swallowed. "She going to be alright?" Elise wasn't sure if she actually asked it or just thought it as she stepped in front of the gurney and snatched a set of headphones and a crumpled paper from the floor to clear the way. She placed the headphones in an open space on the old equipment shelf and unconsciously stuffed the paper in her jacket pocket. Her eyes darted to her purse, which lay on the floor of the anechoic chamber. She must've dropped it when she saw Tierneigh.

She held her breath as she slipped back into the test room, grabbed it off the floor, then hurried to follow the EMTs as they guided the gurney down the hallway toward the front doors.

Elise was grateful the rain had stopped, as they approached the back of the ambulance. She watched Chris pull the two back doors open. He and the other EMT positioned the still unconscious Tierneigh in the back of the ambulance, then Chris leapt out onto the pavement, jogged to the driver's side door, and hoisted himself behind the wheel.

He started the engine as he called out to Elise, "You coming to the hospital, ma'am?"

Elise nodded. She turned and signaled to the security guard that she was leaving, then ran around scattered puddles to her car. Sirens and lights were fully engaged now, and she saw the EMT's head through the back window, as he bowed over Tierneigh, grow smaller in the darkened surroundings. It took all her focus to call Tierneigh's sister, Maryelle, stating carefully what happened and that she'd meet Maryelle at the hospital.

Elise willed her eyes on the road and angrily brushed tears off her cheeks as her headlights skirted blurred walls of cornstalks. She flew through the four-way intersections that just that night had intimidated her, temporarily convinced that she'd see headlights if there were other vehicles on the road. She didn't remember much more until she found herself in the Mt. Harmony Hospital's Emergency Department.

Two female medical assistants in royal blue scrubs stared at a wall monitor in one corner. Not far from them, a young security guard sat at a metal desk, focused on some kind of manual. To her right, an older man held his arm in a makeshift bandage as he watched a small television play hospital info ads. The air was close and stuffy. Then she saw her.

Tierneigh's sister stood near a window, arms crossed in front of her. Her face was pale, and she stared through a streaked window at the artificially lit parking lot outside. Maryelle was her friend's sister, just two years younger than Tierneigh, and the feeling was almost dreamlike to see her like that. Elise's memories, since she'd been in Mt. Harmony, were nothing but happy times with Maryelle. This didn't make sense.

They hugged and Maryelle whispered in Elise's ear, "I got here just as the ambulance drove up. They've taken Tierneigh in. I'm waiting for Mom and Dad now." Her tears caused her cheek to stick briefly against Elise's when she pushed herself away. She cupped her hands on Elise's shoulders and looked her in the eyes. "Tierneigh called me, you know, and said she was going to be late getting home." She dropped her arms to her sides, then just as quickly crisscrossed them in front of her. "She was staying with me tonight. Said it'd be closer for the open house at your office tomorrow."

Elise nodded. The office was the last thing she could think of right now.

Maryelle continued. "They said it's going to be awhile…waiting for tests and all. Why don't you go home." It was more of a statement than a question. "You look exhausted."

Elise felt a sudden weakness take over her, as if Maryelle's compassion, in the midst of her own misery, gave her permission to feel, and she couldn't respond.

"Would you like me to call Cole and have him pick you up?"

Elise shook her head and mumbled, "I'm about five minutes from here." She felt her stomach start to shake but got ahold of herself. "Yes, I think I'll go home, but I don't want you here by yourself."

Maryelle pulled a pink encased cell phone out of her sweater pocket and tapped her find-a-person app. "Mom and Dad are going to be here any minute."

Elise thought briefly about staying but just as quickly decided against it. The family needed time together alone. "Okay, but promise me you'll call if you need—or hear—anything."

"I will."

Elise didn't remember the drive home, but feeling secure in her husband's arms provided her emotions the permission they needed to explode. "It was awful, Cole," she said, as they stood by her car in their driveway. "I found her on the floor of the anechoic chamber. She was unconscious, and those stupid cords were around her legs. She must've fallen and hit her head on something."

Cole led her up the walkway, up the three porch steps, and through the open door. They turned right, into their spacious dining room. He helped Elise lower herself onto a beige tweed, cushioned chair, at the dark walnut-stained dining table. A cut-glass vase of sunflowers Elise had placed in the center of the table a few days ago seemed way too cheerful now. She then noticed one of her favorite floral mugs full of chamomile tea waiting in front of her. Her nose was stuffy from crying, so she couldn't smell the calming aroma, but she saw the curl of rising steam and was grateful. She was only mildly upset that it wasn't on a coaster. Deci and Belle, their white, short-haired kitties, trotted toward Elise, heads tilted up and eyes wide. Deci's black markings and Belle's orange markings rippled on their backs as they rubbed against her legs.

"I'm sure she'll be okay, honey. It was good you were there and found her. Maryelle told me what happened."

Elise's eyes darted around her. "I need my phone. Where's my purse?"

"Don't think you came in with it," said Cole, also scanning the space around them. "Must still be in the car. I'll go get it."

She took a sip of tea, then let out a shuddering breath as Cole strode in a few moments later and set her purse on the table, careful of the cats weaving under her chair. "Brought these in, too," he said, lifting an arm with three gift bags dangling from it.

Elise mumbled, "Those are from the training. One's for Lucy, and two are mine. Tierneigh gave me an extra one."

"You need to get some sleep, sweetheart."

"How can I sleep?"

"Finish your tea and come on up to bed. You can read some of the things you brought home." He rifled through one of the bags, pulled out a single piece of paper, and frowned. "Research papers always put you to sleep. The light won't bother me."

"I don't know." Elise wondered if she had the strength to climb the stairs.

Cole watched her finish her tea, then grabbed one of the bags and her purse. He put an arm around her waist. "Come on," he said, as he led her up the stairs to their bedroom.

Elise's head barely hit the pillow when she was soon in a deep, uneasy sleep. In her mind's eye, she saw vague faces coming at her, then veering off at the last second. Voices droned in the background, but she couldn't make out what they were saying. She tried to concentrate, but couldn't understand, and the voices were getting angry with her. Her body jerked and her eyes fluttered open.

"Mroww."

It was a deep, guttural meow. She whispered, "Deci?"

"Mroww."

A clattering racket downstairs, followed by thumping footsteps, made her bolt upright.

She rolled over and slugged Cole's arm.

"Yeee-ow!"

"Cole, someone's in the house!"

The energy Elise lost earlier came back tenfold. She switched the bedside light on and raced to the top of the stairs, her anger taking over any fear for her safety. She flipped the stairway light on and her jaw dropped at the sight below her. The front door was wide open and the braided entryway rug flipped halfway over the doorstep. She grabbed the banister to keep from falling and was halfway down the staircase when she froze again, only to see a dark figure sprawled on the porch steps. They jumped up and ran toward the street.

She pointed. "There!"

But Cole was already past her, running out into the middle of the street. He stopped under a yellow streetlamp and yelled, "Hey!" Both hands were in tight fists, as in a rugby tackle position. The rev of a vehicle could be heard and a screech of tires. Neighbors' porch lights flipped on as they also ran out their front doors.

Cole yelled, "Call 911!"

At least three different neighbors nodded and ran back into their homes. Elise, who had already called the emergency number, disconnected her call and went to his side, staring at his deep red cheeks, puffing like a bull.

He looked at Elise and between puffs asked, "You okay?"

"Yeah…you see anything?"

"Thin. Wearing a hoodie…and dark pants. He jumped in a truck, I think, parked down there." He pointed to a spot a few houses away. "Didn't turn his headlights on, but I'm pretty sure it was a pickup…maybe with a shell."

For the second time that night, Elise found herself talking to emergency personnel. Flashing red and blue lights from a Mt. Harmony Sheriff's car lit up the homes in dizzying oscillations. Neighbors moved inside their homes now and peeked anxiously from their windows, more in response to the breezy chill that was too much to put up with anymore, than anything else.

They watched as Sheriff Noah Reed, who had just been in Elise's office that day, asked Elise and Cole to wait outside while he and his partner searched their home. As soon as they received the "all clear," porch lights clicked off, and Elise and Cole shuffled back into their home.

They stood now, arms crossed against their chests, staring at the two men.

Noah swung his arm in front of his chest. "Looks like the intruder was interested mainly in this room."

Elise and Cole grimaced at two of their beautiful chairs, flipped on their sides, half on the hardwood floor and half on the oval braided rug under the table. The vase of sunflowers on top of the table was on its side, and a trickling stream of water dripped softly off one end. Belle lapped at the puddle on the floor.

Elise whispered, "Belle, no!"

Belle skedaddled to her safe place under the window seat.

The two gift bags lay on their sides, contents strewn all over. Deci batted one of the bouncy balls between her paws. Elise glanced at her dark oak hutch at the end of the room, next to the kitchen door, and strode over to it. She opened the two glass-front double doors, and scanned the glassware arranged inside, then opened the lower cabinet's four doors, but everything looked as it should. The hutch had been a wedding gift from her parents, and she felt very protective of it. "Everything looks okay here."

Noah turned toward Cole. "You kept saying 'he.' Are you sure the person was a male?"

"Can't be certain, but seventy percent of me says yes."

"And you said you locked the front door when you went to bed, right?"

Cole's eyes gazed at the ceiling, and he took a deep breath. "Actually, I'm not sure."

"What about the front storm door?"

"I think we left that open. Really, Noah, I'm just not sure."

Noah turned to his partner. "Could you check the doors and see if they've been jimmied?" Noah had been writing in a small notebook but paused and looked briefly at Cole. "Okay…and you said he jumped in what looked like a black or dark blue truck, but didn't turn his headlights on?"

"Yes. From the streetlights, I could make out the shape of a truck. I think with a shell on it, but that's about it."

Noah continued. "Can you take one more look around and tell me if anything's missing?"

Both Elise and Cole were too tired to do any real search. "Don't think so…at least at this point," said Elise. Her arms hugged her jittery stomach as she scanned what used to be her beautiful dining room.

The new deputy to Mt. Harmony, a man in his midthirties, with short blond hair, introduced as Deputy Ted Bradley, walked back in from the front porch and gave a thumbs up to Noah, signaling that the storm door was okay.

He then pointed to the gift bags and their scattered contents. "What're those for?"

Elise explained the training she'd attended and the usual handouts and promotional items distributed at those kinds of events.

Stone-faced, Noah spoke into the microphone attached to the front of his shirt that connected to the radio on his belt, then focused back on Elise and Cole. "We've got a car in the area that's going to keep an eye on your house tonight. I'll call you if I get any updates. You can call me or stop by the office anytime, okay?

"Thanks, Noah…Ted," said Cole.

"G'night, you two. Oh, Cole. You gonna be at rugby practice Saturday?"

Elise tried to stop her eyes from rolling but didn't quite make it.

Elise insisted they keep the first-floor lights on for the night, and Cole didn't argue. With everything cleaned up now and locks double-checked, Elise and Cole climbed the stairs for the second time that night to their bedroom. Deci and Belle padded behind them.

***

Elise rolled over in bed, reached for her cell phone on the bedside stand, and squinted against the light on its face. Five a.m. Cole's soft snoring changed to gurgling as he rolled over, then eventually to just occasional little puffs.

Resigning herself to no further sleep, she slipped out of bed, slid her feet into gray, well-worn, bedroom scuffs, and padded toward the bathroom. She touched furniture and walls along the way to help guide her in the darkness. Her mind fought with itself to just stay in bed, curled up in a little ball, but today was her open house, and she needed to find out how Tierneigh was.

After a warm shower and hot coffee, Elise felt as ready

as she'd ever be. She dressed in black slacks and a gray crewneck sweater that would be fine with her white lab coat. She wasn't in the mood for any of her colorful fall sweaters but did give in to the burnt sienna maple leaf earrings she bought years ago, to celebrate her first fall season in Mt. Harmony.

She fed the cats and left a note for Cole so he wouldn't double-feed them (a trick they learned worked, if they cried and rubbed against his ankles enough), grabbed the two gift bags they'd left on the dining room table, almost as a dare that they'd still be there in the morning, and started to get into the feeling of her usual morning routine. It was safer that way. Elise readjusted the braided rug in the entryway about a half inch with her toe, took a slow deep breath, and opened the door.

The sky was still relatively dark, and the air was crisp. A streetlamp glowed through her driver's side window as Elise called the hospital while she started the car. She listened to the ringing through her car's speaker, turned on the heater and buckled herself in. Having no luck getting an update on Tierneigh, she sent Maryelle a short text to tell her she was up and to contact her any time, then called Susan Andres's cell phone, hoping she was on her way to work. It turned out, she was already there.

"Elise!" Susan cried into the phone. "A deputy's here, telling me I can't go into my office or the anechoic chamber!"

"A deputy?" asked Elise, stunned. "Where are you now?"

"At work, outside the front doors. I tried to get into my office, but they're not letting me in!" Susan lowered her voice to a whisper. "No one's telling me what the heck happened here last night."

Elise forced herself to relive the events with Susan, about finding Tierneigh and how their coworker and friend was now a patient at Mt. Harmony Hospital. She couldn't bring herself to get into the home break-in news just yet.

"I have to talk to the Mt. Harmony's Sheriff today," said Elise, "so I'll ask if they know what's going on out there. If you find out anything, let me know, okay?"

"Absolutely. Oh, my gosh, today's your open house, and Tierneigh was supposed to be there. I'll go talk to Gloria, the sales rep manager, and see if she can send someone else. She'll probably call you, too, to make sure everything's covered."

Elise heard the whoosh of the lab's front door and figured Susan must've yanked it open. "Thanks, Susan. Talk to you later."

A flutter of nerves crawled through Elise's stomach as she glanced at the car's dashboard clock. Almost seven. About ten more hours to get through, then she could have a good breakdown, but right now, she needed to get to the office. Amy and Lucy were coming in early to set up for the open house, and they needed to know about Tierneigh, and that another audiologist would be coming in her place.

Vivid red, yellow, and orange streaks appeared just above the horizon, but the beauty went unnoticed, as Elise pulled into her office parking space. A few seconds later, Amy's light blue sedan pulled into the space right beside her. Elise gave her business partner a quick nod, grabbed the gift bags, and took a deep breath as she exited the car.

Amy yawned at Elise, then walked with her in silence to Lucy's gray hatchback, where their office manager was transferring trays of goodies from the back seat of her car to a wheeled cart. She slammed her car door shut, grabbed the cart, and took a couple steps, but stopped short when she saw Elise's face.

"What's wrong? You guys had a good time last night, right?"

"Oh, yeah," said Amy. "I'm just kinda tired."

When Elise didn't respond, both Amy and Lucy turned to look at her.

"I've got something to tell both of you," she said, her voice soft, "but let's get inside the office first."

Amy and Lucy exchanged glances, then followed with the cart of food, as Elise unlocked the side door and turned on the lights.

Lucy rolled the cart past her coworkers and into the waiting room, as the two audiologists put their purses and bags in their respective offices, then the three congregated again in the front office area. Lucy plopped down at her desk and turned her computer on, then swiveled to face Elise and Amy, who now were leaning on the raised counter next to her. It was the usual spot where patients stopped to make appointments, pay bills, or just converse.

Elise soberly filled them in on Tierneigh's accident, the break-in at her home, and her conversation that morning with Susan Andres.

"Whoa," said Lucy, rolling her chair backward, as if creating space between them would lessen the impact she felt.

Amy moved to rest her back against a wall for support, her face pale.

Elise slid around the end of the counter and peered at the patient schedule on Lucy's monitor. She glanced between that and her cell phone, reading a text she had just received from Susan.

A new rep, Dr. Ian Peters, should be here soon to fill in for Tierneigh.

She read the message to her friends, then straightened and pointed to the two gift bags she'd placed on the counter next to Lucy when she walked in. "Not that we're in the mood for this right now, but those are gift bags from the training. One's for you, Lucy, and one's just an extra. There's some basic information on the new hearing aid chip you might want to look at."

Lucy slowly stood and took both bags by the handles. "Yeah, I'll check it out. I'll put them up here in the cupboard for now and take a closer look in a few minutes." She placed them on the first shelf of a wall cupboard near her desk and closed the door.

"I want to run over to the hospital," said Elise. "I think we have about a half hour before the first patient comes. Maybe I can catch someone and find out about Tierneigh."

The side door clicked shut before Lucy or Amy had a chance to respond.

Chapter Six

═══ | ═══

Elise found Tierneigh's hospital room with no problem, thanks to a quick text from Maryelle, but she couldn't go in. According to Jen, the midforties, capable-looking nurse assigned to her friend, Maryelle was speaking with the doctor now, and per hospital policy, she couldn't give Elise any information about Tierneigh, even though Jen knew her through the audiology services Elise and Amy provided for many patients there.

"I understand," said Elise, more than a little disappointed, even though she expected it. "Would you please let Maryelle know I came by and ask her to call me if she needs anything?"

Jen patted the pockets of her royal blue scrubs and pulled out a pen and small pad of paper. "Of course, Dr. Harte. What's a good number for you?"

Elise gave her both the office number and her personal cell phone number, even though she knew Maryelle already had them. It wasn't a bad idea for the nurse to have them, too, just in case.

Elise glanced at a round white plastic wall clock in a small waiting area just across from Tierneigh's room, and hurried for the stairs down to the first floor. She had just walked out the hospital's main doors when her cell phone vibrated in her pocket.

"Maryelle! I was just up there. How are you?"

A middle-aged man and woman, smoking under the No Smoking Within 15 Feet of All Hospital Entrances sign, stopped their conversation and gazed at her with half-open eyes.

"I'm okay, I guess," Maryelle said. "They want to do more tests. Said something didn't look consistent with their first diagnosis."

"What wasn't consistent with what?"

"Not really sure. Might be some internal swelling or bleeding. I just have to wait."

"Okay. Please, if you need anything—I'll be at my office, just down the path over there." Elise unconsciously nodded in the direction of her office building. "I can be there in two minutes."

"Thank you, Elise," she whispered.

Elise squinted against the rising sun as she walked the narrow cement path back to her office. A cool breeze felt good on her face as she approached the side door and pulled it open.

Lucy sat at her desk with her back to the door, talking to Amy, who was standing in front of her, on the hall side of the high counter.

Lucy turned when she heard the door, and both women spurted, "How is she?"

Elise's eyes darted through the window to the waiting room. She saw a handful of patients helping themselves to drinks and breakfast goodies, checking brochures and watching the "How We Hear" video on the TV monitor.

She lowered her voice. "Nothing new to report. Doctors are doing more tests. Maryelle said she'll keep us updated. Is the new rep here yet?"

"Good, and yes," said Amy, as Lucy stood and greeted another patient at the window. Amy lowered her voice. "Dr.

Ian Peters is in your office, and the rep manager, Gloria Strauber, called. I told her Dr. Peters was here. She said you can call her if you need anything."

Elise now instinctively fell into professional mode, mind focused on her patients. She tapped the Dr. Downs picture, then jumped when Jake stepped out of the first test room behind her.

"Jake?"

He smiled. "Hello, Dr. Harte."

"Good morning," she said, a little hesitantly. "Is Nicole here? I didn't realize you were coming in today, too."

"They didn't tell you?" He nodded toward the front office, his eyes half-closed. Elise chalked it up to a late night at the training. "Nicole's not feeling so good. She called me this morning and asked if I could come in for her. Hope it's okay."

"Oh…sure," said Elise. "No problem. If you talk to her, tell her I hope she feels better, okay?"

"Will do. Thanks, Dr. Harte."

"And thanks for coming in."

"No prob."

Elise stepped into her office and extended her hand to the smiling man who was standing in front of the off-white wall to her right, sometimes known as the "I Love Me" wall. It was where professionals usually hung their diplomas, certifications, and any other accomplishments patients might want to know about.

Dr. Peters was shortish and thin and in his early forties, from what Elise could judge. He had short blond hair, wore a white lab coat, and reminded her of a scientist/spy she saw once, on an old '60s mystery TV show.

"Hello, Dr. Peters. Thank you so much for stepping in at the last minute."

"It's great to meet you, Elise. Please call me Ian—and I'm glad I'm able to help."

Elise pulled her jacket off and reached to hang it on a hook on the back of her door. She grabbed her white lab coat, just as a slightly crumpled paper floated to the floor.

"I think you lost something here," said Ian. He grabbed the paper and held it out to her.

Elise's mind flashed to Tierneigh lying motionless on a gurney. She smoothed the paper with unseeing eyes, pulled open the middle side drawer of her desk and dropped it in. "Would you like some coffee before we get started?"

Elise's years of working closely with people, learning about their lives, their families and work or home situations, came as second nature now, and because of that, it centered her. She encased herself in her own indestructible bubble when she was with a patient, listening, guiding, and sharing in their personal concerns and achievements as a result of her chosen profession. She didn't have a chance to talk to Amy again until just before lunch, when the last patient of the morning left.

"Next patient's scheduled in an hour," said Lucy. "You all go get some lunch while you can. I'll turn the waiting room TV off." But instead of turning it off, she turned the volume up. "Hey, come here, quick!"

Elise and Amy bolted for the waiting room with Jake and Dr. Peters right behind them.

"Someone must've changed our video to a TV station," said Lucy. "It's the news."

A local news personality was standing in front of the E. S. Hearing Labs building, holding a microphone. "A near fatal accident at this well-known hearing aid manufacturer's headquarters occurred last night, when thirty-seven-year-old, Dr. Tierneigh Brown, audiologist and sales representative, was involved in a reported, fluke accident in the lab's sound-treated test room, also known as an anechoic chamber."

"Near fatal? What a horrible thing to say," cried Amy.

Elise could not pull her eyes from the headshot of a smiling Tierneigh next to the reporter. Her stomach roiled.

"The audiologist was found barely conscious at E. S. Hearing Labs late last night…"

"I'm going to the hospital," said Elise, yanking open the side door and disappearing up the pathway.

"Right behind ya," said Amy.

Breathless from taking the stairs to the third floor, both women hurried down the disinfectant-smelling hallway, but stopped short when they saw Sheriff Noah Reed with Grady Weber, reporter for the Mt. Harmony Herald, in the small waiting area across from Tierneigh's room. Grady was leaning forward, attempting to catch Noah's every word. In response, a solemn-looking Noah took a step backward.

"Sheriff Reed…Noah…what's going on?" Elise glanced at the reporter and nodded. "Grady."

Grady, in his signature white shirt and bow tie, had interviewed Elise and Amy numerous times over the years, regarding hearing and balance issues.

Noah opened his mouth to speak but stopped himself. He turned to the young reporter. "I'll talk to you later, okay?"

"Oh…sure, Sheriff. Bye, Dr. Harte. Dr. MacNeal." He nodded, then turned and loped down the hallway, glancing back at the group a couple of times before stepping onto the elevator.

Noah turned toward Elise and Amy as soon as the elevator doors closed. His amber eyes drilled into each of them in turn. "This has to stay between us, and I'm not kidding, alright?"

They nodded solemnly, eyes frozen on him.

"I'm here because the paramedics thought the cords around Tierneigh's legs weren't normal."

Amy's eyebrows shot up. "Is that all? That's an occupational hazard for anyone who works in those sound-treated rooms. Sheesh, I fell just the other afternoon. My ankles got tangled in the cords when I was just trying to pick up in there."

"I know, I know, but listen up here." He stared at Amy. "I shouldn't be going over this with you, as it is."

"Sorry," she whispered.

"The EMTs notified the Bluestem deputies because the scene looked suspicious, and they called us." His eyes shot over to Tierneigh's hospital room door. "She was brought to Mt. Harmony because they could treat her head injury better here…and possibly, for her safety."

Elise couldn't take her eyes off Noah. What was he talking about? She forced herself to stay quiet.

Noah's eyes darted between the two women. "They're doing more tests on Tierneigh. She had two head wounds. One from hitting her head on one of the speakers, and…"

"And?" prompted Elise.

"And one consistent with blunt force trauma. Someone intentionally hit her."

"I need to sit down," said Amy, one hand on her stomach.

Noah extended an arm toward three beige, molded plastic chairs close by. Amy sat with her head down, hands clasped in her lap. Elise sat next to her, her own hands clenched in fists on shaking knees.

"Someone hit her?" Elise could barely get the thought out. "What do you mean?"

"Means we have more to investigate. We're in constant contact with the Bluestem Sheriff."

"I appreciate you telling us, Noah," said Elise.

Noah nodded slightly. "I'm telling you, so if anything comes back to you about that night, you need to give me a call. And I knew, with you so close by, you'd want to keep an eye on her. Also, until we can get more information, you two need to be careful, understand?"

"I think so," said Elise.

Amy looked up. "Me, too, I think. But, Noah, what does this have to do with the cords around Tierneigh's legs?"

Good question, Elise thought, as her eyes searched Noah's face.

"We're not sure...yet. Like you said, Amy, it might've just been an accident, but the EMTs didn't know that. Their concern brought up other issues, which is where we are now." Noah stood just as his radio buzzed. He reached for it, nodded a goodbye to the women, and headed toward the stairwell.

Elise and Amy watched him leave, then rose to their feet and slowly headed for the elevators. They walked back to their office, contemplating in silence what they'd just heard. When they reached the side door to the office, Amy grabbed the handle and swung the door open, but both froze at the sight in front of them.

Jake's eyebrows shot up from his bent position over the two gift bags, their contents spread all over the counter. His hands slapped to his sides like iron to magnets. "Oh...hi. Uh...just wanted to see what...uh...you all got last night."

Elise broke her stance first and stepped into the office. "Didn't you and Nicole get gift bags, too?"

Amy followed, as she eyed the office manager's chair. "Where's Lucy?"

"Uh, she should be back anytime." He lifted his arm in an awkward gesture toward the front door. "Had to take some paperwork for a patient to the MD's office across the way."

Elise opened her mouth to ask why he didn't take it

over, when the front door swung open and scheduled afternoon patients entered the office. Jake immediately manned the window. "Hello, Mr. Hildebrand? Welcome! I have a little paperwork for you, if you'd please fill this out and sign the last page. Dr. Harte will be right with you." He repeated the same greeting for the next patient, who was scheduled with Amy, handing both patients clipboards with paperwork and pens.

Elise and Amy glanced at each other, then headed for their respective offices.

The sun had set and the darkness outside, with the lights on in the office, allowed Lucy to assess her reflection in the glass front door. She saw her contented smile, even after the long and busy day.

"Hey, no food left," she called out. "I think today was a success!"

"I think we did well, too," called Elise from her office, a little less excited, under all the circumstances.

Amy stepped into the hallway from her office and opened her mouth to talk when a sudden thunderous pounding shook the office.

"Oh, my gosh!" yelled Lucy.

The three scuttled to the side door in time to see Jake's black pickup screech out of the parking lot with head-splitting, low-frequency stereo noise emenating from its speakers. Lucy turned back to her desk and pointed to her cup of tea. "Look! My tea's still vibrating!" The top of her tea shimmied in circles to the beat of the music.

"Remind me to get on him about that ridiculously loud music," said Amy. "He knows better than that," she added, referring to the damage he was probably doing to his hearing in real time.

The noise receded as Jake drove further away, and Amy took a deep breath when the quiet returned, though she was still perturbed. "And by the way, what did you think about him and those gift bags?"

Lucy's head jerked toward Amy, eyebrows raised. "Gift bags?"

Amy filled her in about catching Jake rummaging through the bags when she and Elise had returned from the hospital.

Lucy's eyes widened, and she waved a hand in the air. "I was wondering what happened. I came back from the MD's office and saw him putting the bags back up on the shelf. Didn't he and Nicole get their own bags last night?"

Elise looked at her. "That's what we asked, too, but he never answered."

"Weird," was all Lucy could say and picked up her purse.

"Oh, and I meant to ask," Elise added, "why didn't you have Jake deliver the paperwork instead of you going?"

"I was going ask him, but he'd just stepped into the restroom, so I decided to take it over myself. I thought I'd be back before the patients came, or at least he'd be here to greet them."

"Yeah," said Elise. "He was. It was okay. Thanks. Goodnight, Lucy."

Lucy waved and stepped out into the darkened parking lot, lit by a few black metal lampposts.

"Hey, I'm coming, too," said Amy, running after her to catch the door. She paused and turned with concerned eyes. "Goodnight, Elise."

Elise's eyelids drooped and the corners of her mouth raised slightly. "Have a good night, Amy."

Peace and quiet. She clicked the lights off and, for a moment, enjoyed—if that was the right word—a moment of quiet reflection. A blue-gray glow filled the office from the muted outside lights but gave enough illumination for Elise to make her way to the waiting room. She let out a breath and lowered herself into one of the cushioned chairs and closed her eyes. Occasionally, at the end of a day, she allowed herself a moment of solitude like this, and if she'd admit it, a little pat on the back for the business she and Amy built and how much she appreciated it. Under normal circumstances, it was gratifying.

A few moments later, she inhaled, slowly pushed herself up out of the chair, and headed for her office. Time to go home. Elise wondered if she should call Maryelle, or wait, knowing that Maryelle would call with any updated news. She decided she'd wait and picked up her purse and workbag that she'd left on her desk.

She took a step into the hallway and reached for the back doorknob just as she felt her purse vibrate. Ugh, she thought. Her sense of obligation winning out, she turned, flipped the light back on in her office, threw her things on the desk, and pulled the phone from her purse, thinking now that it might be Maryelle herself. She was right, but for some reason, her body stiffened at Maryelle's face smiling back at her. She didn't like the feeling that jolted through her.

She tapped the speaker with her thumb. "Maryelle?"

Ragged sobbing made her stomach crunch as she lowered herself slowly into one of the patient's chairs in front of her desk.

"What's wrong? What happened?"

She heard a slow intake of breath. "My sister…she's gone."

Chapter Seven

Friday Evening

Elise disconnected the call after Maryelle convinced her not to come over, saying she had calls to make and just wanted to be alone. Elise felt numb. She stared at one of the framed pictures on her office wall of a country field with rolled bales of hay, the ends of which resembled shapes of ears. As much as she appreciated the humor, it always mildly annoyed her. The ends were shaped as left ears. Where were the right ears?

Rap, rap, rap.

Her body jerked, and she caught her breath. Rap, rap, rap. Down the hall, through the now ominous shadows of the darkened waiting room, a figure loomed on the other side of the glass door.

She forced her wobbly legs to move, touching the hallway walls with one hand to steady herself, until she recognized Noah Reed's squinting eyes, his finger pointing to the door handle. Elise flipped the light switch on and unlocked the door. He brushed by her, hat in hand, then turned to face her.

"Saw your car outside." His face was pale, and he ran a hand across the top of his buzz-cut hair. "By the look on your face, I guess you've heard."

Elise responded with a blank stare.

Noah grasped her elbow and guided her toward one of the chairs. "You alright?"

Her head snapped up. "Of course, I'm not!" She decided not to apologize and glanced at her hands in her lap.

Noah softened his voice. "Listen, before you hear it on the news or someplace else…"

Elise raised her head. He looked so official.

"We're pretty sure that Tierneigh was hit with a heavy rounded object…something that left brown-painted flecks around the wound. Also, we know the basic type of person we're looking for. I can't go into the details right now, but we're confident we should nail this thing down soon."

Elise felt lightheaded, her eyes struggled to stay focused on him.

"Oh, and one more thing. Did you talk to Dr. Susan Andres today?"

Her eyebrows lifted. She tried to swallow, but her mouth was too dry. "Briefly. This morning. We were so busy today, and every spare minute I had, I—I…was talking to Maryelle, or I was over at the hospital."

Noah continued. "The test chamber where Tierneigh was found is staying sealed as a crime scene. Whoever did this intended to harm your friend."

Elise caught her breath.

"We found a note in Tierneigh's office from Susan Andres, asking Tierneigh to come to her office ASAP." Noah leveled his eyes at Elise. "Do you know anything about that?"

"No, I don't. Not really."

"What does that mean, Elise?"

"It means I don't know." She thought hard before continuing. "There might've been something going on with the acoustical engineer, Rick Dayton. Susan was a little concerned about it, maybe."

Noah pulled out a small notepad and pencil. "Is there anything else I should know?"

So much ran through her mind in what seemed like a millisecond. How could Elise tell him that Susan seemed distant to her. Could Susan actually have hurt Tierneigh? And if so, why?

Elise looked at a flickering shadow on the wall as a breeze shifted some of the taller prairie grasses outside. "No, Noah. Not that I know of, right now." The usually soft ringing in Elise's ears sounded like the town's tornado sirens during a storm. She pressed the heels of her hands against her eyes.

"I have to ask you, Elise," said Noah, lowering his voice. "Is there anything you're not telling me, that Tierneigh might've said, specifically about Dr. Susan Andres?"

Elise felt a tickle of sweat run down her back. She didn't move. She didn't talk.

"Okay," said Noah. "Just take care of yourself and tell me if you remember… anything."

Saturday Morning

A thin line of light peeked between the drapes, and Elise could make out the golden glow of the maple tree she and Cole had planted outside their bedroom window when they bought the home twenty-plus years ago. The leaves shivered from a sudden gust of wind, and she subconsciously shivered with them. Then she noticed a warm spot that shifted slightly on her chest.

"I'm sorry sweetie," she whispered to Deci, lifting the limp, warm kitty to another spot on the bed. It was then that she noticed the other side of the bed was empty. Cole must've slept in Becky's old room.

She slipped her feet into her slippers and dragged into

the bathroom with the anticipation of a hot shower clearing her mind.

About a half hour later, Elise pulled on a pair of worn jeans and her husband's old Mt. Harmony football sweatshirt, then checked to see that Cole was, indeed, asleep in their grown, and now moved out, daughter's room. She had tossed and turned alot last night and barely remembered Cole saying something about sleeping in the other room. He was there, and so was Belle, comfortably curled up against his side with one foreleg extended on his chest. Elise noticed what looked like a small smile on her face.

Deci padded downstairs with Elise, then leapt onto the window seat in the dining room, ready to watch her leave.

"Be back in a bit, sweetie."

Mrowww.

She petted Deci, grateful for how much he calmed her. Both cats were short-haired and mainly white in color, but Deci was a little larger, with more black markings, and Belle, with more rusty-orange markings. They were both beautiful and well-loved.

The early morning glow had changed to a "chimney-ash gray," as a local weatherman had once called it, accompanied by sporadic rain. Elise noticed a light on at The Vibe when she drove by, but no customers were there that she could see. She wasn't in the mood to talk to anyone anyway, so drove directly to her office, where she knew she could be quiet and think. She somehow wasn't surprised to see Amy's and Lucy's cars in the parking lot, and actually felt comfort and gratitude for the women she was lucky enough to work with.

"We had a bet that you'd come in," said Lucy, a slight grimace on her face. "We heard the news last night." She and Amy had pulled chairs together in the waiting room, and Lucy met her at the door with a hot mug of fresh-brewed coffee.

Elise saw red-rimmed eyes when she gratefully accepted the mug and breathed in the warm aroma. The three sat in a triangle, taking turns looking at each other in their makeup-less faces and barely combed hair. Lucy and Amy looked like they'd grabbed the first things available to wear as well. The only real light was what spilled through the reception window by Lucy's desk.

"I don't know about you, but I'm mad…and scared," said Amy. "Do we have any idea what was going on with Tierneigh? The news last night said Susan's office and the anechoic chamber are crime scenes!"

Elise could barely speak. "Tierneigh and I kept missing each other. She tried to tell me something at the end of the training." She straightened her back. "But I do know one thing. Something was going on with that engineer, Rick Dayton." Her eyes squinted. "The way he glared at Tierneigh. She looked scared to dea—" She stopped and swiped at a tear.

"I think we need to tell Sheriff Reed about that," said Lucy through clenched teeth. She had taken her shoes off and pulled her stocking feet up on the chair, hugging her knees close to her.

"Actually, I did mention it. Maybe not everything, though." Elise told them about Noah stopping by the office just before she left last night.

The other women nodded their approval.

Amy asked, "Should we tell Noah about the CEO guy, what's-his-face?"

"Theo Wrightman," said Elise. "Remember what Kristin said at the training? She was surprised that Theo'd been at E. S. Hearing Labs for four years already. But I wasn't sure what she meant by it."

Amy filled them in. "Seems there were rumors about Theo bouncing between different companies. Something maybe to do with drugs or something, I think."

"Great," said Lucy with a sarcastic tone.

Amy shuffled over to the coffee pot and held it up with raised eyebrows. The other two raised their mugs, and Amy brought it to them and filled each one up to the top.

"While we're on strange things," said Elise, taking a sip, "what again was the deal with Jake yesterday?"

Lucy jerked in her seat, coffee sloshing over the top of her mug. Amy grabbed a paper towel from a few torn sheets she had brought out and handed her one. "Oh! I forgot to tell you about Nicole!"

"Nicole?" asked Amy, sitting back in her chair once again. "What's she got to do with Jake?"

"I called her yesterday before I went home to ask how she was feeling. She wanted to know what I was talking about, so I told her that Jake said she was sick, and she laughed!"

Elise stared at her. "I don't get it."

"She wasn't sick!"

"What?" Elise and Amy's heads jerked toward her at the same time.

Lucy continued. "Nicole said Jake called her and said that you, Elise, said we didn't need her!"

Elise stared at Lucy. "Why would he say that? And how could she believe we wouldn't need her on an open house day? You're sure that's what she said?"

"Oh, yeah. I was just as surprised."

Elise leaned forward. "And there's still the thing with Jake and the gift bags."

"That was weird," mumbled Lucy.

Amy threw her a sideways look. "What hasn't been?" She straightened in her chair. "They're still here, right? The bags?"

Lucy slowly stood, mumbled, "Think so…" She shuffled

to her desk area and the cupboard just to the left of it.

Elise and Amy followed. They watched Lucy pull the two bags down and, one by one, shake them upside down. Bouncy balls rolled off the counter and broke into flashing colors when they hit the floor, far from amusing this time.

"I don't see anything out of the ordinary, do you?" asked Elise, fingering a red plastic ear-tipped pen as the other two shook their heads.

Lucy said, "Do you think this has anything to do with the break-in the other night at your house, Elise? Wasn't someone going through the gift bags at your place, too?"

Elise felt her stomach squeeze. "No idea, but there's one thing I do know. I'm going to find out what the heck is going on here!"

"I'm with you," said Amy, stern-faced.

Lucy nodded, eyes wide.

"Okay," said Elise, scooting forward on her seat, eyes bouncing between the two women. "First, we have to deal with Jake. I don't think we should confront him just yet, even though that's what I really want to do."

"Why not?" asked Amy. "Him acting like that makes me feel creepy. Especially with someone breaking into your house and all."

Elise nodded. "I need to talk to Susan first. But I don't want Jake in this office anymore, that's for sure. Until we can rule this out as some kind of an innocent thing."

The three started to unconsciously pick up around themselves as they continued to plan.

"Lucy," said Elise, "would you call Jake and Nicole and tell them we won't need either of them next week. I think they've got tests coming up at school that they can be study-ing for, anyway."

"Sure," said Lucy. "If you don't mind, I'd like to stay a little bit this morning and finish up some paperwork from yesterday. I'll make the calls to Jake and Nicole."

"Thanks," said Elise.

"Amy, let's you and I figure out a time to get out to E. S. Hearing Labs and see what else we can find out."

"I'm pretty full with appointments next week," said Amy. "I don't mind going but I might be able to help better if I stay here and see some of your follow-up patients, too."

"Thanks…both of you." Elise forced a slight smile. "Lucy, don't stay long."

***

Elise's burst of determination continued by the time she walked through her front door. She could hear Cole in the kitchen, and the warmth of breakfast smells snuggled around her like her favorite knit poncho on a cool fall afternoon. They walked into the dining room at the same time, Elise from the front entryway and Cole from the swinging kitchen doors in the back of the dining room, wiping his hands on a yellow-and-black-striped dish towel.

"Veggie omelets, extra crispy bacon, blueberry crepes, and dark roast coffee," he said to her unvoiced question. "How're you doing, sweetie? I've been worried about you."

"It smells really good in here," she said. "I wanted to check on the paperwork from yesterday's patients and I…I really just wanted to think. But guess what. Amy and Lucy were already at the office, so we ended up talking a lot of this out."

"Good, I hope it helped. Sit down and I'll get breakfast right out."

Elise pulled out a chair as Cole brought the food to the already-set table. She picked up her fork and looked grate-fully at the spread before her, even though her stomach wasn't quite on the same wavelength, but Cole had gone to so much trouble…or had he? She squinted at the forkful of omelet she held in front of her.

"This looks an awful lot like breakfast from Lake 'n' Bacon."

Cole winked. "It does?"

Elise tilted her head and winked back. She remembered how he always liked to impress her, especially when they'd first dated as students at UC San Francisco. Elise was in the Doctor of Audiology program and Cole in a Master's of Civil Engineering program. They met through Elise's father, who taught civil engineering classes. Cole said later that he saw Elise's picture on her father's desk and knew he had to meet her. After graduation and marriage, they moved back to Cole's hometown of Mt. Harmony, Illinois, when he was offered a position as senior project manager for a major firm based out of Chicago. Cole's position put him in the research and development branch located in Springfield, where a coworker talked him into joining a local rugby team, and where he also met Noah Reed. Elise and Cole's, now twenty-four-year-old twins, Becky and Jon, were born in Springfield, soon after the move from San Francisco.

Elise took a bite of the omelet, closed her eyes, and asked, "Do you know if the kids are still coming for dinner tonight?"

"Yeah. I spoke to them this morning. They're worried about you."

The rest of breakfast was spent quietly, after which, Elise felt a sluggish fatigue take over her body. "I'm going to go lie down for a little bit, okay?"

"Absolutely. I've got rugby practice soon, but I can stay home…if you want me to."

Elise looked at her husband's sad, droopy eyes. "Of course not. I'm okay. You go."

Cole gave her a kiss on her forehead. "I'll have my phone

with me, if you need me."

A few hours later, Elise awoke to voices downstairs. She checked the time on her phone and was surprised to see it was late afternoon already. Activity caught her attention, and she could hear Cole and the twins, Jon and Becky, discussing wonderfully mundane things, like the weather, and unfortunately, Mt. Harmony High School's disappointing defeat in the state's football playoffs.

"What's for dinner?" Jon leaned toward his mother to give her a kiss on the cheek when she descended the stairs.

"Hi, Mom," said Becky, from the dining room. She had flipped on the farmhouse-style chandelier and turned the dimmer down. "How're you doing?" She walked into the entryway to give her mom a hug.

"I'm not sure if I'm numb or in a dream or what. I'm glad you came over," Elise said. Her not-quite-identical twins stood in front of her now, with concern on their faces.

Both were slim with straight, brown hair and Cole's hazel eyes. Jon, who worked as an IT specialist in the field of computer support technology, stood a few inches taller than Becky and wore his hair short. Becky, currently in nursing school, had a more heart-shaped face, her hair falling past her shoulders.

"I'm so sorry about Tierneigh," said Becky, as they walked into the dining room for a pizza and salad dinner that Cole had just set on the table.

"I know we were getting together tonight to talk about your grandmother's birthday party," said Cole, looking at his kids. "And as worried as we are about what recently happened, I think it'll be good to still focus on that. Let's have some pizza and try to kick back a little, okay?"

The kids nodded and took their usual seats around the table. Elise thought she'd give it her best try.

"Actually, Becky, how's school?" asked Cole, beating

out Jon for a slice of pizza.

"Pretty good. I brought my computer over," she said, wiggling her eyebrows at her brother. "I was hoping my wonderful tech brother could take a look at it. There's a lot of online work to do, and I'm having trouble with the school's platform."

"Sure," said Jon, lifting a steaming slice of pizza to his mouth. "What classes are you taking?" He took a bite, a cheese string hanging from his mouth and mumbled, "Yumm."

"I have Wound Staging and Wound Care Lab," she said with a devilish smile.

Jon covered his mouth with his hand and pretended to gag.

"Family time can be so precious," sighed Cole, looking at his pizza a little differently.

"Sounds interesting, honey," said Elise.

Becky grabbed her phone. "I have pictures!"

"No thanks!" Elise, Cole, and Jon all said at the same time.

"Grandma's having her pre-party get-together tomorrow afternoon…and it's already down to one week before the real thing," said Elise, forcing herself to get into the mood. "So how about each of you telling me where you are in the planning? I'll start. The Lake 'n' Bacon said we can get in a couple hours early to decorate, and I had to order a larger cake, because there's over sixty people coming now. I'm hoping one of them is going to be Aunt Ida. Jon, you getting any closer to finding her?"

"I'm trying, Mom." He twirled a pizza slice on his plate with his index finger. "I tracked her to a hotel in New Zealand, but phone and internet service was really iffy." He looked at his mom then with a little more hope in his eyes. "I finally got through yesterday, but I guess she had already left. The hotel person thought she was going to Singapore next. I tracked down what steamer that should've been and left a lot of messages and emails."

"Your grandmother would be so happy if you could find her sister!"

"I know, Mom, I'm trying."

Cole raised his hand. "I've got the country band confirmed—a small group from a town south of here—and they're sure they can get the sheet music for her favorite song."

"You're kidding," said Jon, straightening his back. "You mean, 'I've Got Tears in My Ears from Lying on My Back in My Bed While I Cry Over You?' "

"The very one!" said Cole, over everyone's laughter. "Sung by Homer and Jethro. It's a classic!"

Elise smiled, and the muscles around her chest and back started to relax.

"Okay," said Becky. "Everyone remember, I have a school project that has to be turned in the day before the party, so I'm doing my best, but, Mom, I'm gonna to try to make it to Grandma's tomorrow, too."

"Aha! I knew the excuses were coming," teased Jon. He ducked as a limp pizza crust whizzed by his head.

Becky stuck her tongue out at her brother then turned to her mom. "I've got almost everyone checked off for what they volunteered to do."

"Good," said Elise. "The Lake 'n' Bacon is providing iced tea, soda, water, and the lunch buffet, of course. And Amy said she'd help with the decorations, too."

They continued a few more minutes of general updates, until Becky looked at Jon with exaggerated blinking. "Can you pleeease, look at my computer now, before you have to go?"

He hung his head. "I guess. Let's go upstairs. It shouldn't

take long."

Cole and Elise did a quick clean-up and took mugs of decaf green tea into the living room just across the front entryway, on the other side of the house. Elise switched on a lamp at the end of a gray and beige tweed couch, then curled up on it and hugged a throw pillow with an embroidered H in the middle of it, a Christmas present from her mother-in-law. She stared at the flames in their new gas fireplace, while Cole took a seat next to her.

"I know I've said it each time we do this, but I love this fireplace," he said.

They both paused a minute, admiring the seven-foot wide, white painted-brick fireplace. A beveled oak mantelpiece almost filled the width, with large glass hurricane candleholders on each end. Family pictures and knickknacks dotted the area in between with Cole's pride and joy hanging above it…a fifty-seven-inch TV. Of course, Elise had pictured beautiful wreaths for the different seasons in that spot, but eventually gave in and had to admit she did enjoy it. And yes, rugby games could be watched from the dining room.

Elise stared at the fire. "I like the fireplace, too, but part of me misses the old one, with the crackling and the ashes and everything."

"This one crackles! And look at the great fire we've got in just seconds!" Cole reached for her feet, put them on his lap and massaged them, one at a time. For the next half hour they didn't talk much, and when they did, kept it to small talk. It was nice to relax and hear their grown kids bantering upstairs like they did when they were teenagers…until an ear-piercing scream let loose.

Belle, who'd found a comfortable spot on Elise's lap, dug her claws into Elise's thighs and tore off like a shot to one of her usual hiding places.

"Yeow!" Elise cried out, grabbing her leg as Cole walked

to the foot of the stairs.

He grabbed the banister with one hand. "What's going on, you two?"

"Jon wrecked my computer!" Becky stomped down the staircase with both hands splayed, her brother following, scowling.

"Calm down, I did not," said Jon. "You haven't upgraded your computer. And on top of that, there're bugs. Chill already, okay? Let me take it back to my place tonight, and I'll have it ready for you soon as I can."

"I can't! Assignments have been posted that I need to get into. Daaaaaad!"

"Listen," said Cole, holding up a hand in a stop position. "Let's go look at my laptop and see if you can get in. If so, you can use mine 'til Jon's able to get yours back to you, okay?"

Jon and Cole climbed back upstairs with Becky stomping behind them. Elise closed her eyes, a hint of a smile on her lips.

Chapter Eight

Sunday Morning

Red and green combines rumbled across acres of corn-fields, dotting the scenery in their signature manufacturers' colors, perpetuating the ever-present competition between the companies. Earthy brown dust billowed around seven-foot-high tires, as the grain combines slowly plowed in long, straight lines, back and forth across the fields. Amy always took the opportunity to explain to anyone who'd listen, that the front "snoots" divided the stalks as they picked them up, pulled the ears of corn off each stalk, and fed them into the combine. The empty stalk was then dropped back onto the ground to replenish the soil and serve as a cover crop against erosion. Elise was mesmerized each time she saw the process and found out early on that the harvest didn't stop for Sundays.

Elise and Cole lived on the southwest side of Mt. Harmony, in one of the town's smaller neighborhoods, which butted up against acres of farmland. The contrasts between that life and growing up in such an expansive and active city as San Francisco was equally as interesting and exciting for her, and she was grateful for the experiences. She wasn't quite sure if she and Cole would ever move again, but right now, couldn't imagine anyplace else.

The morning was cool as the sun rose in a cloudless sky. A mild breeze confirmed that Elise's jog would be tolerable, as she stepped off her front steps and zipped up her hoodie. To her right was a two-lane road that separated her neighborhood from acres of cornfields. She chose to turn left and jog through the neighborhood this time, past houses that characterized some of Mt. Harmony's more established two-story homes, with attics, basements, and large front porches.

Elise approached the first intersection that led to the center of town, when a softly fluttering banner, attached to one of the wrought iron lamp posts lining Main Street caught her attention. She slowed to read the notice for the Mt. Harmony Fall Festival, and it seemed that today was the last day. It was early, but she was sure people would be there, so decided to go and check it out. But first she needed to jog one more block over, so she could pass the Coneflower Drive Apartments, where her daughter lived. She didn't intend to wake Becky, but sometimes, she couldn't help being a mom, and just seeing the apartments made Elise feel like she was sort of checking up on her daughter without anyone, meaning Becky, knowing. She could only get a partial view of her daughter's apartment, but that was alright.

Before she turned onto Becky's street, she glanced briefly in the opposite direction toward the church and adjacent cemetery, and pressed her lips together feeling a little disrespectful if she smiled. Decades ago, the town put up a "Dead End" sign at the turnoff to the cemetery, since it was the only road in. It was a source of amusement to the schoolkids, and she never had the nerve to ask anyone the actual history behind it. Someday she'd find out.

Elise jogged past Becky's apartment and appreciated the plethora of gorgeous purple and deep red coneflowers for which the apartments were named. The first time she saw these flowers, she thought they looked like daisies with the center pushed up and the petals pulled backward away from the centers. She learned they were one of many native prairie flowers and made sure she had some around her own home.

Feeling content that all was well with her daughter, Elise continued into town and around the corner onto First Street. She was just two blocks from downtown, when she saw rows of beige canvas tents lining all four sides of the town square. Idling trucks and vans clogged the streets, and merchants scurried to stock their goods before opening time, but found they had to compete with early morning lookie-loos that bobbed this way and that, hoping to get a jump on the best deals of the day.

As Elise drew closer, she heard a high-pitched voice call, "Dr. Harte! Dr. Harte!" She turned to see two smiling women in their late seventies strutting quickly toward her, carrying large purses and empty sacks. They wore matching powder blue sweat outfits with patches on their left shoulders depicting a silver jack and small red ball. The phrase "Jacks of All Trades" was embroidered above it.

"Hello, Mrs. Dean, Mrs. Thompson. Beautiful morning, isn't it?"

"It certainly is," said Mrs. Helen Dean, adjusting the bags on her arm.

"Yes, it is," agreed Mrs. Anne Thompson. "And please, call us Helen and Anne, right, Helen?"

Helen nodded. The women were sisters who lived next door to each other with their respective husbands of over fifty years.

"I'm waiting for that craft tent over there to open." Anne nodded toward a young woman hanging colorful fall wreaths on a tall, white lattice board. Stalks of sunflowers rose from an old silver milk can that had been placed on the ground near the outside edge of the board. "I got the cutest silk flower arrangement in a ceramic pumpkin there for my daughter, and I decided to come back and get myself one."

"Really? I'll have to go check them out," said Elise, gazing at the colorful display.

"We're so sorry to hear about your friend, Dr. Harte," said Helen, adjusting her glasses and squinting. "It's just so awful."

Elise felt a shot of pain in her stomach and gently pressed a hand against it. "Thank you. Yes, it is."

Helen leaned so close to Elise that she could smell the powdery floral scent of her White Shoulders perfume. She spoke low, between tight lips. "Do you know the story, yet? I just can't believe something like that could happen so close to us."

Elise pressed her lips together, knowing she was witnessing the birth of the next subject for town gossip, and decided to take a more guarded route. "No, nothing yet. By the way, how's the jacks tournament coming? I see you're wearing your team sweats. Do you have a game today?"

"No game today," said Anne, her short gray curls swaying as she shook her head, "but maybe practice." She flexed one hand open and closed as if warming up.

Helen nodded at her sister. "And we have a couple of newbies coming. We're doing an 'Intro to Jacks' for them to explain the game and all."

Elise chuckled. "My girlfriend and I played jacks when we were young. By the time I got to 'six-ies,' my hand would be sore from scraping the ground to pick up the jacks. We usually played on the cement playground."

Helen rolled her shoulders back and lifted her chin. "Well, we have tables now…and they're regulation height, you know."

"'Regulation height'? I didn't know there was such a thing," said Elise.

"We figured we had something to say about that, since

getting down on the ground just doesn't make it for us any-more," said Anne, laughing.

"Ever since Anne and I started this a few years ago, it's taken off! And we have our husbands to thank for that!" Both women pursed their red lipsticked mouths and nodded. "This all started years ago, as a joke to get back at them for spending so much time with their sports, that we decided to get our own!"

Anne's eyes widened. "Next thing we knew, we had teams and sweats and official game jacks and balls. And our first full tournament's coming up! Of course, we'll be indoors at the community center."

Helen spouted, "It's been a blast! When are you going to join?"

"One of these days, I'm sure." Elise laughed. She loved the joy and adventurous attitudes of the sisters, and for a few brief seconds, felt somewhat like herself again. "You two en-joy the festival." She picked up her jog once again, as the two women headed toward the craft booths.

Elise found herself melting into the sights and smells as she passed aproned men leaning over smoky grills, adjusting the flames under their cauldrons of soups and chilis. The bursts of warmth calmed her as she passed each station. Scents of cinnamon wafted from tables of homemade apple pies, and baskets of squashes, pumpkins, and assorted fall vegetables delighted her. But the atmosphere still couldn't quell the mild throbbing in her head.

She had intended to jog straight home, but instead, found herself at the corner of First Street and Cardinal Lane, looking at her own reflection in the glass front doors of the Mt. Harmony Sheriff's Department.

"Dr. Harte, Elise, I almost didn't recognize you," said Noah, as Elise closed the door behind her. He looked her straight in the eyes. "How are you doing?"

"Okay, I guess. I didn't know if someone would be here." Now feeling a little self-conscious in her black leggings and old UC San Francisco hoodie, she hesitated. "If you're busy, I can check back later."

"No, I'm okay." He pulled a bottled water out of a small fridge behind the front counter and held it out to her.

Elise smiled her thanks.

He raised an arm toward the room across the hall, grabbed a pad of paper and a pen from the front desk, then followed her into the room and flicked on bright overhead lights. "We don't have a receptionist today, so I need to keep an ear out for the front door."

"Of course. I won't keep you long, Noah. Just wanted to see if you knew anything more about what happened." She sat down at a four-foot-long metal table and took a drink of water. A trickle of sweat snuck between her shoulder blades, and she glanced briefly at the pale yellow walls. "And to tell you about some funny things that…"

"Funny?"

She shook her head. "I mean odd, I guess, but first I have a question for you." It was something she needed to know and had to ask before she changed her mind.

Noah nodded and waited for her to speak.

"What exactly happened to Tierneigh? I didn't want to ask Maryelle. You said before that there were two head wounds."

"Yes. The evidence is pointing to something heavy hitting her on the upper corner of her forehead." Noah lightly touched the spot on his own forehead with his middle finger. "The force made her spin and fall, making her hit her head again on one of the speakers in the anechoic chamber."

Elise felt lightheaded and reached for the water bottle again. She gathered the strength to ask one more question. "Was there anything from the first head wound that tells us what it was that hit her?"

"We don't have the complete medical examiner's report yet."

"Okay." Elise put her hand over her mouth. After a few seconds, she took a breath and slowly got out what she, Amy, and Lucy had discussed the day before, about Rick Dayton and Jake's odd behaviors. "What's bothering me is how Tierneigh was acting. Something was upsetting her that she wanted to tell me about, and it had to have happened on the day of the training."

"Why do you say that?" Noah asked, scribbling on his notepad.

"Tierneigh and I always talked. Even when she traveled." Elise pulled her feet back under her chair.

"She traveled a lot?"

"Yeah, that was her job. Tierneigh was an outside rep for E. S. Hearing Labs, meaning she has a territory assigned to her. She covered about four to five states in the Midwest." Elise waved an arm in the air. "Indiana to Nebraska to Kentucky, and traveled to offices that dispense E. S. Hearing Labs products. She supported the audiologists with training and helped with patients who had more involved problems with hearing loss. Like making recommendations about the lab's hearing aid styles and settings. Those kinds of things."

"Sounds like she was a busy lady," said Noah, turning to a blank page.

"It can be a tough job, mostly because of so much travel and the long days, but she and I usually stayed in contact. A lot. I talked to her at least once a day in just the week before our open house."

Noah stopped writing and looked her in the eyes. "So what changed?"

Elise shook her head, fighting rising tears. "I don't know.

Tierneigh was looking forward to being back in Mt. Harmony...seeing her friends and her sister." She blinked quickly. "We were both excited about getting together, right up to the morning of the training. But something changed, and I don't know what it was."

"Elise, we've already talked to the people out at E. S. Hearing Labs, but I think I'm gonna make another trip." He looked down and flipped through his notes. "What time again did Tierneigh call you that night?"

Elise stared at him. More to delay thinking about that night than anything else. Then she pulled her phone out of her sweatshirt pocket, swiped it, and stopped. "Exactly 9:39 p.m."

"And you got back to E. S. Hearing Labs about ten or a little after?"

"Yes. I went upstairs to Tierneigh's office first, but she wasn't there. I got back down to the first floor and Susan's office about five minutes later. I guess you can check with 911 for an exact time I called them from the landline."

"Think a minute, Elise. You didn't see anyone except the lab person at the front door and the security guard when he brought the EMTs in, but did you hear anything? The person who attacked your friend must've been close by."

A chill shot up Elise's back, and she straightened in her seat. "All I focused on right then was Tierneigh."

"One last question, okay?" Noah closed his notebook and his face relaxed. "Do you know why Tierneigh didn't want to meet you somewhere else? Why did she want to talk at the Hearing Labs if something was bothering her so much?"

"I...I don't know." Elise's head started pounding, and she put a hand to one temple.

I know this is hard, but we're going to find out what happened. Please, leave this to us." Noah stood up and flashed a grin. "And what about this birthday party I'm hearing about?"

"Oh, the party," said Elise, a little less enthusiastically than she meant. She rose slowly from her seat. "You're invited, too, you know."

Noah chuckled as they walked to the front door. "Thanks. I know you've got a lot on your plate, but just be careful, okay?"

"Noah, please let me know what you find out."

His face sobered. "I will, as I can."

Elise nodded and set out for home, glancing only briefly in the direction of the 150-acre park that, in total, surrounded more than a mile of Lake Harmony shoreline. Off to the right, she could see part of the Lake 'n' Bacon restaurant, where her mother-in-law's birthday party would soon take place.

She turned right onto Cardinal Lane and jogged past the train station, then past the high school, a blue and white flag flapping in the breeze by its front entrance. Next came the empty football field, and Elise pictured the night games with bright lights in a clear, dark sky, which she especially enjoyed. The school's band played in her mind, as well as the "yays" or "awwws" of the crowd. She smiled at the square of advertisement on the scoreboard that read "Go Cougars!" on one line, with "Mt. Harmony Hearing and Balance Center" just below it. They were perfect evenings.

Puffy floating clouds seemed to come out of nowhere and cast moving shadows on the fields of green soybean plants and yellow-brown cornstalks, mesmerizing her. It was so beautiful.

The road narrowed, and in a few minutes, she turned back onto Rivers Lane and home. Her circle was done and now in the past, but she didn't kid herself. The conversation with Noah was firmly in the present.

***

The car's tires crunched when Elise turned off the country road, at the mailbox marked "Harte," and onto the graveled drive. She was glad she had her sunglasses on—the sun was so bright—and wondered again if her car's suspension system would hold out one more time.

A small smile pulled at her lips, as she eased her car to the front of her in-laws' farmhouse and parked next to Amy's and Becky's cars. This afternoon was going to be just what everyone needed, but she hesitated, closed her eyes, and sent a thought to Tierneigh that she wished she could be there, too. Was it her imagination, or did she perceive a voice say, I am.

Elise opened her eyes at the rumbling of a combine in the distance, steadily making its way over 450 acres of corn. That must be Frank. Her father-in-law said he'd be harvesting today so the house would be free for the pre-birthday-party meeting. She smirked slightly. As if he really wanted to be there.

For a couple seconds, her mood changed for the better, as she admired the mums and pumpkins displayed around the front of the white, two-story home. A porch extended from the front, around the right side of the home, with more mums placed strategically along the railings. A sunflower wreath hung on the front door.

She exited her car just as another car crunched up the drive. Elise smiled and waved at Lucy, who added her car to the row. Together they climbed the three wooden steps to the front door, knocked, and walked in.

Amy and Becky, looking comfortable in jeans and sweatshirts, were in the midst of holding up dresses on hangers and ooh-ing and ahh-ing over which one Catherine should wear, but stopped mid-spin and smiled when they saw Elise and

Lucy.

"There you are," broadcasted Elise's mother-in-law. A floral house dress with a full-length zipper down the front covered her slightly plump figure, and most likely was for ease of removing it to try on dresses. She sat on one end of her sable brown, comfortable-looking couch, obviously enjoying every minute. Tops and bottoms of white gift boxes with tissue paper lay on the couch next to her.

"Elise, come in here and tell me what you think."

On cue, Amy and Becky jumped in front of Elise, shoving their respective dresses in her face.

"Whoa!" Elise laughed, hands up in defense. She glanced around the room and sat on a matching love seat, that created the "L" shape with Catherine's full-sized couch. A round, orange and brown crocheted pillow felt comfortable against her back. The light yellow walls were cheerful, somehow different from the interrogation room's yellow walls at the police station. She wondered why.

An antique marble top table snuggled in the open spot between the ends of the furniture and supported a shaded, beige, ceramic lamp. Two framed pictures were displayed in front of the lamp, one of Catherine's parents, dressed warm in heavy coats, standing next to an older-model, green and white Buick, and the other, of two smiling young women—Catherine and her sister, Ida—sitting on the front steps of the farmhouse, minus the fall decorations. They looked to be in their late teens, wearing jeans and sweatshirts, each holding a cat, one gray and one black.

Next to that, was a picture of Catherine and her husband, Frank, wearing brightly colored shirts and white pants in front of a monstrously large banyan tree, leis around their necks. The trip to Maui had been a long-awaited vacation for their fiftieth anniversary. There was a slight glint on Catherine's glasses, her thin lips in a wide smile. Her short, gray hair was frizzed, probably from the humidity. Frank's painter's brush mustache hid his teeth, but his smile could not be denied. His high forehead, due to a receding salt-and-pepper hairline, was sunburned.

Two metal folding chairs were set up across from the couch, a coffee table between them, with a lone wooden rocking chair by a side window, that looked over the side porch to the barn and cornfields.

"Well? The red one or the blue one?" Catherine's eyebrows raised as she turned to question Elise.

"As if you're not going to pick your favorite color?"

"The red one?" Catherine laughed in mock surprise.

"Awwww," Amy said. "The blue one's so pretty, but I guess you win, Becky."

Becky danced in a circle, holding a red dress out at arms' length, while laughter erupted from the group.

Elise recited the updates from her family dinner the evening before, especially about Jon's close calls with finding Aunt Ida.

Amy, still standing, smiled at Catherine and nodded at one of the pictures on the marble-top table. "You said your sister grew up with you here in Mt. Harmony, right?"

"Yes, I did. Right here on this farm. Our mom was so darn worried when it looked like Ida wouldn't marry...you know how it was in those days, but Ida persevered. I always thought it was her crazy sense of humor that saved her. She played so many tricks on people that I thought they were happy to see her start traveling."

"Was it really that bad?" Amy sat down now, next to Elise.

Catherine threw a hand up in the air and laughed. "Oh, you bet. She once threw bird seed up on crabby ol' Mr. Kershwin's metal roof on the front porch. You never heard such a racket! Ida said she didn't do it...and no one actually saw who did it, so…"

"Oh, no!" said Amy, clapping a hand over her mouth, laughing.

"Ida couldn't wait each year for April Fool's Day," Catherine continued, enjoying the audience. "But we got used to the usuals…like petroleum jelly on the doorknobs and telephone messages to call Mr. Ly-en with the number to the Chicago Zoo on it."

"What started her traveling?" Amy asked, still laughing.

"An old school friend dared her to take a trip on what they used to call a 'tramp steamer.' Now they're known more as freighters or steamships that take passengers. They tend to travel to exotic places and for less money than the usual cruise ships."

"Sounds like someone else I know, who can't refuse a dare." Amy's eyes slid toward Elise.

Elise stared back. "Who…me?"

"Didn't Cole tell us one time how you all went to a night baseball game when you were in college, with a bunch of friends? You ended up at a nearby, very historic hotel with seven floors, wasn't it? And you went down an indoor chute that was used for a fire escape?"

"Oh…well, somebody kinda dared us."

"Uh-huh…my point!"

Lucy, who had taken a seat in one of the folding chairs, leaned forward. "What happened? I didn't hear about this one."

Elise relaxed slightly at the welcome memory. "Well…we decided that rumors of the fire escape we'd heard about needed to be checked out…and, uh, ended up on the top floor near a square hatch in the wall, near the floor."

Amy prodded, "Go on." All eyes were riveted on Elise.

"Well, one of our friends went first, and I was second. You had to sit on the floor and push the hatch with your feet.

The chute was so steep, my feet dangled straight down, and I almost didn't do it, but somebody pushed me, and I was down at the bottom in a shot! I remember it being pitch dark, and I was straight as a board, my arms pressed against my sides for dear life, actually shooting past slits of light at the different floors. Then I remembered..."

"Remembered what?"

"That there were five more people behind me, and we never checked to find out how it ended! Some of the guys were big, and I pictured the bottom doorway locked and those big bodies slamming into me!"

Lucy bounced on her seat. So what happened?"

"Well, like I said, we hit the bottom fast. There was a flap door...and we rolled, literally rolled, out like human cannonballs, onto an asphalt parking lot. An attendant was standing there in his black pants and white shirt, very nonchalantly pointing his finger at each one of us, counting, as we rolled out."

Lucy said, "And you didn't get caught...beyond just the attendant seeing you?"

"No. I remember wondering why the moon was bouncing all around in the sky, though. Guess I was dizzier than I thought! We high-tailed it, everyone zigzagging as we ran through the parking lot, toward one guy's old paneled truck, and took off."

Catherine laughed and her glasses slid down her nose. She pushed them up with her index finger. "Sounds like something Ida would've done! Lucky you all weren't hurt!"

The doorbell chimed, and Becky jumped up. "I'll get it." She peeked out the front window and waved the woman in. "It's Deborah, Grandma.

They grinned their hellos as Catherine's neighbor, a short, mildly rotund woman, walked in, rocking side to side with each step. Her gray hair tightly curled next to her round head.

"Darn hips. I see most everyone's here," she said, plopping down with a breathy ugh on one of the metal folding chairs, which let out an ominous screeching sound. She put a large, cat-hair-covered carpet bag on her lap and rummaged through it while the others watched. "There they are," she mumbled, pulling out a wadded ball of tissue with one hand. She held it out to Elise. "Dr. Harte…Elise…I knew you'd be here. Could you please look at these for me?"

Elise tentatively reached for the crumpled tissue and carefully pulled the corners open. Two hearing aids lay inside.

Deborah looked Elise straight in the eyes and firmly announced, "They aren't working!"

"Oh…I'll check them at my office tomorrow, if that's okay, and give you a call with what I find out."

"That'd be perfect, honey, thank you. I was hoping to have them for the birthday party. They have one of those systems at the Lake 'n' Bacon that my hearing aids can work off of, so I can hear what's going on better."

"Yes, the loop system," Elise said, referring to a means of hearing speech more directly, usually in public venues, using the telecoil in one's hearing aids. "I know the restaurant installed it pretty recently, and it's been so appreciated."

Becky stood. "I'm going to grab some more iced tea. Can I get some for anyone?"

Lucy's hand went up. "Me! Wait, I'll come with you."

"I'd like some, too, please," said Deborah, with a grateful smile.

Amy turned to face her, knowing that watching faces helped if there was a hearing problem, and spoke just a touch louder. "Deborah, I heard your daughter might be visiting soon, is that right?"

"Marcella? I mean Marcie…that's what she wants to be

called now. As a matter of fact, yes. She's coming back to Mt. Harmony in a couple of days, and she'll be here for Catherine's birthday party. I was so happy about that."

"That's wonderful!" Catherine sighed, her eyes in an unfocused stare. "I remember when she was just a baby." She jerked back to the present, as Becky carefully walked in from the kitchen, eyes focused on the tray she carried, full of tall, emerald green glasses of iced tea.

Deborah accepted a glass, took a sip, and smacked her lips. "Now, I've got quite a few decorations I can bring for the party, if you still need them. And did I tell you what I heard about that neighbor of mine, Elmer Knolls?"

That got the conversation headed toward the latest town gossip, with party preparations sprinkled here and there. The group never brought up the incident at E. S. Hearing Labs, for which Elise was very grateful.

Eventually, the antique grandfather clock by the front door announced the time with four deep bongs.

"Oh my gosh," said Amy. "I need to go. Have to figure out what we're doing for dinner. Troy's helping a neighbor with the harvesting." The hint was taken. Glasses were gathered and taken to the kitchen and the extra chairs folded up.

"Thank you all," said Catherine with a big smile, her shoulders jiggling. "I'm so excited!"

Elise smiled back at her. "It's going to be fun. Tell Frank I'm sorry I missed him." She gave Catherine a kiss on her cheek.

The group waved goodbyes to each other as they climbed into their respective vehicles, revving their engines to life. It reminded Elise of the start of a mini-Indy car race as they followed each other down the pitted dirt drive to the main route, and back to their respective homes.

Chapter Nine

═══ 1 ═══

Mt. Harmony Hearing and Balance Center
Monday Morning

"Your first patient's here, Dr. Harte," said Lucy, peeking around the doorjamb into Elise's office.

"Susan's still not answering her phone," Elise mumbled to herself, clunking the phone's handset back into place. "Thanks, Lucy."

About forty-five minutes later, Elise finished the diagnostic test protocol and directed her patient Alan, and his wife, Lyla, into her office to review the test results. Elise explained the different aspects of each subtest, what the overall results indicated, then the implications and recommendations for any other possible referrals.

"I had no idea you could tell so much from just a hearing test," said Alan, a sixty-eight-year-old, retired schoolteacher. He was shortish, with thinning brown hair, and had an engaging smile.

Elise thought he must've been the kind of teacher that everyone wanted for their class. She was lucky enough to have had one for her high school biology class, but never realized then that even great teachers had challenges that could affect their lives and cause hidden depression.

"Well, I guess this is making sense now. My wife's been

on me for years…and the kids and grandkids make fun of me." His eyes dropped to the clenched hands in his lap. "They don't mean to be hurtful, but I found myself not wanting to be around them anymore. I get words mixed up, and they'd laugh. I'd ask them to repeat what they said, and they'd just roll their eyes, so I quit being around them." He glanced sideways at Lyla. "I pretend I don't hear 'em at all, so they'll just leave me alone."

Elise could hear the hurt in his voice. "Alan, believe me, you don't know how many times I've heard that." She leaned forward. "And I appreciate you bringing your wife in today."

Elise let Lyla hear what hearing loss, like her husband's, sounded like by way of a computer simulation.

She looked at Elise and frowned. "I didn't know…" Then Lyla expressed some of her own concerns, such as not understanding how Alan could seem to hear her one time, but not another.

"We hear a range of frequencies…or pitches…with vowels generally in the lower pitches and consonants in the higher pitches."

Alan and Lyla both nodded, following the information.

"If someone has hearing loss in the higher pitches, they can't hear certain consonants, but can hear the vowels fine. That's why people might think a person doesn't really have a hearing problem…because they still hear low-frequency sounds, but can't understand the exact words."

Elise reached for a small, sturdy gray box and snapped it open. "I have some hearing devices I'd like to try on you, Alan, so you can hear what it sounds like. They've been programmed according to your test results."

Elise fitted the devices to Alan's ears. He watched her raise a paper between them, so it blocked his view of her lips. She spoke at an average volume. "Alan, was there much traffic out there this morning?"

Behind Alan, his wife rolled her eyes and mouthed, "He won't hear you."

"No, not bad," he answered, speaking at a normal volume.

His wife's face froze, eyes wide. "You heard that?"

Alan kept his eyes on Elise. "Of course, I heard that."

Elise put the paper on her lap and continued with her recommendations for hearing devices, noticing that Alan was relaxing and nodding his head. She explained strategies for him to use in different situations, as well as strategies for family and friends. It was the last part that he was uncomfortable with.

"I'm not going to ask them to do anything. They'll just laugh at me."

"We'll take one thing at a time, Alan. The first is to order these new hearing devices for you and give you time with them. Remember how I said you can pair them with your cell phone so you can hear whoever's talking right up through the hearing devices?"

Alan stared at her, the corners of his mouth curling up in a smile.

Elise continued. "As well as the TV…and a whole lot more that we'll be going over when they come in. And you've got the advantage of that new chip that's been released from E. S. Hearing Labs, but in the end, this is going to be your decision, okay?"

"Okay, Dr. Harte. I'm going to trust you. I'll give it a try." He straightened his back and raised his head. "So when am I going to get these things?"

Elise smiled as she removed the demo devices and spoke a little louder, looking directly at him. "Thank you, Alan. I'm grateful for your confidence in me. And in answer to your question, very soon. Let's go find Lucy and make the next appointment."

A few hours later, with reports from the morning now completed, Elise turned her attention to evaluating the hearing aids Deborah Miller had given her at her mother-in-law's pre-birthday-party get-together. She took care of the obvious things first, like cleaning and checking them for moisture, which could cause the devices to work intermittently, then checked the specific components, and finally, compared computer read-outs with the results from Deborah's most recent audiological evaluation.

Amy stopped at the doorway. "Are those Deborah's hearing aids?"

"Yeah."

"They looking okay?"

"So far so good. I'm going to recommend she come in for an updated hearing eval though, to check all the bases...make sure nothing's changed."

"Good idea," said Amy. "I'm heading over to the hospital cafeteria for a quick lunch. Want to come?"

Elise checked her desk drawers, wrinkled her nose, and said, "Sure."

"Also, I had a cancellation, so I can take your afternoon patients if you need to do anything." Amy raised her eyebrows at Elise, guessing she had a few things in mind to do with E. S. Hearing Labs.

"Actually, yes, that'll help." Elise reached for her office phone. "Give me a second. I'm going to try Susan again right now." But, again, the research audiologist didn't answer, so Elise left a message that she was driving out to the labs after lunch, in hopes of talking to her.

The walking path to the hospital was surprisingly quiet. No other people at the moment at all. The sun was warm and beautiful and both Amy and Elise took advantage of the few minutes of peace, with their hands in the pockets their lab coats, walking in quiet and their own thoughts. The over-sized hospital doors swooshed open automatically as they approached, and it was then that they finally saw a few other people. Two older women in dark pink smocks with "Volunteer" pins attached to their lapels accompanied a wheelchair with a woman holding a newborn, a pink balloon tied to one of the back handles. They couldn't help but smile, and at the same time, couldn't help the feeling of satisfaction knowing the baby had had her hearing screening done.

A tall, middle-aged man stood at the information desk to their left, talking animatedly with a cranberry-smocked hospital employee. Elise and Amy veered right, toward the back of the lobby, when Elise suddenly slowed her pace. The gift shop. She loved hospital gift shops. So many cute little things to look at. But then she remembered Susan and picked up her pace again. Amy was already at the top of the stairs, hand on the banister, twisting to see where Elise was.

"Coming."

Amy chuckled. "I figured it was the only way to get you past the gift shop…if I just kept walking."

"Aha! Now I know your trick…it won't work next time."

When they reached the bottom of the stairs, they continued straight, down the cream-colored corridor, then left down another corridor.

Elise cocked her head. "So here's where everyone is."

Low rumbles of conversation, dishes clanking, and the familiar squeak of employees' rubber-soled shoes on the highly buffed vinyl flooring became louder as they neared the cafeteria. They breathed in warm smells of cooked food and tried to identify what was on the menu for the day.

Amy sniffed. "Meatloaf?"

Elise shook her head. "I think chicken pot pie."

They passed a small bank of vending machines for hot

and cold drinks, two microwaves, and two refrigerated cases with premade sandwiches and desserts for those in a hurry, or for when the cafeteria was closed. They approached the propped-open double-glass doors, and quickly surveyed the day's offerings, as well as how long the lines were. The shortest line was at the "hot food" bar.

"Must be the meatloaf," Amy mumbled.

They immediately turned in the direction of the salad bar and got in line. Amy handed Elise a gray fiberglass tray, and they both gathered paper plates, napkins, and plastic-ware as they shuffled forward, looking ahead at the salad choices.

Just ahead of them, a tall-statured nurse turned, pressed her lips together, then said, "Dr. Harte, Dr. MacNeal...I heard the news about your friend! I'm so sorry."

Elise felt her stomach knot. "Hi, Bethany. Thank you."

Bethany grabbed the tongs, lifted lettuce onto her plate, but froze mid-lift. "Do you know what happened? Dr. Harte, I heard you were the one who found the woman on the floor of that creepy test room!"

Amy glanced at Elise, then turned to the nurse. "There's really not much we can say right now."

"Oh, I understand." She took advantage of her captive audience for a few more seconds, just in case one of them changed their mind and decided to tell her something, but then gave up and dropped the tongs back into the lettuce. "Just know we're all thinking of you."

Elise was grateful for the concern. "Thank you, Bethany."

Heads down now, Elise and Amy got through the line, then took the short walk to the cashier.

A woman in her fifties, wearing a pink hospital smock and matching hairnet, sat on the edge of a tall stool in front of her cash register, both feet resting on the cross bar beneath her. One hand, covered in a clear disposable work glove, hovered over the register.

Her eyebrows raised as Elise and Amy approached. "Dr. Harte, Dr. MacNeal!"

Elise smiled. "Hi, Lynn, how are you?"

"I'm fine...but how are you two? I heard what happened!"

"We're working through it, Lynn. Hey, saw in the Herald that your daughter got an award in her science class! Tell her congratulations for us!" Elise didn't like taking advantage of a situation like that, but it did help get them through the checkout without further conversation about Tierneigh.

They finally took a few steps into the dining area and searched the room for a place to sit. Luckily, the majority of people had left with their lunches, so it was easy to find a table to themselves.

The dining area was small compared to most larger hospitals, with about twenty tables of varying sizes. The walls were painted white on the top half and taupe on the bottom half. Large yellow sunflowers were painted on the top half, in an attempt to brighten up the windowless eating area, which was where Amy got the idea for sunflowers in their own windowless testing room back at their office.

"I guess we could've gone back to the office to eat," said Amy. "But then you run the chance of getting interrupted with work or a phone call or something."

"Yeah. It's okay. People care...that's the main thing. Guess I didn't think word would get around so fast. Then again, it is Mt. Harmony."

They finished their lunch in peace, then headed back to the office.

After a quick check for phone messages, or any other pending work, Elise exchanged her lab coat for her black lightweight jacket, and found herself again on the back road to Bluestem and E. S. Hearing Labs. The drive gave her time to think of how she was going to approach Susan with her questions. It bothered her that Susan had hesitated telling her about Tierneigh at the training, and couldn't believe there'd be anything to it. But, at the same time, just couldn't shake the way she felt.

The transformation at E. S. Hearing Labs was remarkable. Even though Elise had been there before, the way it looked today was a far cry away from the way it had looked the night of the training. No decorations, gift bags, or food and drink tables. Just an average manufacturing plant with employees scurrying down halls and the sounds of elevator doors dinging open and closed. Elise noticed updated pictures on the walls that she must've missed the other night, of smiling people wearing E. S. Hearing Labs products, next to plexiglass displays of awards over the years for design, style, and function of the products.

She stopped at a smiling picture of Dr. Tierneigh Brown from a year before, receiving her award for "Sales Representative of the Year."

Elise felt her eyes start to water, but caught herself when she heard her name called.

Tessa looked more relaxed today, in black jeans and a red cowl-necked sweater. "You wanted to see if Dr. Andres was available, correct?"

Elise swallowed as she walked toward the receptionist. "I did, thank you."

"She's testing right now, in one of the smaller booths. She should be done in about ten minutes or so."

"Okay. I'll be right back then." Elise decided to find a restroom, so turned down the south hallway, toward the main training room, where they'd gathered just a few nights before.

As she approached the door, she could hear women's

voices echoing inside, talking louder than usual, as people tend to do when they were the only occupants.

"Yeah, it was crazy," said one voice. "So then, Mr. Wrightman said they're watching Dr. Andres and…"

Elise froze, wanting to hear more, but another woman was approaching, and she didn't want to look suspicious, so she pushed the door open.

Two young women, wearing white lab coats and protective glasses on small cords hanging from their necks, stood in front of the mirrors, washing their hands, looking at each other in the mirror as they spoke. Both were petite, one with long black hair pulled into a low ponytail, and the other with very short brown hair and glasses.

The woman with the ponytail abruptly pressed her lips together and glanced at Elise without saying anything more. Both women then turned to the automatic hand dryers. Elise smiled briefly at them when she entered the room, but they shot each other a quick look and dropped their eyes to the floor.

Elise crossed to the nearest sink and pulled a comb out of her purse, using the mirror above the sink to watch them, but was disappointed when the women scooted out the door without another word.

A few minutes later, Elise walked back toward the reception desk and checked the time on her cell phone. Still some time. No one was at the desk, so she decided to walk up the north hallway to find the testing room where Susan was supposed to be working.

"Hmmm," she mumbled when the CEO, Theo Wrightman, strode out of one of the smaller test rooms next door to Susan Andres's office, still draped with yellow police tape.

"Hello," Theo mumbled as Elise approached him.

His white shirt and tie from the training had been replaced with a red polo shirt with "E. S. Hearing Labs" embroidered over a chest pocket. He paused, unwrapped a stick of gum, and popped it in his mouth. Elise noticed he was frowning, his gaze focused just past her shoulder. She positioned herself slightly to his side, so she could look down the hall without being too obvious, to see what he might be looking at. The only person was the ponytailed lab tech from the restroom, waiting for an elevator.

Elise turned to face Theo and held out her hand. "Mr. Wrightman. I'm Dr. Elise Harte. I was here for the training the other night."

He nodded at her, seemingly still deep in thought, but Elise continued, her hand still extended.

"I had a few questions about the new chip that I wanted to ask Dr. Andres about, and she said I could stop by. Do you happen to know where she is?" Elise knew any conversation she and Susan might have eventually could come back to the chip, so she didn't feel she was lying.

"Oh...well...glad to meet you." He didn't seem to notice her hand, so Elise slowly pulled it back to her side. "I think she's down the hall just a little further, in one of the other test rooms." He nodded toward the bank of heavy doors that lined the far hallway.

Elise took another tactic. "Thank you. I also wanted to tell you how awful we all feel, for what happened here with Dr. Brown."

"Doctor who? What?" This time he looked her in the eyes.

"Dr. Brown. Tierneigh Brown."

"Oh, yes, yes." He puffed out his chest. "It's really going to put us in a bind now with this new chip dropping. The timing of this business is scheduled to the second. We don't need any more problems."

Elise couldn't hide her disgust if she'd wanted to. The

icy stare she leveled at him made its point.

Just then, a weighted test room door swung out into the hallway and thudded against the wall. Elise heard Susan's voice drift out into the hallway.

"There ya go," said Theo, wagging a hand toward the door, leaving Elise gawking at his retreating back.

She tried to temper her shock at his reaction to Tierneigh's attack and forced her attention back in the direction of the research audiologist's voice.

"Thank you again for coming in, David. I appreciate it. This went well today. I can't explain the previous test results we got, but today's are in line with what I would've expected."

A man stepped backward out of the test room and into the hallway. Elise, who had walked up to the test booth, found herself right behind him and quickly raised both hands in defense, touching the back of his heather pullover, to stop him from knocking her over.

He jumped, caught his balance, and twirled around. His quarter-zipped collar was slightly askew, and he reached to straighten it. Elise noticed his close-cut beard and recognized him as the person who'd been talking to Tierneigh at the training. David Nubrey, she thought. An MBA student and one of the test subjects for the new hearing aid chip.

"Oh, I'm so sorry!" he said. "Are you okay?"

"I'm fine." She smiled. "It's my fault. I didn't pay attention to how close I was to the door."

"Dr. Harte," said Susan, "you've met David, right? I mean formally, not from literally bumping into him just now." She laughed, knowing they were both alright. "He's one of our volunteer test students from the university."

"Sort of," she said to Susan, then turned to David. "I saw you the other night at the training, but we didn't get a real chance to meet. It's nice to see you again."

David smiled and cocked his head. "You're Becky Harte's mom, right?"

Elise stopped short. "Becky? Yes, she's my daughter."

"That's what I thought," he said. "Well, I won't hold you." He then turned on his heel and strutted down the hall toward the reception area.

Elise stared after him. "Huh," she said, then turned toward the research audiologist. "Have a couple minutes?"

"Yes, I do," said Susan, as she opened another weighted door and waved Elise into the patient's side of the hearing test room. "Just have to straighten up a bit."

Susan sidestepped her way around the booth, straightening cords and cleaning the usual headphones and other equipment, before rehanging them on wall hooks.

"I'm sorry to interrupt you," said Elise. "I know there's a lot going on. But first, how are you doing?"

"I think I'm still in shock. About losing Tierneigh, and the fact that something like that could actually have happened...here." Susan lowered herself into a black, cushioned chair. She tried to blink tears away. "I feel like a robot in here, just going through the motions. Are there any updates?"

"Not that I'm aware of. And I check constantly." Elise leaned her shoulder against one of the steel gray, acoustically treated walls. "I hate to bring that night up, but...can you tell me the last time you actually saw Tierneigh?"

Susan stopped winding headphone cords around a wall hook and closed her eyes. "I had that small group of people you saw, showing them the anechoic test chamber just before the training started. Tierneigh came to the door and asked if I'd seen you or Amy. I told her I hadn't...and that was about it."

Elise pressed further. "Did she say anything else? I got the distinct feeling something was upsetting her."

"I agree." Susan raised her eyes to Elise. "I got the same

feeling, but no, she didn't really have a chance. I think I told you before that Rick Dayton stepped up behind her, and Tierneigh jumped about a foot, then told me she'd be back later and took off." Susan's eyelids dropped slightly. "So you never talked to her, either?"

Elise shook her head, deciding how much to say, wondering at her own hesitation. "We never had a chance to talk. There were so many people around. So what's the deal with him anyway?"

"Who, Rick?" Susan's eyes jerked to the floor, then back up to Elise. "Rick and Bob Bell, you know, the head accountant here?"

Elise nodded.

"They've been getting pretty friendly lately, which is unusual. For a while, I thought it was my imagination, but then I found out other people noticed it, too. They never used to hang out with each other, and maybe it's all this hype about the new chip and all, but they've been acting pretty chummy all of a sudden."

Elise's eyebrows lowered. "I'm not sure I understand what you're saying."

"Rick and Bob were never that great of friends, but lately, they've had their heads together, and they'd stop talking when anybody came close to them. I hate to sound paranoid, but lately, I felt like they've been watching me...and maybe even Tierneigh, but I don't know why."

That got Elise's attention, remembering what she just overheard in the restroom. "Why would they be watching you two?"

"No idea," answered Susan. "It's just been creepy. I chalked it up to all the pressure lately." Susan paused, as if deciding whether to say something more or not. She lowered her voice. "The chip was released, you know...before some of the final test data was finished."

Blood drained from Elise's face. "What?"

Susan continued. "I wanted to recheck some of the results, but they weren't happy about me delaying everything, with the training and the big release happening."

"Results...like, from patient error or something?"

Susan stared directly into Elise's eyes. "Actually, a lot of random errors...across different test subjects. Things just weren't consistent, and it's not like it was just one person, or all of them. Follow-up results didn't jive with the original results after I applied the statistical designs. I looked for patterns...outliers...anything, and asked a few people back for retests. But then Rick started asking questions." Her eyelids dropped slightly, and she frowned. "We work closely with each other because of the acoustic support I need, especially for the anechoic chamber."

Elise's eyes narrowed. The look in Susan's eyes made her uneasy, as she continued.

"Then, all of a sudden, Bob's down here questioning me, using some of the same words Rick was, so obviously they'd been talking to each other. And it's the way they talked to me. Like they didn't trust me, or they thought I was hiding something. I'm trying not to be paranoid, but they were just plain creepy. And, Elise...I'm telling you this in all honesty...I know you're promoting this chip at your business...and what I was uncovering could be consequential to you. I'm so sorry."

Elise couldn't feel her legs, or her arms. She spoke while she could still talk, trying to convince herself there was an upside to this somewhere. "Maybe there's a reasonable answer." She stared out the open door. "Maybe..." But she stopped, not able to think of one.

Susan's eyes dropped to the floor, but the intensity in her voice rose. "It got even creepier when I talked to one of the lab techs a few days before the training. She said Rick and

Theo were in her part of the lab one morning, and she heard them talking. She was at her station, working on some custom ear plugs, and heard them say something about me and Tierneigh, but she won't tell me what it was."

"Did you confront them? Rick...or Theo? Ask what the heck was going on? Which lab tech was it?"

Susan forced a laugh. "Hey, you get a private eye license along with your audiology one?"

"Sorry, this is upsetting."

"I know...I know... The tech's name is Addison. Dark hair, petite...like a size two or something. Early twenties. And no, I didn't talk to Rick or Theo yet. It shook me up too much."

Elise met Susan's eyes. Elise paused, deciding what else to tell her. "You just be careful...and speaking of weird, I was just talking to Theo in the hallway."

"Really? What'd he...?"

Squeeeech.

Neither woman moved. Their eyes locked on one of the wall-mounted speakers and the recognizable sound of rigid chair casters, scraping against a linoleum floor.

Chapter Ten

Susan turned her head away from the window that separated the two sides of the test booth and mouthed to Elise, "The microphone's on," referring to the two-way communication system that can be activated from the audiologist's side of the test booth.

Elise leaned forward to look through the window, but the lights were out, and it was too dark to see anything. She bounded out into the deserted hallway and yanked on the chrome handle of the audiologist's side of the booth. Empty.

She clicked the black desk lamp on, so Susan could see her from the other side, grabbed a black headset with an attached microphone and whispered, "Susan. Can you hear me?"

"Yeah...through the speakers. And you can hear me, right?"

Elise nodded. "Did you leave the sound field mic on when you finished testing?" She referred to the two-way speaker system.

"I always turn it off...the minute I'm done with a test," said Susan, who had now come to the door and stood staring at the knobs and buttons on the audiometer. "At least I think I did."

Elise stepped into the hallway again and jerked her head both ways. No one was visible, but something on the floor caught her eye. It was a small, shiny, half-crunched foil paper.

Elise picked it up as Susan stopped beside her.

"Gum wrapper or something?" asked Susan.

"Looks like it. Do you remember seeing it when you were last testing in here?"

"This floor was clean," said Susan, a concerned look on her face. "Someone was in here listening to us."

Elise could only nod. She stepped back into the audiologist's side of the booth and noticed a small desk clock next to the audiometer. She tried to shake off the disconcerting feeling invading every inch of her body and mumbled, "It's later than I thought." She looked at Susan and put more effort into her voice. "Do you know if Gloria's upstairs? I need to ask her about the change in sales reps. Ian Peters came out to help us with the open house, but he didn't know if he could add us to his already full client list."

"Not sure," said Susan. "You know where her office is?"

"I think so. Elevator to third floor, where the other managers' offices are, and turn right…then it's on the left…right?"

"Yeah, but no." Susan chuckled. "Second floor. They put her there to be closer to the reps. Everything else is correct. This really burns me up, though. I'll let you know if I find out who our eavesdropper was. Be careful, okay?"

"I will."

Elise decided to take the stairs instead of the elevator, since it was closer and quicker, and reached the second floor in less than a minute, but stopped short when she saw someone ducking under police tape to exit Tierneigh's office. David Nubrey!

She held her breath and watched as he stepped out into the hallway, glanced briefly around him, then strode quickly toward the elevators holding a yellow folder in his right hand. Her first reaction was anger, that someone was intruding on Tierneigh's domain, and she wasn't there to defend it.

She pushed the door open, causing a click, then a whoosh sound from the pneumatics attached to the top. David jerked his head slightly toward the sound but caught himself and picked up his pace.

Elise caught up with him as he stepped into the elevator, and their eyes met briefly as the doors slid shut. She stood frozen, deciding whether to follow him, when a woman stepped out of an office just past the elevators and on the other side of the hall from Tierneigh's office. Elise recognized Gloria Strauber, the woman from the training. She remembered the short, chestnut hair and wispy bangs that hung just above her eyes and didn't think too much about it, but noticed that, today, she looked a little different. Gloria had dark circles under her eyes, and she looked like she'd forgotten to comb her hair after getting caught in a strong wind storm. Elise presumed it was probably a side effect of the training activities the other night and the fall weather. The rep manager held her red-framed glasses in her hand. A charcoal-colored flannel scarf was draped around her neck.

Elise forced a smile. "Gloria?"

The manager put her glasses on, stared at Elise and nodded.

"I'm Dr. Elise Harte, from Mt. Harmony Hearing and Balance Center."

"Oh, of course, Dr. Harte." Her lips parted for a quick blink of a smile. "Are you here to see me? Dr. Peters helped you with your open house, correct?"

"Yes, he did. I wanted to thank you again for sending him to us so quickly."

"I'm glad it worked out. Come in where we can talk."

Elise followed Gloria into a small, somewhat messy, office, where the manager waved her hand toward a cushioned chair placed in front of an oversized oak desk.

"Please, sit down."

"Thank you. I hope I'm not interrupting anything," said Elise, lowering herself into the chair. She ran her hand along the top edge of the desk. "This is a beautiful desk."

Gloria snuggled into a matching oak chair with casters and rolled herself up to the desk. She folded red manicured hands on top. "Thank you. It's a little big for this room, though. They tried to give me one of those small metal desks, but this is one I saved from my grandparents' farm in Minnesota. Just another piece of furniture relegated to the barn. What can I help you with today?"

"I wanted to ask if Dr. Peters could continue to be our rep…at least for the time being. We've been very busy, and it would help immensely."

The phone rang and Gloria put up a finger in a "just a minute" signal. She mouthed, "This will be short," then turned her attention to two computer monitors, her hand clicking a mouse with blurring speed.

Elise relaxed against the chair and perused the room. It had off-white walls and gray linoleum flooring. A drooping philodendron, propped up with plant stakes, sat on the floor behind Gloria, to the side of a small window that looked out over the front of the building. Numerous silver-framed certificates of achievement covered the wall to Elise's left. The room was small enough that she didn't have to get up to see them better. Each seemed to be from a school she wasn't familiar with and referenced a range of different business classes. The dates were either small or blurry, so she couldn't tell how long ago Gloria's schoolwork had been completed. Not that it really mattered, but it was one of the things Elise liked to know. She knew, with the continuous advancements in audiology, it was imperative to keep up with the profession, no matter when a person graduated.

Her eyes roamed to the other side of the room to a picture that hung on the wall by itself. It was an enlarged photo of an older couple in jeans and work shirts, on each side of a smiling ponytailed teenage girl, arms around each other's waists. A two-storied, yellow farmhouse was behind them. Elise loved these beautiful farm scenes, so different from city life. It must've been summer, based on the shorts and tank top the teenager was wearing.

Gloria disconnected her call but kept her eyes on the monitors. "Sorry about that. What were you saying now?"

"About Dr. Peters," said Elise. "I was wondering if he could add our office to his client list...for the time being. I'd really appreciate it."

"I don't see why not," said Gloria. She stood and walked toward the door, an obvious sign the visit was over. "I'll let him know he's assigned to you for at least the next few months. Thank you for stopping by."

"I appreciate it," Elise said once more.

So, that was that. She relaxed slightly with one worry off her mind. The next was just getting on the road and back to her office.

Elise shivered a bit under the overcast sky as she walked out the front doors and headed for her car. A cool breeze swept through the parking lot, and leaves swirled and scraped across its surface. She was alone as she walked toward her car and felt the need to snuggle the collar of her all-weather jacket closer around her neck.

Keys in hand, she clicked her green SUV's side door open, then stopped to look at the building's windows. It's funny when you get that feeling that someone's watching you.

This time, she didn't notice the combines on her drive back to Mt. Harmony, or the way the wind ebbed and flowed in the soon-to-be-harvested cornstalks. Her temples throbbed, and it wasn't just the corn dust in the air. It was more a feeling of irritation and confusion…and worry. It ate at her to think Susan might be in some kind of trouble now, too. She believed Susan's concerns and was convinced the research audiologist couldn't be part of anything underhanded…or unethical…right?

"Oh!" She jerked the steering wheel to avoid an opossum making a wobbly dash across the road, then straightened the car and checked her mirrors. Luckily, no other vehicles were on the road. She pulled her foot a little off the gas, not realizing until then, she'd been slowly increasing her speed, as she was deep in thought. She needed a plan.

Elise blew out a long breath, as she pulled the car into her office parking space and felt the comforting familiarity of her office…her second home. Her mind switched mental gears to the afternoon's work ahead, but just as quickly switched again to an unexplained high alert. Something was off.

She saw the Mt. Harmony Sheriff's car when she pulled into the parking lot, with the fleeting thought it was probably Noah about his custom ear plugs, but scowled when she realized the car was not only askew, but parked unusually close to the side door. What was that all about? She then watched, dumbstruck, as the side door opened and Noah walked out holding a handcuffed audiology student's right upper arm.

He opened the backdoor to his patrol car, guided Jake into the backseat, slammed the door shut, then climbed in behind the wheel, all in the course of thirty seconds, without ever acknowledging Elise.

The police car rolled forward, and the scene seemed to drop to ultra-slow motion as it passed her, as she sat with her mouth agape.

Jake's head and back were rigid, but she was sure that, for one split second, his eyes darted in her direction before his body slumped forward and shivered, as if he were crying.

Chapter Eleven

Mt. Harmony Hearing and Balance Center
Monday Afternoon

Elise shot out of her car, ran for the door, and yanked it open. She took one step inside then froze, feeling the door knock her in the back. A quick glance through the reception window indicated an empty waiting room, at least from what she could see of it from that angle. She turned to Amy and Lucy, who were standing near Lucy's desk, their faces frozen, eyes wide.

Amy whispered, "We're alone. And whatever it was that just happened, happened pretty quickly, Elise." Both her hands rested clenched together on top of her head, as if she was in utter shock. Then she dropped them in front of her, palms up. "And Jake didn't seem surprised at all."

The look Elise gave her coworkers made them cringe. "What was he doing here?"

Lucy had one hand on the back of her swivel chair for support. She cleared her throat. "He said he needed to pick up some schoolwork that he left here...but I never saw any-thing...did you?" She looked at Amy, who shook her head. Lucy continued, "It was only a few minutes later that Sheriff Reed came in. I don't know if they were following Jake or what."

Amy took up the story. "Noah told him they were arresting him 'in connection with the incident at E. S. Hearing Labs,' and Jake didn't even buck it. It was almost like he knew it was coming."

Elise closed her eyes and pressed her hands against her temples.

"You alright?" Lucy stepped toward her.

Elise shot a hand up in a stop position. "I'm just…taken aback. And at the same time, I'm not, and I don't know why."

"Know what you mean," said Amy with a slow nod. She raked her hands through her hair, messing it slightly.

Elise's eyes darted out the side door window, not quite sure what she was looking for, but saw the back end of Jake's truck parked on the street and couldn't take her eyes off of it until Lucy spoke.

"Luckily, the patients that were here left before Noah came, and the next appointment's going to be late…oops, I mean, she's here."

A pretty, middle-aged woman, dressed in a jean skirt and a white loose-stitched pullover sweater, walked in the door, and immediately their demeanors changed to business mode.

"Hello, Pat," said Lucy. "Dr. Harte will be with you in just a few minutes."

"I'm early, no rush." Pat smiled as she sat down and pulled a cell phone out of her rust-colored shoulder bag and swiped its screen.

Amy followed Elise down the hallway. "Elise, you don't look so good. You okay taking this patient?"

"Yeah, I'll be fine. But I need to talk something out with you. Can you meet me after work somewhere…coffee, glass of wine, anything?"

"Sure. I have to run an errand now, but why don't we meet at the Lake 'n' Bacon…about six thirty?"

"Perfect."

It was just after six o'clock when Elise finished her patient reports. She made one last call to the Mt. Harmony Sheriff's Department, hoping someone could update her on Jake, but no one could…or would. She'd probably hear from the town's grapevine before she heard from the police anyway, she thought, as she squeezed her eyes shut, then tried to focus on a call to her husband. When the recorded greeting stopped, she said, "Cole, honey, I'm going to meet Amy for a drink after work, okay? We have something we need to talk over. Call me if you need anything."

Twinkling white party lights lined the Lake 'n' Bacon's roof and gave a festive air to the cool evening. Elise pulled into a spot next to Amy's car, her coworker still behind the wheel, head down, a blue-gray glow from her cell phone lightly illuminating her face. The slam of Elise's car door brought Amy's head up. She nodded to Elise, said a few words into her phone, then threw it in her purse.

"Troy says hi," Amy said, as she exited her car and fell into step beside Elise. She noticed the serious look on Elise's face and tried a proactive approach. She looked at the sky and said, "What a beautiful night."

Elise looked at the emerging stars in the dark blue sky, the previous clouds now gone, and relaxed just slightly.

They walked through double oak doors, where they were greeted by a young woman wearing a white blouse and black skirt, holding oversized menus. Contemporary music played softly in the background at a volume Elise's dad would say was "good for atmosphere."

She breathed in the mildly sweet smell of fried walleye and seared vegetables, but the aromas didn't seem to entice her appetite. They passed a narrow wood-paneled hallway with a sign in the shape of an arrow on the wall announcing the "Prairie Room."

Amy pointed. "That's where the birthday party's going to be, right?"

"Huh? Oh…yeah," Elise mumbled, regretting her lack of enthusiasm as she said it.

The women were shown to a table next to an oversized window, with a gray-painted wooden deck on the other side of it. Lake Harmony, built decades earlier to be the water supply for the town, lay just beyond. Spots of pink and green pastel flood lights were trained on the water, adding a soft ambiance, and strings of white lights outlined a dock to the right, giving just enough illumination to see a group of Canada geese huddled in the tall grasses near the shore.

The women took off their jackets, hung them on the backs of their chairs, and gave their order to the waitress, then quietly gazed out the window in pseudo-trances until their drinks arrived.

Amy's fingers twirled the stem of her glass of chardonnay on the table. Elise followed suit with her glass of merlot. At the last minute, they ordered Lake 'n' Bacon's famous cucumber sandwich hors d'oeuvres to share and were surprised at how hungry they actually were.

"So what happened today?" asked Amy in a forced whisper, breaking the spell and getting right to the point. It was best not to beat around the bush with Elise.

Elise, also speaking low, let it all out. She filled Amy in on what she'd learned from Susan Andres, including the antagonistic feelings from Rick and Bob, Theo Wrightman's cold attitude about Tierneigh's attack, what she overheard from the lab techs in the restroom, and the incident in the test booth when she and Susan were sure someone was listening to their conversation.

Amy took a slow sip of wine and stared at the empty hors d'oeuvres plate. "I remember seeing them together."

"Who?"

"The three of them…Rick, Bob, and Theo, at the training, and I'm pretty sure I saw each one of them give Tierneigh the evil eye."

"I saw that, too," said Elise. "It makes sense it would've upset her. It must've had something to do with why she wanted to talk to me."

"But about what? And why did she want you to come back to the lab and not meet somewhere else?" Amy took another sip of wine as a ploy to stop talking when a waitress walked by with a small group of people. When it was clear, she continued. "And why were they treating her that way? And if Susan's feeling the same way, what could it mean?"

"Those are a lot of good questions," Elise mumbled, as she turned to stare out the window again. "And now, Jake. I guess we need to take one thing at a time. Either Tierneigh and/or Susan did something to make them mad…maybe?"

"Or…" Amy straightened in her seat, "the men did something that they think Tierneigh found out about and told Susan. You said the only thing Susan mentioned was how odd her data was. About results that didn't jive…and you said Susan was trying to retest people to hopefully find the problem, even if it was a little late in the game."

"But Susan said she never got the chance to talk to Tierneigh," Elise countered.

Amy's gaze drifted out the window and focused on small dots of lights from homes on the far side of the lake, then came back to watch the water fill in footprints from a young couple walking hand in hand on the sand. "That water must be chilly," she said, shivering. She pulled her eyes back to Elise. "So how can we find out what's going on at E. S. Labs?"

"I don't have a patient 'til nine-thirty tomorrow morning." Elise took another sip of wine. "I'd like to stop at the sheriff's station before I come into the office. But I'd really like to go out to E. S. Labs again."

"Are you sure? Until we know who attacked Tierneigh, we really have to be careful. What exactly do you want to go out there for?"

Elise's body slumped. "Truth be told, I feel like one of those tornado watches. You know, where 'conditions exist that could result in a tornado,' and you just have to be aware. But I'm also fighting against moving to the next level."

"The tornado warning?" Amy grimaced.

"Exactly…that a tornado's been sighted, and the only thing you can do is take cover. At that point, everything's out of your control. Right now, conditions seem to exist, and I want to do what I can to deter those conditions from moving out of our control."

"I understand, but you really need to be careful, Elise."

"I know. I will."

They raised their glasses to their lips.

Elise took a sip. "That hit the spot."

"I can tell," said Amy, pointing to a spot on Elise's white shirt…something she didn't often wear.

Elise looked down and moaned.

Amy giggled. "You want to go check out the room where the birthday party's going to be, and see if you think it'll be big enough?"

"Sure."

Chapter Twelve

Tuesday Morning

The rising sun's pink glow reflected off the Mt. Harmony Sheriff's Department's glass doors and made Elise squint, along with the sudden gust of cool wind that hit her face and made her eyes water. Great. They were going to think she'd been crying and she wanted so badly to project a more confident, in-charge attitude, in comparison to the nervous and distraught person she felt she'd embodied the last time she was here. She hoped the dark gray suit she wore today would help.

Her hand pulled on the cool metal handle, and she stepped inside.

"Morning, Lauren." Elise strode toward the receptionist, who quickly hid a half-eaten snack bar under the counter.

"Hey, Dr. Harte," said Lauren, standing up. "What can I do for you?"

"I was hoping I could talk to Noah. And please, call me Elise."

"Sure thing, Dr. Harte. Sheriff Reed ran out for something and ought to be back any minute. Why don't you have a seat in that first room there." She pointed to the same room where Elise and Noah spoke just two days before.

A whoosh caught their attention when Noah pulled

open the front door and tried to catch it with his foot. One hand clutched a white bag, decorated with the "Sweet Shop Bakery" logo, and the other hand held a cardboard carrier full of hot drinks.

Elise lurched forward and grabbed the drinks for him.

"Thanks," he said, now inside and taking the drinks back from her. "I've been expecting you."

He turned to Lauren. "Pass these out for me, okay?"

The receptionist nodded, eyes already searching the contents of the white bag.

Turning toward Elise, he said, "Have a seat in the first room there. I'll be right back."

Elise complied, and Noah was back in less than a minute, carrying a folder, a pad of paper and a pen. She noticed a couple drops of coffee on the front of his uniform shirt. Probably easier to get out than wine.

"I guess you want to know about Jake."

Elise pulled both sides of her jacket tighter around her and steadied her eyes on him. "I'm concerned. And very confused. I'd appreciate anything you can tell me."

"Actually, you saved me a phone call."

"Oh?" She let go of her jacket, grabbed the sides of her chair, and scooted forward.

"We have proof that Jake was in Susan Andres's office— at least outside the anechoic chamber—sometime that evening."

Elise froze mid-scoot and stared.

Noah rubbed his face with his hands, then looked directly at her. "We found a print on the door to the anechoic chamber."

She finished her scoot. "A print? Like a fingerprint?"

"No...more like an ear print."

Elise's eyes widened. "A what print?"

"An ear print. They can be just as important as finger-prints, especially in this case, where the match is perfect."

"I still don't understand."

"Someone with a malformed right ear pressed that ear against the door...as if trying to listen for something. It matches Jake's right ear perfectly."

Elise closed her eyes, remembering Jake's dog-bitten ear. She slumped against her chair, then jerked forward like when she was a teenager in California and realized just how sunburned her back really was. "But I don't get it. Couldn't that have happened anytime?"

Noah shook his head. "We checked with the building's cleaning crew. They clean that room every night. Mainly vacuuming, but they also wipe down the test room doors and door handles. They cleaned right after Dr. Andres's last tour group, and the room was cordoned off soon after Tierneigh was taken to the hospital...at about ten thirty. His ear print places him at the scene and at the time in question."

"What about an alibi? Does he have one?"

"He told us he stopped for some fast food after the training, but it didn't pan out. We checked, and the two people working the restaurant that night said no one came in at all during that time, and there were no receipts indicating a possible drive-through order."

Elise put her elbows on the table, her hands over her eyes. "What is Jake saying about all this?" In her mind, she wondered if Jake understood how thick and sound-treated the anechoic chamber door was and how hard it would've been to actually hear anything. She dropped her hands to the table.

"He's not talking. His parents are coming with an attorney and probably bail money."

"Can I see him?"

"Not a good time right now. I'll tell you when, okay?"

"Thank you, Noah." She pushed against the table to stand, then grabbed it and sucked in air.

"Elise, you okay?"

"I'm okay, thanks."

But she was far from feeling okay. Her body felt numb as she tried to put one foot in front of the other to leave, her mind racing. Could Jake actually have murdered Tierneigh? She barely breathed until she was settled in her car and started the engine, but reflexively turned it off. She shook her head against the idea of going out to E. S. Hearing Labs, started the car, and headed straight for her office. And it was a good thing she did.

Elise always felt sneaky when she came in the back door, as if she intentionally wanted to avoid people, but this time, that actually happened to be the case. She mentally tapped her Dr. Down's picture, picked up the handset of her desk phone, and "inter-officed" Lucy.

"Hey, I'm here. Is Grady out there? I just saw his car in the parking lot."

"Morning. Yeah, you can't miss that thing," Lucy whispered, referring to the lime green Ford Ranger, that was a moving advertisement for the Mt. Harmony Herald.

No exterior space was left untouched, from images of cornstalks and soybean plants, to "Read the Herald" scrawled in canary yellow and fire engine red letters down each side door, to the sign on top with an image of a Mt. Harmony Herald front page, slanted to look as if it was poking up through the cab's roof.

"Said he stopped by just in case you were available. He's in the waiting room and your first patient'll be here in about half an hour. Oh, and Grady's watching the video about closed-loop systems. Says he could use one in his office, especially when he's talking to groups of people, in case some have hearing problems."

"We'll have to hold him to it," said Elise. "Has he bugged you with any questions about Jake?"

"Not yet."

"Good. Be right there. Not much I can tell him except I'd really like not to get into it."

"No kidding."

Elise straightened her workspace, checked herself in the hand mirror she kept in her desk, then shoved it back in the drawer. She traded her gray blazer for her white lab coat and headed for the waiting room.

"Good morning, Grady." She held out her hand for a brief handshake with the young man, noticing that he was looking stylish in his signature bow tie and brown suede jacket.

His thin lips grinned wide. "Thanks for giving me a few minutes."

He followed Elise down the hall and into her office. She sat on her side of the desk as Grady bounced into one of the chairs on the other side.

His body continued to bounce as he spoke. "First off, I wanted you to know I'll be there for your mom-in-law's birthday party on Saturday. I know Uncle Mike'll be there, too," he said, referring to the owner of the paper, "but I'm the one officially doing the story. I was supposed to go out of town for the high school playoff game, but you've probably already heard that the Bobcats lost." Grady slouched in the chair for a moment. "So we're done 'til next year."

Elise grimaced. "I heard...and they had such a good season. I'm glad you and your Uncle Mike will be at the party, though."

Grady pulled a paper from his satchel and bounced on the seat again. "Also wanted to show you the ad we worked up for you for next month. I know I could've emailed it to you, but I like doing these things in person, if you don't mind.

It has the Thanksgiving theme you wanted."

He held a printout of the proposed ad displaying a bundle of beige and tan cornstalks tied with a red sash, placed on a backdrop of orange hues. Pumpkins, colorful fall leaves, cranberries, and acorns were scattered on the ground. Smiling pictures of the audiologists and Lucy crossed the top of the picture, with the appropriate contact information at the bottom.

"Looks great, Grady!" Elise was more pleased with it than she thought she'd be. "Dr. MacNeal already saw this, and gave her okay, too, right?"

Grady nodded. "Absolutely...and, uh, while I'm at it..."

Elise steeled herself for what she suspected was coming.

"I was wondering if I could just ask you a few questions about all the stuff going on lately. 'Specially 'bout your student, Jake...Cagney, isn't it?" He stopped bouncing, leaned forward, his face searching hers. "Guess the police arrested him right here in your office, right?"

Elise didn't flinch. "Unfortunately, Grady, there's nothing I can say about it. The whole incident is still under investigation."

"Was there a connection with Dr. Tierneigh Brown? Jake knew her, right?" He looked at notes on his cell phone. "They worked together at E. S. Hearing Labs, right? Do you know if there's someone there I can talk to?"

Elise's voice stayed firm. "I suggest you contact Mr. Theo Wrightman, the CEO, and see what he says, but I wouldn't expect too much right now."

"Yeah, guess not." He swiped something on his phone and bounced again in his seat. "Oh, almost forgot...I saw Marcie at The Vibe this morning but didn't think to ask her about this. She still knows people at E. S. Hearing Labs and can probably tell me something."

Elise's eyebrows rose. "Marcie Miller? Deborah Miller's

daughter?"

Grady met her gaze with a question on his face, as if he didn't realize he was talking out loud. "Oh, sorry…yeah. Marcie used to work at E. S. Hearing Labs, a few years ago." His eyes dropped to his cell phone again. "That's when we were…kinda dating."

Elise saw an immediate opportunity to flip this interview around. "So, how long did she work at E. S. Hearing Labs?"

"A few years, I guess, after college. But she kept getting overlooked for promotions, so went to a competing lab…Lewelling Labs…east of here." He pointed in the appropriate direction. "Almost to Indianapolis."

"I hope she's had better luck there," said Elise.

"Yeah, she likes it. I wish she'd move back here, though." A wistful smile passed over his face, but he bounced again, now looking directly at Elise. "She said she really got a surprise the other day, when she saw Rick Dayton walk into their building."

Elise's face froze, and she barely got out, "Rick? From E. S. Hearing Labs?"

"Yeah. I don't know a whole lot about him, but she said she never liked him, and she was hoping he wasn't there looking for a job. Marcie said she stopped at E. S. Hearing to see some of the people she used to work with and mentioned seeing Rick. Guess he told them he was taking the day off to go to some car races at the Brickyard," he said, referring to the famous race track in Indianapolis. Grady scooted forward on his seat, and his face became even more animated. "They were really bugged at him for taking a day off in the middle of this 'to-do' about a new chip."

"Maybe he just forgot to mention Lewelling Labs," said Elise.

"Maybe, but Marcie said, knowing him, it was probably

something sneaky."

"Why would she say…?"

Just then, Lucy rapped on the doorjamb. "Your next patient's here, Dr. Harte."

"Guess that's my cue, huh," said Grady, rising from his seat.

Elise smiled, as she stood. "Thanks again, Grady. The ad looks great." She took a couple steps toward the door. "Will you be seeing Marcie again?"

"Probably, why?"

"I'd like to talk to her. Could you ask her to give me a call?"

"Sure. Hey, I'll text her right now. What's your cell number?"

Nice try, thought Elise, amused. "Oh, just ask her to call the office number, okay? Thanks, Grady. See you at the party."

★★★

Among Elise's afternoon patients, was a forty-one-year-old man with constant ringing in his ears, also known as tinnitus, and a fifty-five-year-old woman with occasional dizziness. Both required in-depth audiological evaluations. Elise counseled each patient regarding their results, noting that her reports would be sent to the appropriate healthcare teams. She then scheduled follow-up appointments to review reports received in return, as well as to discuss any possible follow-up audiological services needed.

The sun had slipped unnoticed below the horizon when Lucy's voice preceded her appearance at Elise's door. She had a cranberry Berber jacket slipped up one arm and was wiggling to get the other arm covered. "That's it for today, Dr. Harte. Dr. MacNeal just left. Her first patient's at eight tomorrow morning and yours is at nine."

"Thanks, Lucy. You leaving now?"

"Yeah…gee, it's dark out already." She maneuvered her head to look out Elise's back window. "Oh, and Marcie Miller called. She said, that Grady said you wanted her to call you."

Elise's attention immediately left audiology reports. Luckily, she'd just finished the last one, so now homed in on what light Marcie might shed on Rick Dayton.

"Did she leave her number?"

"Yup," said Lucy, already pressing a yellow sticky note to Elise's desk.

"Thanks. You have a good evening. Go ahead and lock up, and turn out the lights, okay?"

"Okay. See ya in the morning."

Elise grabbed her cell phone and tapped in the number for Marcie Miller, who answered with a quick "Hello?" She seemed out of breath, and traffic noise was definitely competing with her speech.

"Marcie. It's Elise Harte. Welcome home and thank you so much for calling. You sound busy!"

"Hi, Elise! Yes, it's nice to be home with my mom," said Marcie in a jovial voice, "but she's given me a ton of errands to run before dinner, which is in half an hour!"

Elise laughed, too. "My mom's in San Francisco right now, so I don't have that problem, but I do miss her, and my dad." Elise paused for just a split second, as she tried to push aside memories of pot roast dinner with her family. "Actually, I have your mom's hearing aids, and there was something I wanted to ask you, as well. Would you be able to meet me at The Vibe for some dessert later?"

"Oh sure, that'd be nice. How about in a couple hours? I'll tell Mom her hearing aids are ready and meet you there."

"Thanks, Marcie. See you soon." Elise disconnected the

call, switched her white lab coat for her blazer on the hook on the back of her door, and grabbed her purse and work bag, intending to scoot out the back door. Plans were already forming in her mind for a quick dinner with Cole, and an even quicker run to the coffee shop to think through her questions before Marcie arrived...when her cell phone buzzed.

"Ughhh...never fails." She plopped her things on her desk, then froze when she saw the call was from the Mt. Harmony Sheriff's Department.

"Hello?"

"Elise? It's Noah...I just wanted to check in with you."

Elise's voice dropped a little tentatively. "I'm okay, Noah. What can I help you with?"

"Well, I wanted to let you know that we just released Jake on bail. He's going to stay with his parents out in Bluestem."

"Oh," said Elise, lowering herself into one of the chairs by her desk, not quite sure how she was feeling about this. "What does this mean exactly?"

"Well, Jake's able to do pretty much what he wants to do, until his court date," said Noah. "He can go back to school, put in his work hours..." He let the sentence hang in the air.

Elise couldn't help but ask, "So there wasn't enough to hold him until a court date?"

"No. His parents have a lawyer, and he's questioning the ear print. Jake's not talking, so we'll see where this goes, but he's still a strong suspect. Elise, are you going to let him come back to work at your place?"

Elise stared at the doctorate diploma on her wall. "I'll have to talk to Amy about that, but I don't see how we can, under the circumstances."

"I understand," said Noah. Elise visualized him nodding

his head.

"Thanks for letting me know." After a minute of Noah's pleas for Elise to be careful and let his department take care of this, she disconnected the call.

She walked to her side of the desk and sat down, needing to make a couple more calls. The first one to Amy confirmed her own feelings about not letting Jake come back to the office until things were settled, one way or another. She asked Amy to call Lucy and let her know, in case Jake tried to contact the office, even though she doubted he would.

The second call was to Susan Andres, who was just getting ready to leave for the day.

"Elise, I feel the same as you. We just couldn't let Jake come back to either of our places, under the circumstances. I'm so torn. I don't like to judge people before we know the truth, and I like Jake. He's shown real promise with audiology, but we have businesses to think of, and…"

"And what, Susan?"

Susan dropped her voice to a whisper. "Hold on while I close my door. It's been so awkward using a temporary office."

Elise could hear the roller chair squeak on the linoleum floor, a few footsteps, the click of the office door closing, then a few footsteps again.

"Okay. I don't think anyone else is around, but just to be sure… I hate to say it, but what if Jake had something to do with what's been going on here? What if he's been part of something, and Tierneigh found out about it?"

"What do you mean? How could he?" Elise whispered back.

"Honestly, I hate to be paranoid, but it's almost like someone's trying to sabotage this chip. I found more inconsistencies with the test data. It's taken me days, but I've narrowed it down to specific test subjects and the days they were here for testing."

"And?" prompted Elise.

"Jake was here on the same days."

Elise paused, then said, "Are you saying, you think he did…what? Something to the test results? That's a big leap." Elise shook her head.

"I know, but it's sure a crazy coincidence," said Susan. "Then, there's the fact that he had access to the data."

"What do you mean, 'access to the data'?"

"The test data is on a shared drive here at the lab," explained Susan. "Only managers can access it, but anyone could get into it from my office, and a couple of side areas with computers that we use as audiology stations. I've allowed access for the students, or other audiologists directly involved with the project."

Elise's mind was racing. "I need to ask you something," she said, hunching over her desk, still whispering. "How well do you know Rick Dayton?"

"Rick?" Susan paused. "I've known him a few years. He knows his acoustics, and he's done a great job with the anechoic chamber."

"Did you know he stopped by Lewelling Labs, near Indianapolis, last week?"

"Our competition?"

Elise told her about talking to Grady Weber earlier in the day, then added, "I'm meeting Marcie Miller tonight, so I'll see if I can find out anything else."

"Oh, Marcie…tallish, straight black hair with a part down the middle, right?"

"Not sure, I haven't seen her in a while."

"Yeah, she used to work here. This is all so weird. I'll see what more I can find out about Rick on this end."

"Thanks, Susan."

Cole called soon after Elise got home and said he was

running late and to go ahead and eat, which worked out fine. She warmed up some leftover cauliflower pizza in the microwave, then left for the coffee shop.

The Vibe was relatively quiet. Soft instrumental music played in the background, and the TV was off. The lighting was dimmed slightly to create a more relaxed feeling for the evening hours. It was empty except for Steve, the high school student working the counter, and one man who Elise thought was one of the new high school English teachers. He looked to be in his thirties, was thin with dark hair, and sat in the corner by himself, engrossed in writing in what looked like a journal. A smile was on his face. Elise smiled, too. It's always so nice to enjoy what you do.

She took a sip of her pumpkin spice latte, stared out the window, and watched the cars go by. She thought of the first time she came into the coffee shop after she moved to Mt. Harmony. She was immediately drawn to the small-town atmosphere and friendly people. Not that she didn't love San Francisco, and always would, but there was something about this town.

That day, she'd heard a fire engine's warning siren rev up but stop, just halfway into its first cycle. She remembered thinking, wow…this really is a small town! She laughed later, when she found out that the fender-bender had happened right in front of the fire station. No one was hurt and, yes, the town was definitely larger than what she pictured in her mind that day.

She switched her thoughts to her conversation with Susan. Rick Dayton really bothered her, and she hoped Susan could find out more about him. Elise unconsciously smoothed her hair with one hand and was scribbling notes on a yellow napkin with the other one when Marcie walked in.

"Elise, hi! Oh my gosh, I feel like it's been years!"

Elise stood to hug her, both women sincere in their pleasure to see each other. "I think it has, Marcie." Elise noticed that, yes, her eyes were still the beautiful dark blue that she remembered. "How are you? Your hair's so long! How's your new job? Or is it not that new, anymore?"

The room echoed with the sound of chairs scraping the linoleum floor. Elise sat down, but Marcie continued to stand while she slipped her marled brown wool poncho over her head. She brushed her long, black hair back over her shoulders, laid the poncho across the back of her chair, and sat down.

"Yes, I've let my hair grow. And the job, well, it always seems new to me...there's so much to learn. Actually, I've already had one promotion, so I'm happy with that. I miss being closer to my parents, though. Someday, I'd like to move back this way."

"So is it, what...? About a two-hour drive to Mt. Harmony?"

"Yeah, more like just one and a half from where the lab is, and I don't live far from that, but Mom and Dad are getting older, and that weighs on me, especially if there's an emergency."

Elise thought of her parents in San Francisco. A non-stop flight could get her there in decent time, but getting around the airport, renting a car, and dealing with traffic, could add hours. Her shoulders drooped slightly, and she pointed to the display case.

"Dessert's on me. Let's check out what Laura's baked today."

It didn't take long to finish off slices of homemade pumpkin pie.

Marcie closed her eyes. "That was wonderful. Laura's pies are the best."

"I agree," said Elise, sliding her empty plate away from

her and glancing at the notes on her yellow napkin, which were now covered with pie crust crumbs. "Marcie, as you know, I spoke to Grady, and he told me something you brought up about Rick Dayton, at E. S. Hearing Labs."

"Oh, yeah…him."

"Can you tell me about it? I'm just being a little nosy, I guess, but he's helping Susan Andres with the acoustics in the test booths, and I was wondering what you thought about him."

Marcie furrowed her brows. "What do you mean exactly?"

Elise slouched against her chair, hoping to come across more nonchalant than she felt. She cocked her head. "I guess I'm wondering if you think he's someone you could trust. That might not be a very nice thing to insinuate about anyone, but Dr. Andres's work is so important, and I'm hoping he understands how important it is."

"Oh, well, I guess he would. I didn't actually work with him when I was there, but I did hear a little gossip. It mainly had to do with a divorce that didn't go so well, and that he was always in a bad mood. People that worked more closely with him said it was hard to be near him because he was so grumpy all the time…about the divorce… and money issues."

"You mean with alimony or something?"

"Yeah…that and all the time he spent at the Brickyard. I guess he liked to gamble on the races, and his wife got tired of it."

"Grady said you actually saw him the other day."

Marcie's eyes grew wide. "I did! I sure didn't expect to see him at Lewelling Labs!"

Elise tried to push a little more. "What day was that? Do you remember?"

"Umm, yeah. It was a week ago…last Tuesday."

"I wonder why he was there?" Elise hoped she sounded more innocent than she felt.

"I really don't know. I was just hoping it wasn't for a job or something."

"I heard he told the people at E. S. Labs he was going to a race at the Brickyard, and never mentioned that he was stopping at one of their competitors."

"Yeah, that's what I heard, too," said Marcie, now wiggling in her seat and looking around the café. "Maybe he didn't want to deal with the questions he'd get."

Elise took the hint. She pulled a small, gray zippered case out of her purse and handed it to Marcie. "Here's your mom's hearing aids. All cleaned and fixed."

Marcie relaxed as she took them, then winked at Elise with a sly smile. "Thank you. I really missed them."

★★★

Cole was settled on the living room couch when Elise walked in the door. A fire crackled in the fireplace, and the light from her computer spotlighted his face. No other light was on, so she clicked on one of the beige ceramic table lamps at the end of the couch.

She stood still and announced the obvious. "I'm home."

Cole grunted his acknowledgment, deep in thought on whatever it was he was focused on.

She turned, walked into the dining room, dropped her purse and workbag on the table, then pushed the swinging doors into the kitchen. She wanted some hot tea. Cole didn't like tea, so she made him hot cocoa.

"Here ya go." Elise set both mugs on the coffee table.

Cole's hand reached for it without looking up.

"Make sure you get the right one, and don't spill anything on my laptop," said Elise, lowering herself slowly next to him. The warmth from the fire was comforting.

"What are you looking at?"

"Just some rugby news…"

"Can I run something by you?"

"Sure." He closed the laptop. "Becky just called. She's bringing my laptop back tonight."

"Good."

Cole looked her in the eyes. "Ready."

Elise pursed her lips. "Well, my mind's going all over the place, and I'm trying to stop from losing it altogether. A week ago, I was getting ready for an open house, to bring new information and products to my patients. I was excited about your mom's birthday party, and you know how much I love the fall here." Elise swiped at a tear that seemed to come out of nowhere. "Now, one of my best friends is gone and everything seems upside down. Something bad's going on at E. S. Hearing Labs, Cole, and…I might be promoting something to my patients that's not what it's supposed to be!"

Cole settled his hot cocoa on a coaster and swung an arm around Elise's shoulders. "The police are looking into this. Let 'em find out what's going on at the lab. You have good instincts, and you have a great co-owner in Amy—and a great front office person in Lucy—that everyone with a business like yours envies. I feel strongly that, if something comes out about that chip that isn't what you expected, you'll handle it, and your patients will trust your decisions."

Elise leaned over to give her husband a peck on the cheek when they heard the front door open, then click shut.

"Hey, what's going on in here? Mom, you alright?"

Chapter Thirteen

Tuesday Evening

Elise swung her feet to the floor and stood to give her daughter a kiss on the cheek. "I'm fine, honey. Just talking some things over with your dad. How're you doing? Want some hot cocoa?" Elise headed for the kitchen, already anticipating the answer.

Becky chuckled and called out, "Yes, please!"

She placed her dad's computer on the couch and plopped in the overstuffed chair near him, letting her purse drop to the floor. "Jon brought my computer back, so I don't need yours anymore. Thanks for letting me use it, Dad."

Her eyes looked tired, and her hair was pulled back in a messy ponytail. She wore a loose, oversized Mt. Harmony sweatshirt and black leggings. She had kicked off her shoes and pulled her bright red sock-covered feet to the side of her on the chair.

Cole smiled. "Glad it helped."

Elise came back with a mug of cocoa for Becky, and soon all three sat staring at the fire, their hands wrapped comfortably around their warm mugs.

Becky groaned. "I'm still sorta stressed about school and all. I need to stop at the store on the way back to my apartment to get some little stuff, for my report. Then I have to turn in a printed copy and submit one online. It's such a pain."

Elise pulled her eyes off the fire and looked at her daughter. "Why don't you go check upstairs in the office, and see what we might have that could help?"

"Thanks." Her face brightened. "I was hoping you'd say that." But in the middle of getting up, Becky stopped herself and looked around the room. "Where're Belle and Deci?"

"Ewww!" Elise shuddered. "Please…it's Deci and Belle. Get the order right."

"Gets her every time." Cole guffawed.

Becky looked at her mom with a weak attempt at hiding a snicker. "Oh, and can one of you take me home tonight?"

Elise felt a slight crunch in her stomach. She still wasn't used to her daughter calling any other place "home" than the home they were in right now.

"Sure…I can," she said. "Not that I mind, but where's your roommate tonight?"

"Hope needed my car to go to her boyfriend's dad's home, and I'm not sure when she'll be back. Guess he pulled a muscle in his leg or something and wanted Hope to work her physical therapy magic on him. Her boyfriend's there already. He said he didn't want to leave him." Becky picked up her cocoa, tilted her head back, and dripped the last few drops onto her tongue before she placed it back on the coffee table. "And before you say anything, yes, he was checked out by his medical doctor and physical therapy was recommended."

Cole laughed and Elise made a face.

Becky continued, "Have either of you heard from Jon lately? How's the Aunt Ida front?"

No one admitted to hearing from Jon since the last family meeting, and they all agreed that the promotion to manager at a major tech company in Springfield was keeping him busy. Besides that, he was sharing a rental home with two friends he knew from high school and had just met a possible future girlfriend. Elise relied quite a bit on Jon for the latest information on cell phones, computers, and other technology, and their interfacing capabilities for people who are using hearing devices.

"I'll try to give Jon a call later and see if there's any update on Aunt Ida," offered Cole, as their daughter climbed the stairs in search of needed school supplies.

About a half hour later, Becky thumped down the stairs carrying an E. S. Hearing Labs's gift bag half-full of supplies to help her with her project. She raised the bag in the air. "Okay if I take this, Mom?"

"Sure," said Elise. "Did you get the bouncy ball and ear pens, too?"

"Of course." Becky laughed. "But I need to go home and get working on this thing."

She kissed her dad good night, and a few minutes later, Elise pulled into the Coneflower Drive Apartments parking lot, where Becky and her roommate had lived for the last two years. The apartments had outside access with four apartments to a section, two upstairs and two downstairs. An outside stairway connected the two buildings. The same format was repeated for five more buildings, three on each side of the road, totaling twenty-four apartments in all.

Elise and her daughter chatted about the upcoming birthday party as they climbed the cement plank stairs to Becky's apartment. Elise noticed that she had a little trouble with the lock on her front door, jiggling the key quite a bit, and brought it up.

"We've all been having trouble with these locks, Mom. Management's supposed to be checking 'em out for us."

"Well, I hope it's soon. I don't think I like that," said Elise.

"Oh, Mom…"

Becky opened the door, and Elise followed her daughter through the somewhat sparsely furnished, but comfortable, living room area, to a small dining area that held a round white table on which Becky deposited her things.

"Do you want any tea or anything?" she asked, somewhat half-heartedly.

"No, thanks." Elise did a quick survey of the area. Dirty dishes in the sink, crumbs on the kitchen counter, clothes strewn on the couch. Don't say anything…don't say anything.

She turned her back and took a few steps toward the front door. "I need to get home, and you need to start on your school stuff."

They stepped back out onto the landing and gave each other a hug.

Elise whispered, "Goodnight, sweetie." Voices carried in quiet evenings, and she wanted to be thoughtful of the neighbors. "Good luck with the—" She stopped when she heard a door creak below them.

Elise peered over the black wrought iron railing and saw a young man come out of an apartment on the first floor in the building section across from Becky's. He turned and walked toward the parking lot.

Something was familiar about him.

Becky looked down as well, then back up at her mom. She moved to close the door.

"Wait," whispered Elise. "Is that David Nubrey?"

"Huh? Dave?"

"He lives here?" Elise wasn't sure why she was so surprised. Quite a few students lived in these apartments.

"Yeah, why? Do you know him?" asked Becky, eyes half-closed.

Elise was too intent on the door not closing all the way

behind him to answer. It drifted open into the apartment by a couple of inches. Her eyes shot out to the parking lot just in time to see—and hear—an older-looking, green foreign car exit the lot, turn right onto the main drive through the complex, then left onto Second Street. The view was one advantage of an upstairs apartment.

A horrible thought snuck into Elise's mind, and she flashed to David sneaking out of Tierneigh's office at E. S. Hearing Labs with a folder in his hand. Her eyes squinted. Don't do it.

She glanced sideways at Becky, whose eyes grew wide in response.

"Mom, I know that look. What's going on?"

"I just want to make sure his door closes good. You have to think safety, you know."

"Mom!" Becky's whispered voice raised in intensity.

"I'll be right back. The layout's like your apartment, right? Watch out for David."

"Watch for who?"

"David."

"Mom!" Becky's eyes popped out of her head. "What are you doing?"

Elise skittered down the apartment stairs and glanced at the front door peephole of the apartment directly across from David's, just below Becky's. Luckily, it was late, and the dim yellow glow of a few strategically placed lights barely illuminated the area.

She could hear Becky in the background, hissing, "Mom…Mom…" but all she could think of was Tierneigh.

Elise stood at David's door and used the back of her hand to give it a little push. A high-pitched creak made her wince as it swung open. She peeked in. A small light was on, just to the right of what looked like the living room. Probably a light over the stove, she thought, if this was like Becky's apartment.

She stepped in, then carefully pushed the door closed, but not all the way, in case she needed a quick exit. She turned and saw sparse shadows of furniture in a relatively small living room and grimaced at the stale smell of fried eggs and bacon in the air.

Just beyond the living room was another small area that looked like it would hold a dining table for two but, instead, held a one-person desk and chair with an open laptop.

She tiptoed a few feet forward, eyes scanning side to side. What looked like amateur paintings of cornfields and silos dotted one wall, though in the dim light, could've been great works of art, but she doubted it. Textbooks haphazardly covered the floor around the desk that Elise felt drawn to.

She tiptoed in that direction, then spied a yellow folder that was propped between the computer monitor and a heavy-looking block of a book. The folder looked an awful lot like the one David had in his hand when he left Tierneigh's office.

She reached for it—

"Mom! He's back," hissed Becky in the doorway.

A rumbling noise grew steadily louder in the background. Becky bounced up the stairs in her stocking feet, grabbing the railing to pull herself up faster.

The room took on the spooky aura of the state fair's funhouse as headlights fell on the closed blinds at the living room windows, sending shards of yellow-white light at all angles.

Elise dashed for the door, closed it as well as she could behind her, then hugged the outside wall as she heard the thud of a car door closing…way too close for comfort. She tiptoed in the opposite direction, to the back of the building, then turned and glanced up through the open stairway to where Becky's door was barely cracked open. She couldn't see if Becky was there, but gave a thumbs up just in case, then started a stealth-walk around the back of the building and out to the parking lot.

Just as she passed the last window, a dog inside the apartment let out a heart-stopping bark. Elise jumped, smacking her hand to her chest, and ran as fast as she could.

Once inside her car, she slouched down in her seat, took a deep breath, and called Becky on her cell phone. She didn't want to start the car yet and draw attention to herself, in case anyone was watching.

"Mom! What're you doing? Why'd you go in there?"

"Honestly, Becky, I'm not sure. But I saw David at E. S. Hearing Labs, coming out of Tierneigh's office…which still had police tape across it."

"Did he see you?"

"I was in the stairwell and was just about to open the door when I saw him through the window. I think he heard me when I opened it, and I followed him down the hallway, but he never turned around. I know he saw me after he got on the elevator, though. He had something in his hand when he came out of Tierneigh's office. A folder. Maybe it was something he already had, but I don't believe it. So, why'd he go in there?"

"Don't know, Mom," said Becky biting her lower lip. "Did you see anything in his apartment?"

"Yes. There was a folder that looked just like the one he was holding then, but I couldn't grab it in time."

"Oh, Mom," said Becky. It was good Elise couldn't see her daughter's eyes rolling.

"Don't worry about me, honey. You need to work on that report, okay?"

"Okay. Be careful, Mom."

"I will. Oh, Becky…"

"What?"

"Do you normally see David coming and going?"

"I might not see him, but I always hear his car. It's one his parents gave him, and it's kinda rumbly."

"I noticed," mumbled Elise. "And one more thing. Can you remember back to last Thursday night? Do you remember him coming home…and when?"

"Not right now, I don't."

Elise noticed a hint of exasperation in her voice.

"If I think of anything, I'll call you, okay?"

"Okay. Love you, honey. Bye."

★★★

Later that night, after two cups of chamomile tea, Elise rolled over in bed for the umpteenth time and reached for her cell phone on the bedside stand.

One a.m. Sheesh, if she was awake enough to go downstairs and make more chamomile tea, she'd be even more awake just trying to get its calming effect to get her back to sleep. Somehow that didn't make sense.

She squeezed her eyes together and tried a breathing technique that was supposed to help you fall asleep. It seemed to work, because she drifted off after a couple minutes, but it was a restless sleep.

In her mind, she saw acres of sunflowers with white cottony clouds drifting above them in a powder blue sky. Figures stood in the distance. They turned to look at her. She squinted and recognized Susan, her face stern. Next to her stood Theo and Rick, both glaring at her. David smirked and waved. Cole, Becky, and Jon were in the opposite direction, waving at her to come over to where they were. She mouthed to them, I can't…I have to watch these people…and patients are waiting…

Elise jerked awake again, but this time it was from two lumps of fur trying to snuggle against her ribs, one on each side, her arms at awkward angles around them. The warmth emanating from Deci and Belle calmed her body, but was not enough to stop her mind. She pictured the time between Tierneigh's call and when Elise found her. The attack must've happened between about 9:45 and 10:15…at the latest. Where was everyone?

Jake Cagney: Police put him at the scene of the crime because of his ear print. His alibi of being at a fast-food restaurant didn't hold up.

Susan said she left at 9:20. She'd insinuated possible data sabotage, but Elise absolutely refused to believe that Susan, or Tierneigh, could be involved in something so reprehensible.

Susan said she saw Rick leave the building by the front doors a few minutes after nine, when she was walking with the last tour group toward the anechoic chamber. Didn't mean he couldn't have snuck back in through another door, though. Like the one at the end of the hallway near Susan's office and the anechoic chamber.

The sound of a train's horn interrupted her thoughts. Sharp tones, like a high-frequency pipe organ, cut through the air and grew louder as it approached, then dropped to low-frequency tones, as it receded. Her breath fell into a shallow rhythm, while restless sleep finally took over again.

Chapter Fourteen

Wednesday Morning

Her mother-in-law's favorite Homer and Jethro song blared, and Elise felt her body almost levitate over the bed. She slapped a hand on the cell phone, but instead of turning it off, the phone flipped off the bedside stand, ricocheted off the floor, and came to a stop somewhere under the bed still delivering its twangy song.

Cole groaned.

"Sorry," Elise mumbled as she threw back the comforter, slid down the side of the bed onto the hardwood floor, located the phone, and turned it off. "Go back to sleep, honey. It's way too early."

Cole mumbled something unintelligible and fell back into a soft snore.

Why did she set the alarm for five a.m.? Then she remembered...she had an early patient at the office. She hadn't planned on tossing and turning all night, and under normal circumstances, could think things through better in the mornings. The plan now was to get some coffee, sit by herself somewhere nice and quiet, and think.

Showered and dressed, Elise forced herself to swallow a stale cinnamon roll she found behind the milk carton in the refrigerator. Now, where was her purse? Yes, on the dining room table. So, where was David Nubrey that horrible night? Stop it.

She walked across the entryway to the living room, thinking she might've left her workbag by the couch, and at the same time tried to bring up the day's schedule in her mind. People were coming in who were going to want answers to what's been happening. And what her involvement might've been.

The workbag was right where she thought it might be, and she relaxed slightly. The mind's not completely gone…yet.

She allowed herself to picture a steaming dark roast coffee waiting for her at The Vibe, so said goodbye to the cats, locked the front door, pitched her things into the car, and was on her way. The morning was cool, damp and overcast. The same as her mood. How fitting.

Elise slowed the car as she passed The Vibe, glancing in the windows. Laura always opened early, and right now it didn't look too busy. She almost pulled into one of the diagonal parking spaces, but then thought the better of it. Probably better to find somewhere she'd be sure to be alone.

Her stomach rumbled in reaction to the tasty food she knew she was passing up, which caused her to glance sideways at the passenger seat, and her shoulders dropped. No lunch. And the hospital cafeteria was out. There was a good chance she'd expose herself to more uncomfortable questions there, so she decided to circle back to the small grocery store on the west side of the square. They opened early, and she could probably get in and out without anyone noticing.

She pressed her foot on the gas and drove the short distance into the small, asphalt parking lot on the side of the store, and pulled into a space near the front doors.

A display of yellow mums caught her attention as she approached the grocery store's glass double doors. She picked up a pot, appreciating its fragrance, and held it in her arms as she pushed the right side door open with her back. She walked down the black-and-white speckled linoleum aisle and approached the refrigerated case marked "Food-To-Go," only briefly noticing two gray-haired women in powder blue sweats a few feet away, fingering plastic containers of pumpkin and pecan pies, on a round display table.

Elise had just reached for the refrigerator door handle when she overheard one of the women say, "Well, she was looking into her husband's life insurance, you know."

Elise stopped so quickly she had to grab the mum with her other hand to stop it from falling. Her jaw tensed as she steadied herself and glanced over at the women. The "Jacks" ladies from the fall festival downtown were standing just a few feet to the side of her.

"What do you mean?" Helen asked, as she slid pies around on the table with one finger.

"Well," said Anne, my friend Marilyn overheard two men talking at the coffee shop about it. She was supposedly deciding on the best way to get the most insurance out of her husband's demise."

"Anne, you're kidding! I can't imagine such a nice person as Dr. Harte acting that way." Helen picked up a pumpkin pie and held it aloft, as her eyes squinted to find even the most minuscule flaw. "Well, if she can think like that about her husband, what about her best friend?"

The pain Elise felt as it shot though her chest took her breath away. The mums started to shake in her hands. She slowly raised the flowers between the women and her face and carefully inched backward down the aisle she just came down.

"And did you hear that one of her students was arrested for murder the other day?"

"Yes!" Anne shook her head. "I just can't believe it!"

Helen tsked and lowered the pie. "What a thing…two people in that office involved in horrid crimes." Her tone suddenly softened as she cocked her head toward Anne. "These pies are perfect for the luncheon today, don't you think? I really didn't have time to bake, I've been so busy."

"Oh, I agree. These are perfect," said Anne.

Elise's mum was shaking so badly now, she set it on an empty shelf next to her before it crashed to the floor. As she did, something about that movement touched her memory again, but just for a brief second. She shook it off, made sure the mum was safe, then watched the women as they sauntered toward the checkout counter, heads bobbing in conversation.

Elise glanced at the front doors then back at the women. As soon as they were busy checking out, she made her break. She dashed behind their backs, turning her head away, and pushed with both hands against the right side of the double doors. But that side was locked, and her body slammed into the plexiglass, shaking the frame.

"Ma'am, you okay?" asked a young man, as he walked in the other side.

Elise lowered her head, squeezed past him, ignoring the question, and sprinted for her car. Once inside, she contemplated whether to go home and calm down, or just go to the office. She chose the latter. It was still early, and if she went home, Cole would be there, and she'd end up worrying him even more. On top of it, he was busy getting ready for an overnight trip to Chicago the next day. The office it would have to be.

Minutes later, Elise leaned against the back door she'd just locked, closed her eyes, and took several slow breaths. She opened them and clicked the hall light on, providing just enough light to see where she was going, without advertising that the office was officially open.

She unceremoniously dropped her purse and workbag on the top of her desk, then headed for the coffee maker located in the work/break room.

Still using the light from the hallway, Elise grabbed her "I Love Audiology" mug from one of the cupboards, placed it on the small platform, and dropped her favorite dark roast into the basket. She pushed the start button and focused on its little red light, willing herself to be patient.

But as it gurgled to life, she sensed a small geyser working its way upward, not from the coffee maker, but from a fissure in her stomach. What nerve of those women! It was ridiculous gossip, and probably already over and done with, but still, what horrible things to say! And who else had they been talking to?

The nutty aroma of brewed coffee averted her thoughts for a few seconds as she lifted the mug to her lips, feeling the steam tickle her nose. But within seconds, her shoulders slumped again as she shuffled down the hall toward her office. An unacknowledged Dr. Downs watched from her wall photo, as Elise ignored her for the second time that morning.

She dropped her coffee cup on a torn piece of paper on her desk, now an official coaster, pulled her desk chair out and clicked the computer on, ready to check the day's patient schedule. The corners of her mouth curled into a slight smile when she saw the first name, appreciative that the large majority of her patients were lovely people.

Elise assembled what she needed for her first appointment, including the new hearing aid demos and important patient information regarding their use with other devices. Her eyes fell on a copy of Susan's research article just as her office phone pierced the silence with such clatter that she about jumped out of her seat.

She yanked the handset to her ear. "Dr. Harte," she snapped, a little more shortly than she meant to.

"Elise, it's Susan. I had just a minute to call."

"Oh, Susan." Elise relaxed slightly against the back of her chair. "I'm sorry… didn't mean to sound so awful. How are you?"

"I'm okay, I guess. Well, not really. I'll get right to the point. Did one of the lab techs tell you that Theo suspected me of intentionally sabotaging data on this chip?"

Elise could hear the intensity in Susan's voice and decided that truth was the best response. "I overheard a partial conversation in the restroom the other day, but it was only partial and thought everyone was just upset."

"You heard that and didn't say anything to me?"

"Hey, you should hear what I just heard about me at the grocery—"

"I couldn't care less about that right now!" Susan snapped, then took a breath. "I'm sorry, Elise, but I just don't know what to think. I'm trying not to jump to conclusions, but is there anything else you're not telling me?"

"No, Susan. You know what I know." Elise truly believed the research audiologist and felt guilty at even wavering from the usual admiration she had for Susan's work. She added the copy of Susan's research to the patient's packet.

"Well, that just set me off. What gall they all have! After the work I've put into this project."

"Look," said Elise. "Can you check into something there for me?"

"Into what?"

"It's about what happened to Tierneigh. I'm sorry, but I need to know something. Seems Tierneigh was attacked between about 9:45 and 10:15, Thursday night. I want to confirm where Rick, Bob, and Theo were around that time. And add in David Nubrey, if you can."

"Well, I know about Rick. He let everybody know he left the training a few minutes after nine and met a friend at a bar."

Elise mumbled, "He has one of those?"

"One of what?"

"A friend," said Elise. "I'm sorry, I didn't mean it the way it sounded."

"Yeah, you did," said Susan, and they both giggled, releasing a little bit of tension.

"Well, would it be a friend who would lie for him?"

Susan paused, then mumbled, "Don't know." She raised her voice slightly. "I'm pretty sure I did see him head for the doors when he said he did. That was when I was taking the last group to the anechoic chamber. And Theo…I heard him talking the other day, and I'm sure he said he was here, in his third-floor office."

"What?" Elise didn't expect that. "Why was he there so late?"

"Said he had a late phone meeting with a possible investor overseas."

"Hmph."

Susan continued. "And did you say David? What's he got to do with this?"

"Probably nothing. I just can't put my finger on the way he acts sometimes. So that leaves the accountant that we don't know about, right?

"Yeah. Bob." Susan let out a long breath. "Gossip's running around here like crazy, but not so much about him. I guess I shouldn't be surprised that I'd be part of it, too."

Elise heard the side door rattle open, followed by a flood of lights, and Amy and Lucy's light banter with each other. All signs the day was starting.

"Susan, you going to be alright?"

"I'm trying. I'll see what I can find out about Bob and David, okay?"

"Thanks. And I'll see what I can find out from the Mt.

Harmony Sheriff's Department." Elise scanned the day's schedule once more and saw Noah's name down for an afternoon appointment for a remake of one of his custom ear plugs. Good.

"Okay. Talk to you later."

"Right," said Elise, and she clunked the handset in its cradle.

"Thanks for making the coffee," said Lucy, stopping at Elise's door. "Your first patient's here."

Elise took a deep breath and cleared her mind as best she could. "Be right there."

***

Noon came upon them faster than expected, and since Elise was minus a lunch, Amy volunteered to pick something up for the both of them at the hospital cafeteria. When she got back, she and Elise grabbed two folding chairs, usually stashed in the hearing aid work room, and set them up outside the back door. Tacos and sunshine were welcomed after the morning's dreariness.

Elise filled in an astonished Amy on the latest events, including David Nubrey's strange behavior, Rick Dayton's money problems, and Susan's recent annoyance with her. She ended with the grocery store incident from that morning.

Amy wiped her mouth with a paper napkin, her eyes wide at all the information. "That's crazy! Can't wait to see what your afternoon's gonna be like."

"Gee…thanks."

"And it sounds like the pressure's really getting to Susan."

"I know," said Elise. "But until we find out what happened to Tierneigh, and why, we're all going to be looking twice at each other."

Amy blinked wide eyes at her.

"I didn't mean you!"

"I know. I was just trying to lighten the mood here." Amy glanced at her watch. "Hey, I have a patient in ten minutes."

She gathered the trash, while Elise folded the chairs and brought them back inside the building, suddenly getting an idea. She had a little time before her next patient, so walked to the test room across the hall from her office and stopped in front of a poster-sized, laminated picture of an ear's anatomy that hung on a hook. It was usually used for patient education, when explaining how a person hears and/or where a problem may be occurring, but this time would be different.

Elise grabbed it off the hook and took it to her office. She flipped the anatomy side over on her desk and exposed the clean, white backing. Next, she cut out pictures of Rick Dayton, Theo Wrightman, and Susan Andres from brochures and papers from the training and taped them in a line across the top. She told herself that Susan was there only to mark timelines and not as a real suspect. A second line included Bob Bell, a hand-drawn attempt at David Nubrey (since she didn't have a picture), and to her great dismay, Jake Cagney. She printed his picture out from a social website she knew he used. Underneath each picture, she wrote brief notes and the times they said they left E. S. Hearing Labs the night Tierneigh was attacked.

"Dr. Harte, your patient's here," said Lucy, leaning around the doorjamb. Her eyes grew wide at the rogues' gallery on Elise's desk, but neither woman said a word.

Elise nodded and Lucy headed back to her desk as Elise replaced the ear picture on the wall of the test room, anatomy side out.

The next few hours morphed into manageable chaos. Usually, by the end of the day, the office staff would come together, even for just a few minutes, to check in with each other, but today seemed more than just a little off. For one thing, she never saw Noah Reed.

Amy's door was closed, so Elise walked to the front of the office and waited as Lucy hung up the phone.

"Didn't I have Noah on my schedule this afternoon?"

Lucy swiveled to face Elise. "Yeah, but Dr. MacNeal saw him. He came in early and saw you were busy, so asked if she could see him. She did the impression for the remake."

"Oh," said Elise, her eyebrows scrunching together. "Did he say anything about wanting to talk to me...or anything?"

"No, he didn't. And...ahh... your last patient cancelled...and..."

"And what?"

"There's a few more cancellations for tomorrow, too."

Elise glanced at the schedule on Lucy's computer and saw quite a few blank spaces. "How many?"

"Enough to maybe give you a break to rest tomorrow?" Lucy raised her eyebrows as if looking on the bright side might be a good thing.

"Why'd they cancel?"

"No excuses. Just said they had to."

Elise felt her stomach sink. "Is this too much of a coincidence with everything that's been going on lately? Do people think I'm involved in something...nefarious...or something?"

"Oh, no, Dr. Harte. Noooo...I'm sure there were things that just came up."

Just then, Amy's door flew open, and out walked a tall, middle-aged woman with short graying hair. The woman turned and pressed her lips tightly together. She looked Elise up and down, then strode out the front door.

Bewildered, Elise turned to Amy. "What was that all about?"

Amy lowered her eyes to a chart she was holding. "What was what about?"

"Your patient's attitude."

Amy walked back into her office and returned, holding a copy of the Mt. Harmony Herald. "Might have something to do with this."

Elise took the paper that was folded in half. "What? I don't see anything."

Amy grabbed the paper and flipped it over. Elise's jaw dropped at the headline.

"Mt. Harmony Hearing and Balance Student Arrested for Alleged Murder." By Grady Weber, Reporter.

Angry tears welled in her eyes.

"It'll be over soon," said Amy. "Come on. Let's sit down and figure this out."

Since it seemed they were done for the day, the women shuffled into the waiting room, locked the front door, turned out the light, and sat in semi-darkness. The office lights glowed from the hallway and through the reception window at Lucy's desk. It was enough for Elise to see her coworkers watching her intently, sympathy in their eyes.

"What?" said Elise.

"Come on," said Amy. "Tell us what we can do. What would Marion Downs do?"

Elise glanced toward the picture of the woman she admired so much. "Dr. Downs would demand to know what was going on…and fix it."

Lucy spoke up. "Look. I think you could use a break. Dr. MacNeal and I will take care of the office tomorrow, okay? It looks like it's going to be kinda light, as it is."

"Good idea," said Amy. "My office cupboards need to be

cleaned out, and I can be here in case anyone does come in."

Elise closed her eyes. After a long minute, she opened them. "How long does it take to get to Indianapolis?"

Amy's eyebrows lowered. "A few hours, give or take, why?"

"Less if I stop somewhere before that, like maybe…Lewelling Labs?"

"Lewelling La— Ohhh," said Amy, nodding her head. "I'm not sure I'd want you going there alone, though."

"Actually, if I go alone, I might not look too conspicuous."

"What's at Lewelling Labs?" asked Lucy, eyebrows raised.

"Some information, I think, that might be worth looking into."

"You sure?" said Amy.

"Yes, I'll be fine. The ride will be good for me. I may go out to E. S. Hearing Labs first, though…make a day of it."

"Okay, if you're sure." Amy stood and looked around the office. "I think I'll get going then. You just be careful."

"I will. Oh, before you go, would you make impressions of my ears for the new demo ear plugs I need? You don't have to wait. Just put the goop in my ears, and I can take them out." She was referring to the soft silicone mixture inserted into the ear canal and bowl of the ear, which hardens in a few minutes to make accurate ear impressions for different products.

"Sure, no problem." Amy headed for the work room. "Come here and I'll do it right now."

Elise followed and sat on one of the stools as Amy opened and closed drawers, gathering the impression material and tools she needed.

They heard Lucy call out from the front office. "Orders

are in from the open house, so I'll check them in and call patients tomorrow for appointments."

Elise called back, "I hope they come in."

"Hey, I know some of these people really well. They'll come in. Goodnight!"

Just minutes later, Elise was alone in the office. Lime green, silicone goop filled her ears. A white string hung from the bottom of each ear, attached to a small foam block inserted into the ear canal first to protect the ear drum. Elise walked around the office, checking that doors were locked and lights out as she waited for the goop to set. She went back to her desk, sat down, and gingerly tapped the middle of one ear, but the goop wasn't ready. She noticed a few green spots on her finger and brushed them off with her other hand. Just a few more minutes.

She slowly rotated the chair to look at the bookshelf behind her, wondering if she needed to buy an updated version of her five-inch-thick audiology reference book, but the space it usually took up was empty. Her eyebrows lowered and she stared. What was it that was niggling at her?

Elise turned back to her desk to see her cell phone spinning in jerky circles on the smooth desktop. A gray-haired, smiling face shimmied on the face of the phone.

Aunt Ida! Elise grabbed the phone and tapped the green dot to answer. She raised her voice. "Aunt Ida? Hello? Hello?" She pressed the phone to her ear, but still couldn't hear anything. "Hello? Aunt Ida? It's Elise!" Why couldn't she hear her?

Elise tried to pull the phone away from her ear, but felt it resist. "Oh, no!" she cried.

The phone broke free, but was covered with splotches of rubbery, green goop!

"Don't hang up, Aunt Ida! Wait!" She slid her fingers between the goop and the back of her ear, trying to get a good grip on the almost-set impressions, but ended up with green sticky strings on her fingers and down the side of her face.

By the time she pulled all the goop and foam blocks out, Aunt Ida was gone. Green sticky blotches covered her fingers and smudged the front of her phone. She grabbed a tissue to wipe the phone off, but created an even worse mess of sticky, torn tissue and green debris.

Elise carefully laid the phone on the desk, covered her face with both hands, and let the tears come.

Chapter Fifteen

Thursday Morning

There he was again, standing by the reception desk. Theo Wrightman wiped his brow as his eyes darted over the heads of two lab employees standing in front of him, trying to get his attention. His eyes met Elise's and froze like laser beams that had found their target.

She mustered a smile and wondered at the odd reaction, as she strode toward him.

He actually shook her hand this time. "Hello, Dr....Dr...."

"Harte. Elise Harte." She nodded a hello at the lab techs. "How are you this morning, Mr. Wrightman?"

"Fair to middling, I guess. Can I help you with something?"

She nodded toward the north hallway. "I wanted to see Dr. Andres. Is her main office open, yet?"

"No, and it's just one more thing putting us in a bind. I think she's using that test room just across from it. The one she was in yesterday."

"I'm sure this has all been a great inconvenience to you," Elise said straight-faced, "especially now with Jake Cagney arrested."

Theo looked at his shoes and mumbled, "Yeah, I heard. I was shocked, but he always was a troubled kid."

She didn't expect that. "Why do you say that?"

"Oh…uh…I thought you knew." A patchy flush rose up Theo's neck. "I knew Jake's parents from a previous job, years ago. We worked at the same plant. Seemed like Jake was always getting into trouble. His parents were relieved when he turned himself around…going to school and all …to be an ide…ideo…audio-ologist."

Elise sighed inwardly and ignored the mispronunciation. "It is a very rewarding profession. You know that he's been helping at our office, besides here with you, on top of going to school, right?"

"Hmm?"

Elise couldn't tell if Theo was truly surprised or not. She thought she'd play along and see where it went. "He's nearing graduation, so at this point, he's getting real-world experience in as many audiological settings as possible."

Theo glanced at his watch. "Well, good seeing you, Dr. Harte. Have a meeting to get to." He strode with determination toward the elevators behind the reception desk.

Elise counted as he smacked the elevator button four times with the palm of his hand before the doors finally slid open and he disappeared.

Well, thought Elise, as she did a slightly dramatic, old black-and-white movie flip of her hair, then strode up the north hallway, anxious to talk to Susan.

She felt her stomach flip, as she approached the Research Audiology door, yellow crime scene tape still taut. No one was around. She turned her attention to the door across the hall, tapped on it, grabbed the handle, and cautiously pushed it open.

"Elise, good morning." Susan rose from her computer, a tentative smile on her face.

"Am I interrupting anything?"

"No, no, come on in. Just looking over data. It's such a

pain not to be able to get into my office. I got your message. Have a seat." Susan extended her hand toward a second office chair, concern on her face. "You sounded upset."

"Yes, I guess I am." Elise lowered herself into the chair and crossed her ankles under her. "I need to ask you something more about Tierneigh…and Rick…and maybe about your data. Thought it was best to just come see you and not talk on the phone, under the circumstances."

"Oh. Okay. Yeah, I'm still not sure who was listening to us when we were in the test booth. Maybe it was innocent, but—"

Elise interrupted, doubting any innocence. "I was hoping you could help me understand exactly why Rick had this crazy attitude toward Tierneigh."

Susan opened her mouth as if to talk but closed it again.

"And are the accountant and Theo involved in this, too? And do you know exactly why, for sure, there's all this negative attitude toward you?"

Susan's eyes grew wide as Elise spoke, then her face saddened. "I know I told you about the inconsistent test results I found, right?"

Elise nodded.

"I don't have anything to really base this on, but I've had the feeling they either think I'm lying or…"

"Or?" Elise prompted.

"Or, I guess, that I don't know what I'm doing, or even worse, that I do know what I'm doing, and they truly suspect me of something that I can't even repeat." Susan looked away from Elise.

Elise leaned forward. She felt her heart start to pound. "Like intentionally sabotaging your own work? Are you serious?"

Susan frowned. "I told myself the behaviors around here were just from the pressure of getting the new chip out…the creating, testing, producing…the marketing. You've seen the ads."

Elise nodded, concern growing in her stomach.

"The pressure's been off the boards. When I found inconsistencies in my test results, my professional life flashed before my eyes. I had no choice but to retest and try to find out what and where the problem was."

"Susan, I'm so sorry." Elise felt relieved in one sense, that her initial instincts about Susan were right, but at the same time, felt her stomach constrict at the confirmation of what she'd been suspecting about the new chip. "Is there anything I can do?"

Susan shook her head. "I just need time…"

Elise stared at Susan. "And now you're short help, with what's happened with Jake."

"I never heard what actually happened with him or why he was arrested."

"Oh. Well, Sheriff Reed told me they found an ear print on the anechoic chamber door, that matched Jake's right ear, but that's all I know."

Susan slumped back in her chair, eyebrows raised. "What?"

Elise explained the ear print. "And I guess Jake's not talking. I wasn't able to see him, and now, like I told you the other day, he's been released until his court date. In the meantime, I've got patients, and you've got data to look at."

They both rose and walked out to the hallway but stopped when they saw Rick standing about twenty feet away, glaring at them. Elise raised her hand to wave in acknowledgement, but he turned on his heel and disappeared.

"Susan, when was it, again, that you saw Rick on the night of the training?"

Susan's eyes jerked to the floor then focused ahead of

her as she started walking toward the reception area.

Elise's jaw dropped, but she had enough wherewithal to close it when she quickened her pace to catch up to her.

Susan spoke, eyes still straight ahead. "I, uh, saw him when I brought the last group of people to the anechoic chamber. He had his jacket on and was heading for the front doors when my group and I walked through the reception area. I presumed he was leaving the building."

Elise lowered her voice. "So that must've been a few minutes after nine, right?"

Susan nodded.

"I don't mean this to sound the way it's going to sound, but I have to ask…when did you actually leave that night?"

Susan stopped walking and turned to face Elise. "I walked out of here with the last tour group…about fifteen, or so, minutes after nine."

Elise couldn't help but stare. What was it she just heard in Susan's voice? Anger? Defensiveness?

"Look, Elise. I really need to get back to work." With that, she turned and strode back down the hallway, never looking back.

Elise's jaw dropped for the second time that morning. The long quiet drive to Lewelling Labs was looking better by the minute.

Chapter Sixteen

Thursday Morning

Elise had decided earlier that she wouldn't mention her trip to Lewelling Labs to Susan, and after that uncomfortable conversation, she was sure she'd made the right decision. She just couldn't put her finger on why. Elise wanted information on Rick, and she knew she could trust Amy and Lucy, so was she admitting that, deep down, she didn't really trust Susan?

Traffic was light and the air cool and clear. Cornstalk tassels glowed golden in the sunlight and reminded Elise of butterscotch candy. Her saliva glands kicked in just thinking about the yellow-orange disks of sugar she'd enjoyed so much as a child. Massive groups of small black birds she'd learned were starlings, swooped up and down and around the fields like never-ending roller coasters, against a cloudless sky, like the roller coaster at the Santa Cruz boardwalk where she and her high school friends would go every summer. She could watch them for hours.

Elise passed shiny metal silos that housed harvested corn and towered against the sky and tried to imagine the families that lived in the two- or three-story farmhouses. How free the children must feel, growing up on farms. Growing up on a hill in San Francisco made her envy kids who could play right outside their own front doors.

Once, a combine rumbled close to the road, and she

thought it had to be as big as a locomotive. She cranked her neck to see the farmer sitting way up behind a wrap-around, four-foot-high window, with a blond-haired boy about three years old standing next to him, both hands flat on the windshield. His eyes were wide, with an even wider smile. He waved at her as she passed. She waved back.

Elise felt pleasantly relaxed by the time she pulled into a parking space in the visitor's section of the Lewelling Labs parking lot. She glanced at the time on her dashboard. Eleven thirty. Perfect.

She scanned the area, and instead of one large building like E. S. Hearing Labs, she saw a complex of three white concrete buildings. One two-story and the others just one-story. Elise guessed the executive offices would be in the two-story building, so she locked the car, pulled her purse strap up on her shoulder, and headed for the main door. A slight breeze chilled her, and she hugged her jacket collar around her neck.

As she approached the front doors, a group of employees walked out, probably on lunch break. They wore IDs on lanyards, or clipped to their outerwear, chatting casually with one other. One or two glanced her way but didn't seem overly concerned at her presence. Elise took their nonchalance as a good sign and entered when one employee held one side of a pair of glass doors open for her. She smiled her thanks.

Ahead of her, a middle-aged, balding security guard wiggled on a metal stool behind a dark wood podium. He grinned "hellos" to the usuals, but when he saw Elise, his back straightened, and he gave her his full attention.

"Hello. I'm Dr. Elise Harte. I'm an audiologist and was wondering if I could speak to someone about your products."

He relaxed slightly and pulled a clipboard out from under the top of the podium. "Where ya from, ma'am?"

"Mt. Harmony. I have a business there and was on my way to Indianapolis." Technically, she was headed in that direction. "I thought I'd take advantage and stop and see the lab and possibly get information about some of the products."

He smiled, turned the clipboard toward her with a blank, lined paper attached, and asked if she'd print her name, the date, and time.

When she finished, he took the clipboard, stood, and waved an arm to the side. "Come this way."

Elise followed him across a clean, white, linoleum floor, toward a reception desk not far behind his station, where a young woman with a long blond braid flipped forward over one shoulder, shuffled through papers on her desk.

"This is Dr. Harte," he said to her, then turned to Elise. "Lindee here will take care of you."

"Thank you," she said with a smile, then turned toward Lindee and repeated her request. "I apologize for not calling first, but I was on the road and realized how close I was to Lewelling Labs, so thought I'd take a chance." Elise crossed her fingers in her mind to make herself feel better about one more slight deviation from the truth.

"Of course," said Lindee. "Let me call our CEO and see if he has a few minutes."

"That'd be great, but I could speak with someone in your sales department, if he or she is busy."

"It's a he...Bill Hooper. I'm sure he won't mind."

After an elevator trip to the second floor, Elise was left staring at a man with light brown hair and glasses, standing behind an oversized oak wood desk. A window filled the wall behind him. Sunlight hit his back, putting his face in a slight shadow, and directly into her eyes. She wondered if that was intentional.

Bill Hooper approached Elise, hand held out. "Well, I'm awfully glad to meet you, Dr. Harte," he said as he enthusiastically shook her hand, almost hurting it. "You said you have a business in Mt. Harmony? You're close to Bluestem, right? Are you familiar with E. S. Hearing Labs?"

Well, he sure didn't miss a beat, she thought, trying to maintain her fixed smile. "Yes, actually, I do use some of their products. I've been meaning to stop by Lewelling Labs, as well, and took a chance this morning. I have basic information from the internet but like to introduce myself in person when I get the chance."

Bill Hooper gave her an even bigger smile, then winked. "E. S. Hearing Labs had a little trouble lately, I hear. We've been getting quite a few inquiries, so I'm glad you decided to look in our direction. Have you ever used our products before?" He pointed to a side table filled with coffee urns and condiments. "Coffee?"

Elise declined the beverage, even though it smelled fantastic to her, and intentionally kept the rest of her conversation vague. She was relieved when Bill picked up the phone, made a request, then said someone named Julie would be there soon to give Elise a quick tour of the plant.

"Thank you, Mr. Hooper," said Elise. "I appreciate your time. I hope I'm not interrupting your lunchtime."

All of a sudden, an extremely loud, persistent, rap…rap…rap caught their attention, causing them both to jump.

"Well, that was quick," said Bill, as he opened the door to a grinning, wide-eyed, Rick Dayton, hand still raised in a fist, obviously not done announcing his presence.

He was casually dressed in jeans, a white tee shirt, and brown leather jacket. His face froze, though, at the sight before him.

"Rick?" Elise was proud of herself that she didn't actually sputter.

Rick's eyebrows were higher on his forehead than Elise thought possible, and his mouth struggled with something close to speech.

Bill slapped Rick on the shoulder and smirked. "Didn't know you were coming today, Rick. I take it you two know each other?"

Rick's eyebrows lowered, but his eyes didn't move from Elise, as a young woman wearing a loose navy jacket walked up behind him.

"Hi, Rick...Bill," she said, then turned to Elise. "Dr. Harte? My name's Julie. I came to give you a tour of our place here, if this is a good time."

"Oh, uh, absolutely. Thank you so much." Elise held her breath and squeezed between the two men and out the door.

She followed Julie down the cream-colored hallway, fighting a horrible urge to look back. *What's Rick doing here? He seems awfully familiar with Bill and Julie...and them in return!*

She followed her guide onto an elevator, then to the first floor, where Julie led Elise down a quiet hallway and out one end of the building. Elise, still in shock, was glad Julie took care of the small talk, running through a brief history of the lab and the people who worked there. As soon as Elise felt she could bring herself to speak without sputtering, she'd ask about Rick's presence, but for now, she tried to turn to a safer subject and asked Julie about the company's production, timelines for delivery, and research behind their products. The young woman's demeanor was that of a well-informed professional, as she answered Elise's questions, while at the same time, explained the different departments and their functions.

They entered one of the one-story buildings from the

front door. Poster-sized pictures of products were displayed, as well as trophies from a local Little League team sponsored by Lewelling Labs. Julie took Elise past open doorways of long, white, workrooms, where lab techs in white lab coats worked in rows, bent over their stations. They looked like they were frozen in place, as they peered through illuminated magnifying glasses. Occasional drilling and buffing noises were the only sounds Elise could hear. She noted that the techs all wore ear protection.

After a few more stops and a quick walk through the other one-story building, they entered the side door of the main building again and proceeded back down the hallway.

Julie paused and waved her hand at an open door. "My office is right here," she said. She walked in, picked a beige burlap bag off her desk and held it out to Elise. "Here's more specific information for you about our products, with names and contact information for the different departments. Is there any other department you'd like to see?"

Elise took the bag and smiled. "Oh, no, I'm fine. I really appreciate your time, thank you. I'll look through this when I get back to my office." Elise paused, then decided to take a chance in another direction. "I did notice that the hearing aid selection seemed limited. Does the lab plan to expand that at all?"

"Yes, we're primarily focused on assistive devices and ear protection, but are soon hoping to update our hearing aid manufacturing department."

Elise nodded, her mind focusing on that tidbit of information. Normally, she wouldn't think anything of it, but the presence of Rick at Lewelling Labs put a whole different light on things.

Elise and Julie walked back down the hallway toward the front of the building, but as they passed what looked like a break room, Elise sniffed. "Ooh, that coffee smells great."

Julie smiled. "Would you like some before you get back on the road?"

"I'd love some, thanks."

A few minutes later, both were sipping surprisingly good machine-made mochas at a round metal table in the good-sized break room. They were alone at the moment, and Elise made a comment about it.

"This is nice for breaks," Julie said in response, "but mostly people like to get out for lunch."

Elise took in the room as she sipped her drink. One wall held vending machines and a counter with a microwave oven. Two other sides of the room held glass display cases that almost filled the walls. Elise wanted to see the displays better, so, coffee in hand, slid out of her seat and walked closer to one end, where she started a slow trek across both wall displays. She saw black-and-white photos of employees from decades earlier, along with pictures of the lab itself, transformed from a small, three-room concrete building over the years, to the current three-building complex. Her eyes lingered on a display of antique hearing devices, ear trumpets and hearing aids from the late 1800s to the 1900s. As always, the old testing equipment specifically caught her attention.

Elise was proud of her profession's history, especially the part audiology played in addressing hearing problems in World War II servicemen when they returned home. She shook the thought aside for the moment and sipped her coffee again, then decided to take a chance.

She turned to Julie. "Does Lewelling Labs plan to have the same kind of technology in hearing aids as E. S. Hearing Labs does?"

Julie paused and looked her in the eyes "Maybe," she said, as she raised her cup to her lips. She stopped, as if she'd just thought of something, and placed her cup back on the table. "Did you hear what happened out there? I just can't believe it."

Elise nodded and lowered her eyes. "Maybe that's why Rick Dayton's here. He works there, you know."

"I know!" Julie seemed more relaxed now and maybe was just a little hungry. Elise suspected she was missing lunchtime on her account. "This is like the third time I've seen him here. I think he's interviewing or something."

"Really?" said Elise, trying not to sound too interested. "Maybe he's—"

But just then, two employees in business suits, a man and a woman, walked into the break room and glanced at Julie, who wiggled in her seat.

"I need to let you get back to work," said Elise.

Julie nodded silently.

They disposed of their trash and walked toward the entrance to the building, where Elise thanked Julie again for accommodating her unscheduled visit.

Elise nodded goodbye to the guard, then strode across the parking lot, head down against a chilly gust of wind, her mind filled with so many questions. She pulled her purse off her shoulder and rifled for her phone, anxious to call Amy and tell her about seeing Rick at Lewelling Labs. Was it really for a job, or was there a more nefarious reason for his visit? Was Bob Bell in on this with him? Did Theo know?

Elise transferred her phone to her other hand as she grabbed her keys with her free hand and clicked her car door open. She threw her purse on the passenger seat just as she heard heavy footsteps shuffling roughly through leaves behind her.

"Hey!"

Elise jumped, whirled around, and reflexively pressed her back against the door frame. A red-faced Rick Dayton strode toward her, both hands curled in tight fists. Elise threw him the meanest glare she could muster, in defense of what, she didn't know, but knew she needed to take some kind of an offensive.

"What are you doing here, Rick?" A gust of wind blew hair across her eyes, and she quickly brushed it back and held it with one hand.

"Me? What are you doing here?" His glare was more than unsettling. "I couldn't believe it when I saw your name on the sign-in sheet at the front door!"

"I have a business, Rick," she said, not hiding her sarcasm, and at the same time continuing with her direct offensive strategy. "What's your excuse? Trying to get away from E. S. Hearing Labs for some reason?"

Rick blinked. "No." That seemed to take him aback. "Actually, it's none of your business. Does Susan know you're here?"

"Susan?" Elise didn't expect that. "What's this have to do with Susan? And you haven't answered my question."

Rick ignored her. "You've been pretty chummy with our research audiologist lately."

His tone of voice caught Elise by surprise. Her jaw clenched and she tried to hide her true anger.

"You looking at leaving E. S. Labs, Rick? You know something the rest of us don't?"

That seemed to hit some kind of nerve and Rick's jaw dropped. "No...no...I'm going to Indy for a couple of days...meeting a friend...going to some races."

"The friend you met the other night after the training?" She regretted it the minute it came out.

His head jerked, and she fought recoiling against his glare. He clamped his mouth shut, turned on his heel and stomped away, fists in his jacket pockets, head down.

Elise watched him for a split second, then just as quickly, realized she wanted to get as far away from him as possible. She jumped into her SUV, punched the lock button, and tried not to look in his direction, in case he was watching. Rick certainly seemed to be capable of attacking someone, or could he actually check himself and walk away like he did just then? And what'd he do? Follow her to Lewelling Labs? She'd seen him at E. S. Hearing Labs just this morning.

Elise glanced at the mirrors, then turned to check the area around her. She was pretty sure it was him she saw in a black sports car, screeching toward the interstate. She punched the radio button and, with deep breaths and Beethoven, began to think.

Once again, there'd been little traffic on her return to Mt. Harmony. Elise convinced herself she was safe…that Rick did what he said he was going to do and drove in the opposite direction to Indianapolis. She commanded her voice texting service to send a message to Amy that she was on her way back to the office.

About an hour later, her phone buzzed, and she immediately recognized Maryelle's number. She tapped the phone button on the steering wheel.

"Maryelle?"

"Elise, hi…yes. You driving?"

"Yeah, got you on speaker. I'm alone. You okay?"

"I'm alright, I guess." The tone of her voice was not as convincing. "You left a message about Tierneigh and data, so I thought about it and remembered something."

"Oh?" Elise eyed some low gray clouds that seemed to appear just ahead of her.

"Yeah, I don't remember her saying anything exactly about data, and whether it was good or bad, but I did remember something else."

"Okay." Elise tried not to hold her breath.

"Tierneigh was bugged about something at work. She overheard someone named Glory…or Gloria…talking on the phone one morning, when she went to see her at her office. Tierneigh said Glory or Gloria was really upset."

"I think it's Gloria, you're talking about. That's Tierneigh's manager. Do you mean upset, like yelling or something?"

"Sort of. Tierneigh said this Gloria said the name 'Bill.' She remembered it, because she didn't know any Bill at work, and she wasn't sure if that's who she was talking to, or actually someone she was talking about. Whatever it was, it was pretty serious." Maryelle's voice dropped. "Does that help you with anything?"

Elise's mind raced. "It does…thank you, Maryelle."

"I'll call if I think of anything else."

"Okay, thanks, and…take care of yourself, okay?,"

"I will."

Elise disconnected the call. Bill was a common name, but what were the chances that Gloria was either speaking to, or about, Bill Hooper, the CEO at Lewelling Labs? What if Gloria found out about Rick getting familiar with people out there? Elise wondered if she could just outright ask her about it.

And what was it that Susan just told her yesterday about Theo talking to investors? It makes sense that Theo'd be pitching Lewelling Labs about the new chip, so was he in on this, with whatever Rick was doing? Or was Rick acting on his own?

The steady monotony of the drive now made her evaluate how naive she'd been in her own life. She went through school, moved across multiple states, started a family, as well as her own business. It was a lot to her, but doable. Besides her family, she was most proud of her business…of meeting her co-owner, Amy, and creating a means to help people in a field she felt passionate about.

What she felt now, though, scared her. And it started

with the loss of one of her best friends.

Her hands slid slightly on the steering wheel. One at a time, she wiped them on her pant legs. Now she felt that everything she loved was being threatened.

She glanced at the dashboard clock. She expected to make it to the office by midafternoon.

The office was empty when Elise arrived. She checked the schedule and found there had been a cancellation. There was also a note on the front door, in case anyone came by, that Amy and Lucy had gone to the hospital to check on one of their patients and would return soon. Occasionally, Lucy would help the audiologists carry portable equipment and such, when a physician ordered a diagnostic hearing evaluation on a patient. So Elise made a cup of chamomile tea and headed back to her office.

She sat at her desk in the quiet and figured Amy and Lucy might be catching a late lunch while they were out. She pulled herself closer to the desk to look at the paper messages that lay in front of her. There was one from Gloria Strauber and one from Deborah Miller that she started to read, when she heard the click of a dead bolt turn, and an office door open.

Good, Amy was back and they would probably have time to talk before the next patient. She didn't know why she hadn't unlocked the doors anyway, when she first came in.

She pushed her chair away from the desk and called out as she walked down the hallway. "Amy, you won't believe who I saw at Lewelling Labs this—"

Her face froze as she approached the open window to the waiting room and stared directly into the baby blue eyes of Jake Cagney.

Chapter Seventeen

═══ | ═══

Thursday Afternoon

"Jake." Elise kept her tone as even as she could.

"Hello, Dr. Harte." Jake's voice was soft and forced. "Can I talk to you a minute?"

Elise watched him roll a key over and over in his hand. She'd completely forgotten that he had an office key.

Elise glanced at the wall clock and tried to keep her voice steady. "This might not be a good time. We have patients coming, and Amy and Lucy had to go over to the hospital."

Now he knew she was alone.

But his eyes were pleading. Elise followed her instincts and motioned him in. They walked uncomfortably down the hall to her office where Elise took a seat behind her desk, Jake in front of it.

"I came to apologize, Dr. Harte." His voice shook, and he dropped his head, then raised it again and looked directly into her eyes. "And I have something I have to tell you."

Elise nodded in an "I'm listening" way, clasping her shaking hands under the desk.

"I know you think I did something to Dr. Brown, but I didn't."

"You said you came to apologize."

"Yeah." Jake's head dropped again. "I'm the one...who

broke into your house…the night of the training."

Elise stiffened. She took a shallow breath and said only one word. "Why?"

"Look, I know this has ruined everything, but I can't stand you thinking I did anything as bad as hurting Dr. Brown."

"What else, Jake." It came out as more of a statement.

"Theo Wrightman forced me to do it."

Her eyes bore into Jake's and anger took over fear. "You need to explain that."

Jake winced. "Theo needed something. And he knows me…or knew me…when I was a kid."

Well, that jived with what Theo said earlier, but Elise wondered cynically if this was really true, or if he and Theo came up with this story for other reasons.

"He made me feel like I was doing something for the company, that it was really important."

"Doing what, Jake?" Elise's eyes didn't leave his.

"Honestly, I don't know why he asked me, but he said there was something really important that he thought you had…and he thought it was something that wasn't true…and could ruin the company."

Elise felt her throat go dry. What was he talking about? She wished someone else was there to hear this, too. "I'm lost, Jake. I still don't get it. What would I have that was so important?"

"Theo thought Tierneigh either told you about something or passed something on to you in one of the gift bags, on the night of the training."

"I don't know what you're talking about." Elise tried to relive that night. Think of any details she might've missed. "Why did Theo ask you to do this?"

His head dropped. "I thought you might've heard that I got in trouble when I was a kid. My parents worked, but they didn't make a lot of money, and I kinda got in with a wrong group of kids. We did malicious mischief kinds of things. I was underage when I got caught and had to do community service."

"And Theo knew about this?" Elise tried to maintain only one level of shock and anger at a time.

"Yeah. He knew my parents, and he kinda insinuated that he'd hurt my career if I didn't help him…with what he thought you had."

"I didn't know anything about your background, Jake. I just know you're a good student and will be successful in anything you put your mind to."

He reacted the way she hoped he would and saw tears pool in his eyes.

"I broke into your house, Dr. Harte, and I'm sorry. But I didn't hurt Dr. Brown. I need you to know that. If you want to call the police, I'll tell them what I just told you."

"I have to let them know, Jake, and I'll talk to my husband. But I think I can tell you that we probably aren't going to press charges."

Now the tears flowed, and Jake stood up. His office key clunked as he dropped it on the desk.

Elise's eyes jerked to the hallway at the sound of a door opening and closing.

Jake mumbled, "I think you have a patient. Do you mind if I leave by the back door?"

"Just one more thing, Jake." Elise's voice softened, and he stopped, but kept his eyes to the floor. "How did your ear print get on the anechoic chamber door?"

Jake raised his head and rolled his watery eyes to the ceiling before looking straight at her. "I was still in the building after everyone left and was curious about it. I went into Dr. Andres's office and turned on her audiometer, then cranked up some speech noise through the speakers. I just wanted to see what you could hear through the door when it's closed."

Elise pressed her lips together to stop the corners from curling up. "And could you hear anything?"

He closed his eyes. "No."

"How come no one saw you?"

"I went out the exit door at the end of the building...just past the stairwell door."

"Okay. Go ahead." She put a hand on his shoulder as they walked into the hallway. "And listen...we'll get through this. Right now, take care of yourself. Don't you have some tests coming up?"

The corners of Jake's mouth fluttered slightly as he glanced sideways at her, then slipped out the back door. She turned to see a wide-eyed Amy standing at the other end of the hallway, mouth open.

***

It was the end of the day, and Lucy had left for home. The audiologists stood in quiet, staring at the makeshift rogues' gallery in the back test room. Both had fists pushed into their lab coat pockets. Elise filled Amy in on what happened at Lewelling Labs with Rick, and then with Jake at the office.

"That creeps me out about Rick," said Amy. "He must've been driving toward Lewelling Labs right behind you."

"I know."

"And you didn't say what Theo told Jake to look for at your house."

"I'm not sure that even Jake knew. Guess I was more rattled than I thought."

"I hate to add to your crazy day, but Lucy asked me to make sure you saw your phone messages."

"I did. I saw the one about calling Deborah Miller about that loop system."

Amy shook her head slightly. "Sorry, but you might have to go out there."

Elise nodded.

"And you don't need to call Gloria, the rep manager, back. I already talked to her and told her you weren't here…that you have to go out to a farm to check their loop system. Oh, and that we're doing okay with Dr. Peters."

"Good, thanks." One less thing, but it reminded Elise to tell Amy about Maryelle's call.

Amy stared wide-eyed at Elise. "She actually heard Gloria say the name 'Bill'? Maybe we need to talk to her. Find out what that's all about."

"If I can think of a way to bring it up, I will," said Elise.

They finally broke themselves away from the pictures, replaced the ear anatomy poster on the wall, and retreated to their separate offices. Elise was able to get hold of Deborah Miller on the first try.

"It's just not working," she said. "That loop system was fine last year when you sold it to us, and we used it at our Pumpkin Fair, but something's wrong now, and we need it for the fair this Saturday! What am I going to do?"

"Actually, I was planning on coming out in just a little bit to take a look at it, if that's all right. If I can't figure out what's wrong, I'll get hold of the technician who installed it. Please don't worry. You use it during the auction, right?

"Yes, we use it when we announce raffle winners. The people who wear hearing aids love it!"

With that settled, Elise remembered that Cole had taken the train to Chicago that morning for a company meeting and would be back the next day. She was tired, and it seemed a hot bath and an old forties movie would be just the thing tonight. But first things first, as she heard a patient arrive who had called earlier requesting an immediate appointment. Amy was busy, so Elise said she'd see him.

"Dr. Harte, I'm just a little discouraged about these hearing devices. I think I should be hearing better when I get around a lot of people talking." The forty-five-year-old man leaned toward her, unblinking.

That comment led Elise to do more speech-in-noise testing, with results showing that he was doing much better than he thought he was.

"You're showing significant progress in retraining the hearing nerve, and your brain, to identify sounds you haven't heard in a while," said Elise. She reviewed information about realistic expectations and the need to wear the devices consistently.

"I wear them every day," he announced proudly, "and I do want to thank you. I'll admit, home life's a lot nicer now."

Elise walked her patient to the front door and locked it after him. She turned out the waiting room lights and tried to brush away a slight, somewhat insecure, feeling about his difficulty hearing in background noise. She couldn't help wondering if there really was a problem with the chip. She rubbed the throb that had just popped up in the middle of her forehead. No. She knew her testing, and after years of practicing audiology, was more than confident she'd recognize a problem if there was one. She'd seen nothing to date with any of her patients' fittings.

Elise packed up her things, turned out her office lights, then decided to leave from the side door so she could say goodbye to Amy. When she got to the audiologist's door, she saw Amy fixated on her computer screen, a stack of patient files next to it. Not wanting to interrupt her concentration on the day's reports, she decided to stay quiet.

Without looking up, Amy's hand did a small wave in her direction, and the corners of Elise's mouth twitched. They'd talk later. The only sound after that was the clunk of the lock on the side door.

Elise tried to ignore the spreading fatigue in her body, and somehow, a second wind kicked in, as she drove out to Deborah's farm. At least for the first five minutes. As much as she tried not to, her mind focused directly on Jake. She knew she had to tell the police what he'd said about breaking into her home and how Theo was behind it. Her jaw muscle clenched as she wondered if Theo could actually think she had been in on something underhanded with Tierneigh…and possibly Susan. How dare he!

Almost to Deborah's, she pushed her sunglasses higher on her nose against the setting sun flickering through walls of eight-foot high cornstalks.

She remembered that moisture in the corn determined the amount of income the farmers would receive at harvest. Too much moisture and money was lost. Like with a computer chip that didn't work.

Stop it, she thought. She had to admit…she was really tired. Her mind darted to a recent ethics class she'd taken…one required to keep her board certification current, and she gripped the wheel a little harder. Stop it. Susan's research showed excellent results at all stages of the chip's production. She had complete faith in Susan and in her own testing and evaluations with patients. She needed to find out what was going on…and soon.

Elise pressed lightly on the brakes as she reached the turnoff for the Miller farm. The sun had dropped below the horizon now, and she squinted against her headlights' reflection on the route sign at the corner of the intersection. She slowed even more, but her mind didn't. According to Jake, Theo told him something might not be "true." About what? The chip? Was Rick involved in this or not?

The car bounced as she turned onto the rutted road, and

Elise tensed her neck so her head wouldn't keep bouncing off the headrest. The worst was not being able to see around her. The cornstalks were so high…somewhere around ten feet, she guessed.

Just then, the car's headlights illuminated a large clearing around the farmhouse. Pumpkins lined dirt walkways around the house, to the barn and other structures, in preparation for the upcoming Pumpkin Fair. Elise smiled. Dancing scarecrows flanked each side of the wooden steps leading to the Millers' porch, which held antique milk cans full of giant sunflowers. Floodlights automatically snapped on and highlighted garlands of yellow, orange, and red leaves, draped on the porch railings. A matching wreath hung on the propped-open front door.

Deborah stepped into the doorway, pushed the squeaky screen door open, and with a wide smile, called out, "There you are!"

Elise exited her car. "Yup, I'm here. To the rescue, I hope!"

Deborah swept her arm in the direction of the barn. "Well, it's waiting for you. I really appreciate this. My hubby's in town. He said to say hi."

"Well, tell him I said hi back when he gets home. The decorations are fantastic!" Elise thoroughly enjoyed the strategically placed signs with whimsical sayings, like "Happy Fall, Y'All!", "Pumpkins, Apples and Hayrides, Oh My!", and "Fall is My Favorite Color."

She laughed at the painted adult- and child-sized farm characters on wooden boards propped upright. Holes replaced the characters' heads, so folks could put their own heads through for funny photo ops.

They passed a horse-drawn wagon, currently minus the horse, with "The Autumn-mobile" painted in fall colors down its side.

Deborah pointed toward a red barn that seemed twice the size of Elise's own house. Two mature, bright yellow maple trees stood on each side of it, lit by yellow flood lights, placed on the ground in front of them. A large arched, wrought iron lamp attached over the entrance lit the way in, in a warming welcome. Elise had learned that yellow lights helped keep the number of swarming bugs to a minimum. She took in the scene, as the two women walked and kicked up small piles of colored leaves. She loved the sound of it, still not taking anything for granted, after twenty-plus years of living in Mt. Harmony.

Deborah waved her arm in front of her. "We'll set up the popcorn and apple cider tables just outside the barn, and the people selling crafts will use the booths we set up inside."

"Sounds like so much fun!" Elise ignored her fatigue and actually felt swept up in the spirit of it all, as they entered the barn.

She sniffed the sweet smell of hay scattered on the floor and admired streamers of pretend colorful leaves that dropped from the rafters. An area of low tables to her right was set up for kids' crafts. It was surrounded by a two-foot-high white fence, with pictures of pumpkins and children playing in piles of leaves. To Elise's left and middle of the barn, booths were filling up with crafts, homemade jellies and jams, as well as honey from local beekeepers. She passed a booth, that according to its sign, would soon be filled with fresh pumpkin, pecan, and apple pies, as well as breads, muffins, and cookies. Her saliva glands kicked in and she swallowed.

Deborah pointed to the back right corner of the barn. "That's where the dance floor and live music will be. We'll announce raffle ticket winners…that's what I want the loop system for…so people with hearing aids can hear over all the noise."

"This looks fantastic, Deborah! I brought a pair of hearing aids I can put on to check it out."

Mild swirls of hay dust covered their shoes, as they walked to the back of the barn where the podium and microphone stood, and within minutes, she found the problem. The switch for the loop system itself was stuck, and not turned on all the way. With one good flip it was fixed. They both laughed, greatly relieved.

"I'm sorry you came out all this way just for that, Elise," said Deborah, concern on her face.

Elise faced her directly. "Are you kidding? I just got a backstage look at one of the best pumpkin fairs in the area!"

Deborah flashed a smile, that just as quickly turned to a frown.

Elise frowned, too. "Is there something else?"

"Well…it's about Catherine's birthday party being on the same day…this Saturday. We wind up a lot of the competitions and raffles around four in the afternoon, when we announce the winners, but everyone I've talked to said they're gonna be at the birthday party!"

Oh my goodness, Elise thought, then said out loud, "What if we move the party from noon to three, instead of four, as originally planned. You can also move the time for the announcements an hour or so later, so people can spend more time here.

"Oh, you'd do that?" squealed Deborah. "Thank you…and thank Catherine, too."

Truthfully, Elise thought three hours was going to be enough for Catherine anyway, and they could get word out, so party-goers could go to both events without feeling rushed.

The two women ambled back to the house, content in the quiet coolness of the early evening.

Marcie, a big smile on her face, opened the screen door

as they approached. "Got everything fixed?"

Elise opened her mouth to answer but was immediately overwhelmed with the spicy scent of fresh baked apple pie, and all she could do was close her eyes and murmur, "Hmmmm."

The two women swooshed past Marcie and into the dining room, where Elise saw three plates filled with the largest slices of pie she'd ever seen. An open carton of vanilla ice cream stood behind them. It couldn't have been a better end to such a stressful day, and Elise was grateful.

Way too soon, a wall clock bonged six times, and Elise realized she needed to get home. It was dark out now, and her time at the Millers' home was so enjoyable that she hated to go.

Deborah and Marcie waved goodbye from the front porch as Elise turned the car in a tight circle, trying not to hit any pumpkins. She then headed down the rutted driveway, guided by red reflectors in front of the walls of cornstalks, and toward the main road. Deborah had told her that people coming for the fair would be parking in an open field closer to the main road. She could see why.

Elise slowed to a stop as she approached the main road and decided she should just skip dinner. The pie had been absolute heaven and, between that and her returning fatigue, she was pushing it just to drive home.

She reached to turn her radio on when a horrendous crashing noise made her grab the wheel.

She reflexively scrunched her head down, and her shoulders shot up. Her eyes bounced in all directions, attempting to see what it was, or where it was coming from, but she couldn't see a thing in the darkness. She took a chance and lowered her window with her left hand, to get an idea of its direction, but the attempt caused a massive cloud of dust and dirt to enter the car, covering her eyes and nose. She swiped her sleeve across her eyes.

What the…?

A throaty, low-pitched sound of cornstalks thrashing made her heart explode in her chest. A combine? Headlights suddenly flipped on, flooding blinding white light on the car and the area around her. She recoiled, tensed her body, and instinctively ducked, expecting to feel a crushing impact.

Her back right wheel had settled into a rut when she stopped and now spun, kicking even more plumes of dust into the air. She jammed the car in reverse, then forward again, as monstrous green cones emerged from the cornstalks and just missed her lurching car, or so she thought. One cone struck the car's left bumper.

Elise's hands flew off the steering wheel, and the car skidded sideways over the gravel. She grabbed the gyrating wheel again and with all her strength, fought against the force of the impact, and finally came to an abrupt stop in a ditch, on the opposite side of the road.

Elise fought rising terror, as dust and chaff engulfed her car.

Chapter Eighteen

Thursday Evening

A shrill squeal erupted from Elise's chest and throat, that momentarily masked two other screaming voices. Fuzzy streams of light from handheld flashlights bounced in the darkness around her, as Deborah and Marcie appeared like ghosts out of the murkiness.

Elise stopped screaming when she put a hand over her mouth to filter the dust just to try to take a breath. A car spinning gravel was heard in the not-too-far distance, then a long screech down the main road. Elise actually considered taking off after it, but realized her legs were shaking so badly, she couldn't move them to drive.

Marcie yanked on the door handle. Her already ashen face was topped with a layer of light brown dust, making her look right out of a science fiction movie. "Are you okay? The sheriff's on his way!" Seeing that Elise was alive and breathing, she slid her cell phone into her dust-covered pants pocket.

Deborah talked between gulps of breath. "We saw the combine lights…and the taillights on your car. The combine looked like it was headed straight—" She coughed and couldn't finish the sentence.

"That was our combine!" Marcie screamed, barely able

to control herself.

Sirens blared in the distance and, within seconds, a sheriff's car, ambulance, and fire truck screeched to a stop. Lights flashed and dust swirled around their vehicles as uniformed bodies jumped out and ran for Elise's car.

Approximately fifteen minutes later, on Elise's insistence that she didn't need to go to the hospital, the ambulance left, but Sheriff Reed's eyes never left her. They had moved to chairs in the Millers' living room, where the lingering scent of apple pie played havoc with her stomach.

"There's not much more I can tell you," she said to Noah. "It could've been an accident, but who was it, and why did they take off?"

They turned to watch as two firefighters stomped up the front steps and spoke to them through the open door. They had found the combine several yards away, in the field across the road. They checked it out, decided there was no immediate hazard, and stated the keys were still in it.

Deborah saw Elise's eyebrows raise and spoke up. "We always leave the keys in the cab."

"Yeah, we do that, too," said one of the firefighters, with the name Ken on his shirt.

"Why?" Elise found her head still a little unsteady.

"Really no reason not to," the firefighter said. "Sometimes a master switch can be turned off to the battery, if they want to do that, but no one ever does. And does this belong to anyone here?" He held up one mustard-colored, leather driving glove.

They shook their heads. Marcie turned to her mom. "Does Dad have something like that?"

Fatigue showed heavy on Deborah's face. "Not that I've ever seen."

Noah's eyes drilled into Elise's, and his voice was intense. "Looks like someone decided to take a pretty serious joy ride. I'd like to take you home in the squad car. You shouldn't be driving tonight." He looked at Deborah and asked, "Okay if she leaves her car here?

"Of course," said Deborah. She patted Elise on the knee. "Anything you need, honey? Want to stay here tonight?"

"No, really, I'm fine," said Elise. She was feeling somewhat better and thought riding with Noah was a good idea at the moment…and that it might give her the opportunity to tell him about Jake.

They said their goodbyes, then Noah walked next to Elise, his hand cupped around her elbow, until she was safely in the patrol car. Her stomach crunched when they passed her car. The dirt, surprisingly, didn't cover everything, and she closed her eyes to the damage evident on the back part of the car.

The drive home was relatively quiet, except for the last few minutes when she told him about Jake's visit to her office, his admission that he was the one who broke into her home the night of the training, and his adamant denial of hurting Tierneigh. She told him that, according to Jake, Theo thought Elise had something that Tierneigh had given her, that "wasn't true" and could hurt them.

Noah turned toward Elise after he pulled up to her home and turned off the squad car. "Hurt him, or the company, or what? You don't know what it was?"

"No. I meant to ask a couple of times, but guess I got distracted. People were coming into the office. I'm not sure he even knew."

Noah looked past her to the house. It looked eerie in its darkness. "Cole's not home, yet?"

"He's in Chicago. He'll be home tomorrow."

Noah was clearly uncomfortable with that news. "I'm at least going to check the house out and have a deputy in the neighborhood tonight."

"Do you think someone's trying to scare me…on purpose? Or worse?" Then she put two and two together. "Was it Theo who did this? Or got someone else to do it?"

"We'll find out. Is there someone who can come stay with you tonight? Or maybe you can stay with your daughter at her apartment…just for the night?"

"Really. I'm alright." Hopefully, she could convince herself of that, too. The last thing she wanted was to bring trouble to her own daughter's door, if someone really was out for her. Deci and Belle would let her know if something was off.

Noah checked the inside of the house, then the outside, and made sure things were locked up. "Don't hesitate to call," he said, as he stepped onto the porch and scanned the neighborhood one more time.

Elise watched him from the other side of the screen door. "I know. Thank you."

The house was ablaze in lights, as Elise and her whiskered assistants checked each corner of the home themselves. Once satisfied, the decision was unanimous to snuggle on the living room couch with their favorite floral quilt, handmade by Elise's grandmother.

Elise's breathing had just dropped into a heavy, even pattern, when her cell phone trilled, jerking her upright. It only took a few seconds to assure everything was alright…no intruders…then she saw her daughter's beaming face light up the screen.

She tapped the phone, closed her eyes, and let herself plop back onto the couch, phone to one ear. "Becky, why aren't you asleep?"

"Asleep? It's early," she whined. "Just wanted to tell you that I got my paper done and turned in."

Elise made every effort to move her lips, but the impact of the day's events now hit her like a combine hitting a…oh…never mind. "That's great, honey." It was an effort just to mumble. "Sure you feel be'ter now tha itz off your plate."

"It was a pain, but I did it."

"Good," said Elise. "Talk t'morrow, k?"

"Oh, and speaking of pains," Becky continued. "There were two thumb drives in the gift bag I took the other night from your room. One was okay, but the other one had stuff on it already."

"That's good, honey," Elise mumbled. "Good it'z all dun."

"'Night, Mom." Becky chuckled. "You sound awful."

"Night. Love you." Elise dragged her finger across the OFF button, and within seconds, soft kitty and human snoring were the only sounds in the house.

Chapter Nineteen

Friday Morning

Elise squirmed against a growing throb in her lower back. Her head felt clammy and dense, like San Francisco fog creeping over the hills at night, consuming everything in its path. There was a noise, but what was it? She kept her eyes closed, but her face contorted. A foghorn? No. Something more high-pitched and repeating, over and over. Deci?

Concern that her kitty might be hurt made her sit up a little too fast and immediately caused her lower back to spasm.

"Yeow!" She grabbed the spot with one hand, which made her teeter on the edge of the couch, then roll, both arms flailing, onto the floor with a painful thump.

She did a quick head-to-toe survey for injuries, then felt a wet nose press against her forehead. Her eyes snapped open to two upside-down, pale green eyes, staring back.

"Deci!" she cried. Her eyes darted around him. "What am I doing in the living room?"

The cat stared, attempting a mind-meld, but Elise ignored him.

She saw her teacup on the coffee table and remembered, as the fog slowly cleared. A quick glance at the wall clock said it was still early, and she had enough time for a shower and coffee, depending, of course, on how long it took to get herself together and actually stand up.

Memories from the night before, how someone had actually tried to hurt her, were pushed aside for the moment.

About a half hour later, Elise walked carefully across her bedroom floor against growing stiffness in her back, holding a pair of brown ankle boots by their tops. She groaned as she sat on the side of her bed and leaned forward to slip one boot on, but in the process, knocked the bedside stand with her elbow, sending small odds and ends scattered on top tumbling to the floor. She stopped herself from saying something she shouldn't while she surveyed the spilled contents around her. Must be the rejects that Becky decided not to take when she looked through the gift bag the other night.

Her eyes followed something small and black that slowed as it crossed the hardwood floor and finally stopped at the wall. Elise squinted. A tube of Becky's lip balm?

Suddenly every muscle in her body stiffened. It reminded her of something else. A thumb drive! It almost looked like a thumb drive. What was it Becky had said last night when she called?

Elise squeezed her eyes and tried to remember. Then, it came to her...that one of the thumb drives she took...had "stuff" on it? And what was it Tierneigh had said? That she couldn't have too many thumb drives?

In her mind, Elise saw Tierneigh drop an extra thumb drive in Elise's gift bag the night of the training.

Her mind ping-ponged to the break-in...to Noah saying it seemed that the intruder, who she now knew was Jake, was only interested in the dining room...coincidentally, where the other two gift bags were.

She let out a long breath. Jake was looking through the bags at the office and almost jumped out of his skin when Elise and Amy walked in on him. Was that what Theo sent him to get? A thumb drive?

She grabbed her phone. "Becky, it's Mom," she said, as soon as she heard the call connect.

"Mom?" the voice barely mumbled, but grew clearer as Becky woke up. "You okay?"

"Yes, honey. Sorry to wake you so early, but I need to ask you something."

"Now?"

"Yes. Please listen. Do you still have that thumb drive that you said was full?"

"The thumb drive? Yeah, I have it."

"You didn't do anything to it, did you? Like erase it or anything?"

"No, Mom," said Becky, now fully awake. Elise could hear bedsheets rustling as she was probably attempting to sit up. "What's going on?"

"Don't move, I'll be right over. I need to get it."

"The only moving I'm doing is for coffee."

Elise fed the cats so quickly their heads spun. She slid their filled dishes across the floor, grabbed her purse and workbag, locked up and ran out the front door, only to stop cold when she saw the empty space in her driveway. Her car was at the Miller farm!

She remembered that Cole had left his truck in the garage, so she ran back into the house, through the kitchen, and hit the garage door button by the door, since her garage door opener was a few miles away, in her car. She sent thanks telepathically to Cole's coworker for picking him up to go to the train station this time, instead of the other way around.

It was a tight fit as Elise climbed into the truck, since their older home had only a one-car garage. It was something they had planned on addressing in the future, but just never did. She adjusted the seat and mirrors and started the engine. Automatic headlights flooded the garage as she backed out into the early morning darkness.

Becky had unlocked her front door so her mom could walk in when she got there. Elise entered the apartment and noticed that the door closed and locked nicely behind her.

"Hi, honey," she said to Becky, who was sitting at the small kitchen table, her laptop open in front of her.

"Hi, Mom. This what you're looking for?" Becky swiveled the laptop in her direction.

Elise crossed the small living room in a few steps, pulled out one of the kitchen chairs, and adjusted the laptop to see it better. A black thumb drive protruded from one side.

"These are definitely test results from speech-in-noise testing," said Elise, squinting at the screen.

Becky leaned across the table and let out a noisy yawn. "I'll take your word for it." She pulled herself back up in her chair, lifted a mug of hot coffee cradled in her hands, took a noisy sip, then said, "Hope remembered David coming home that Thursday night."

"What?" Elise pulled her eyes off the screen and stared at her daughter. "Did she remember what time it was?"

"Yeah, they actually walked in from the parking lot together. Hope was over at her boyfriend's and remembered the time 'cause she wanted to be home no later than ten that night to see some show on TV, but she ended up missing about the first twenty minutes of it. She said David pulled in the parking lot right behind her, so they walked to the apartments together. But she said he was in a really bugged mood, so she didn't say much except hi."

Elise's eyebrows lowered. So, maybe between ten fifteen and ten thirty? "What do you mean by 'bugged'?"

"Hope said he seemed mad at something, so she thought she just ought to stay quiet."

Elise stared at the bottom of Becky's mug as her daughter lifted it to her lips again. The timeline was tight, if David saw Tierneigh after she called Elise, then attacked her, and drove straight home. But it could've been done.

Elise really needed to talk to Amy. And Susan.

Becky's eyebrows raised. "Want some coffee, Mom?"

"No…uh…thanks. I'll get some at the office." She pulled the thumb drive out of Becky's computer and dropped it in her blazer pocket, then grabbed her purse and bolted for the front door. "Call you later…love you."

Elise heard the door lock as she tried to skuttle down the first flight of stairs, still feeling a little stiff, but then realized it wasn't Becky's door she'd heard lock. The noise came from below her. She slowed at the landing, grabbed the handrail to descend the last flight of stairs, and stared at the back of David's black hoodie as he shuffled toward the parking lot, a workbag slung on one shoulder.

She followed him with her eyes as he passed in and out of the yellow-white light from a nearby lamppost.

Without thinking twice she called out, "David!"

David's head swiveled side to side. He then turned around and with raised eyebrows said, "Dr. Harte?"

She decided to take the innocent route. "David, I thought that was you! You live here, too?" She waved a hand behind her. "I just stopped by to see my daughter."

David rubbed the thin beard on his chin. "Yeah, I live here. Was just on my way to an early class." He turned to walk away.

Elise caught up with him and fell into step. "So, you know my daughter, Becky, right?"

David looked like she'd asked him if he robbed a bank. He cleared his throat. "No…yes…well…not really." He stopped as he approached his car, opened the back door, and threw his workbag in.

Elise gritted her teeth. She walked past him and glanced into the car. There was enough light from a nearby lamppost to see a yellow folder on the backseat.

David turned toward her, followed her eyes to the folder, and slammed the door shut, causing Elise to jerk back.

"Nice seeing you, Dr. Harte," he said, unconvincingly, as he walked to the driver's side, slipped behind the wheel, slammed the door, and took off with a skid.

Elise didn't know how long she stood and stared at the car's taillights. She hardly remembered driving to her office. What was his problem? And what was in that folder…presuming it was the same folder she saw him take out of Tierneigh's office? And what was the deal with him about Becky, or was it just her imagination? He was the one who'd asked her if Becky was her daughter out at E. S. Hearing Labs, right?

She pulled into her office parking lot, turned the car off, and tried to push David out of her mind.

Elise knew Amy and Lucy wouldn't be at work yet, so took her time switching on lights and starting the coffee. The normal routine helped calm her, and Marion Downs's picture added to the feeling as she regarded her hero's angelic, albeit, mischievous face.

Elise straightened her back and, at the same time, fingered the thumb drive in her blazer pocket. She acknowledged what seemed like an unspoken understanding with Dr. Downs to continue to look for the truth.

She didn't realize how long she'd been standing there, when the side door squeaked open, and two voices sang "Morn-ing."

Elise turned away from the Dr. Downs photo and watched Amy plop her things on her desk.

Lucy scooted forward in her chair at the front desk, and turned on her computer, then swiveled to face Elise, and with a big smile. "So did you fix the loop system at the Miller farm?"

"Well…"

Amy stopped what she was doing and looked up at Elise's hesitation.

"Yes, about the loop system, but there was another incident I hadn't counted on." She proceeded to tell them about the combine, her ride home with Noah, and the episode just this morning with Becky and the thumb drive.

The two stared frozen at Elise, with mouths open, but Elise's mind continued to churn. "I've seen those numbers before."

"What numbers?" It was Amy who finally spoke. "But, more importantly, are you all right? What about your car? I was wondering why Cole's truck was out there." She nodded in the direction of the parking lot.

"I'm okay. Just really mad that someone might've actually wanted to hurt me. The car's alright, as far as I know…just the back bumper that needs to be fixed…and it's going to need a good washing."

Lucy said, "You okay to see patients today?"

Elise gave her a rueful smile but was grateful for the concern. "I'm good." She looked at Amy. "Let's get some coffee and check out this thumb drive, okay?"

Amy dragged a chair from in front of Elise's desk and plopped it next to her, so both could look at the data on the computer screen. Elise had already plugged in the thumb drive and opened the file.

Amy squinted. "This definitely looks like results from speech-in-noise testing."

Elise rubbed the area between her eyebrows with her finger. "I know I've seen this before."

"How about this morning, at your daughter's?"

"Funny." Elise squeezed her eyes together, then it hit her. "Back up a minute."

"What?"

Elise pointed to a spot in front of Amy's stomach. "I need to get into this drawer."

"Oh."

Amy slid her chair back and Elise pulled open the top side drawer. Nothing. She pulled open the middle drawer…and there it was. The paper the new rep had retrieved for her after it dropped out of her jacket pocket. The memory of picking up that paper and the headphones in Susan's office, when the EMTs were moving the gurney to take Tierneigh to the hospital, was so clear in her mind now. She told Amy the story.

"I can't believe I forgot about this." Elise smoothed the paper out on her desk while they studied it.

"I can," said Amy. "I think you've had a few distractions lately."

"Look!" Elise jumped in her seat as she looked from the paper to the thumb drive numbers on her computer screen. "The research results they gave us at the training match what's on the thumb drive, right?" Her eyes bounced back and forth quicker now. "I mean, the thumb drive data looks official…it says 'For Internal Use Only' at the top, meaning this was supposed to stay within E. S. Hearing Labs."

"But this paper," said Amy, pointing to it, "looks right out of the clinic. Look, there's handwriting on the side." She grabbed the paper and turned it sideways, squinting. "Do you think it's Susan's?"

Elise propped her elbows on her desk and covered her face with her hands.

"What?" said Amy.

Elise lowered her hands and whispered, "Susan said she found discrepancies in the test results. She was retesting people to double and triple check it, which was the right thing to do."

Amy nodded as Elise's finger bounced back and forth between the computer and the paper. "But which ones? I'm thinking the discrepancies were with the internal results from the computer. The paper results are the correct ones, from the original tests, before they were entered into the program.

"So you think someone actually did change them in the computer? Is that why Theo and Rick...and Bob...were acting so weird?"

Elise nodded. "Remember, the differences were inconsistent. Why? It might've been what Tierneigh saw or overheard and wasn't able to follow up on. The thing is, she called me first...she didn't even talk to Susan. She had to have seen the note Susan left for her, saying she wanted to talk to her, but she called me instead."

Amy whispered, "Tierneigh might not've known Susan was retesting. After all, she just got back from traveling four or five different states. I know we've alluded to this before, but I'm more convinced now, whether right or wrong, that Tierneigh didn't trust Susan."

Chapter Twenty

Friday

The rest of the morning seemed almost normal to Elise. She was afraid to even think it could be true. On a normal day at the office, the worst thing that might happen was that a piece of equipment stopped working in the middle of a hearing exam, or you use an electronic buffer to carefully buff a spot on someone's custom earpiece and it hits wrong and flings the thing across the room to roll up to the patient's foot. But that seemed so trivial now.

Elise regarded her coworkers throughout the morning, watching them with different eyes, and appreciating them more than she thought possible. She actually felt a brief moment of calmness, that she hadn't felt in a while.

The patients were kind. No one questioned her, thank goodness, with the majority of conversations focused on her mother-in-law's birthday party and the fair out at the Miller farm. She arranged a staggered lunch with Amy and sent a text to Noah, asking if she could meet him at The Vibe before the main lunch crowd came in. He sent a text back that he'd be there. She told him she wanted to update him on something, but she actually wanted to press him on his trips to E. S. Hearing Labs and hoped he'd be more open with her now.

At about eleven fifteen, she called Lucy from her desk.

"I'm on my way out. Amy will be here until I get back."

"Got it, Dr. Harte."

Elise slipped out the back door and, minutes later, was sitting in The Vibe, across a table from Noah. She was glad the TV was off and tried to relax to the soft jazz playing in the background. Only a few other people were there, and Noah and Elise were able to talk out of earshot of anyone else.

Elise told Noah what she and Amy had uncovered, about the data discrepancy between the official computer program and Susan's original written data. He observed her as she spoke, quietly sipping his coffee, then lowered his cup to the table when Elise stopped talking.

"So you think Tierneigh uncovered something, making her uncomfortable with this newly released technology? And that there was a connection with Susan?"

"Yes. Whether it was right or wrong about Susan. That would explain why Tierneigh called me first."

"But we only have Susan's word for it…that she never talked to Tierneigh."

Elise's eyebrows lowered. "I know, but I trust Susan…with her work, her ethics and yes, I think, I believe her."

Noah nodded. "So you found that data paper exactly where? On the floor of Susan's office or the anechoic chamber?"

Elise leaned forward. "It's a blur, Noah, but it had to be close to the anechoic chamber door." Her eyes blinked twice. "The EMTs put Tierneigh on a backboard, then brought her out the chamber door and switched her to the gurney. I saw the crumpled paper and a pair of headphones on the floor, so I picked them up to get them out of the EMTs' way. Maybe Tierneigh dropped the paper just before whoever it was attacked her." She paused. "I have no idea why the headphones were on the floor." Her mind flashed to rifling through Susan's desktop, looking for the weather radio. "It might've been something I did."

Noah's eyebrows raised as she explained, then continued.

"I'm not sure if this paper was Susan's or not. I think the data was hers, but this paper was a copy, not an original." Elise scowled. "I mean, I know her desk is always a mess, but data is important, and it's usually either on the computer or an original from a specific day's test results."

Noah stayed quiet, eyes still focused on her.

"All I can think of is that she wanted to analyze the results further. Susan must've made a copy so she could be free to make marks on it." She placed her palm on her forehead. "I just don't know. I don't know if it was Susan who dropped it, or Tierneigh."

Noah raised his cup to his lips. "So what'd you do next? After you picked the things up off the floor?"

Elise pushed aside the stab of pain in her stomach. She'd gone over this so many times. Eyes closed, visualizing the room, she said, "I picked the headphones up and put them on the shelf to the left of the door, and I must've put the paper in my jacket pocket." Her eyes popped open. "But there was an empty space that hadn't been there before!" Was that what bothered her when she saw the empty space on her bookshelf, or when she'd looked at the old equipment out at Lewelling Labs? But...so what?

As if Noah read her mind, he said, "So?"

"There was no room when I was there before the training! The shelves were packed tight with old testing equipment. Then, just a couple hours later, there was that space."

Noah leaned forward. "Maybe someone borrowed something, or Susan herself took one of the pieces off the shelf."

Elise's back stiffened. "It was a busy night, and that collection of old test equipment was Susan's pride and joy." Frustrated, she looked at Noah. "I'll call her myself and see what I can find out." Elise could tell Noah wasn't fully convinced this was anything important. "Can you tell me anything about your trips to E. S. Hearing Labs? You've been out twice now, right?"

He glanced around the room. "You know I can't go into it."

Elise ignored him. "What about Rick? Did you talk to him? Or to Theo…about Jake?"

Noah rolled his eyes. "We talked to Rick the first time, the day after Tierneigh was attacked. But we've interviewed most all the employees. I was told Rick was in Indianapolis, at the races, the second time I went out, so that supported the story he told you when you saw him at Lewelling Labs."

"So, do you know why he was there…at Lewelling Labs?"

"Elise, it's not a crime for someone to visit another lab. You did it."

Elise felt taken aback, but then she saw the glint in his eye and decided to ignore the comment.

"We brought Theo into the station for questioning, because of what Jake told you."

She didn't try to hide her surprise. "You did? What'd he say?"

"He admitted sending Jake to your home, after I assured him you weren't going to press charges. He said he was aware of talk about the chip and how effective it was…or wasn't…and he suspected that Tierneigh had passed that information on to you. He's adamant that the chip is good, and he panicked. I told him I was going to tell you this, so just keep things under wraps for a while, okay? He's just grateful you're not pressing charges."

Elise thought about the thumb drive Tierneigh had passed on to her the night of the training. So something definitely happened that day, and her friend thought she'd uncovered something monumental.

Elise pushed. "Okay…so what else?"

Noah pressed his lips together, then decided to go ahead. "Theo admitted he just didn't know what was going on with this discrepancy with the data. His first instinct was that Susan was involved, since she was in charge of it all, then somehow Tierneigh came into the picture, and whether he showed it or not, he said he was really upset about the attack. Said it threw him for a loop and that he's trying to get to the bottom of it."

"And you believe him?"

"So far, but I'm keeping my options open. And that's it. All I can tell you."

"Did you confirm Theo was in his office when Tierneigh was attacked?"

Noah paused. "You interviewing me?"

Elise glanced down at the table, and when she looked up, saw the corners of his mouth twitch.

"Theo admitted to being in his office late. Said he was trying to get someone from overseas that had left him a message. Said he tried to get back with them, but never did. He said he didn't hear a thing in his office, being on the third floor, and I believe that. He didn't even know the EMTs came, until they were gone, and the security guard told him what happened. And, yes, we checked his phone records."

"Did you ask if anyone saw him leave, just in case he was lying?"

Noah cocked his head with a hint of a smile. "Yes, Detective Harte. No one saw him leave the building…but…"

"But, what?

"He could've left by one of the side doors, at either end

of the building."

Elise suddenly remembered what the one lab tech told her. About leaving by the front door when it was late, where there were more people around...so sneaking out one of those other doors, undetected, could possibly work. Especially late at night.

"Aren't there security cameras around the building? Can those be checked?"

"There's a camera at the front door, but unfortunately, not at the two side doors."

"Did you talk to the lab techs and the other managers?"

"I've told you what I can, Elise." Noah's voice was firm now. "The main thing, concerning you, is that Theo got the message about never pulling a stunt like that again."

Elise thanked Noah, then left The Vibe, far from satisfied. Her mind was preoccupied when she walked in the office's back door, and she felt frustrated that she couldn't get more information out of Noah. She knew he accommodated her as much as he could, but she needed answers that she was sure he had.

Elise shook her blazer down her arms, exchanged it for her lab coat hanging on the back of her office door, then heard the soft squeak of Amy's door opening.

"Thank you, Anne. You have a good day, now."

Lucy's voice followed. "Bye, Anne. It was good to see you."

Within seconds, Amy stood in Elise's doorway, her face solemn. She dangled the ear anatomy chart next to her leg. "Something happened while you were out."

Elise froze. Now what?

"Anne Thompson came in. You know, one of the 'Jacks' ladies?"

Elise nodded and relaxed slightly. She walked to her chair behind the desk and sat down. "Was she okay?"

"Oh yeah. She was okay. I needed to do an updated hearing eval." Amy waved her free hand toward the test room across the hall. "Her hearing hadn't changed. It's just..."

"What?"

"I was showing her where most of her sensorineural issues were on the ear anatomy chart, when she brushed against it and knocked it off the wall onto the floor."

Elise slumped against her chair and closed her eyes, afraid of what was coming next.

"Yeah," said Amy. "It fell with our rogues' gallery facing up."

"Oh...no!"

Amy pushed the chart across the top of the desk toward Elise, who stopped it with the palm of her hand.

Amy smirked. "Oh, yeah. She saw it. But, actually, she was pretty good about it."

"What do you mean?"

"She actually kinda perked up, like she was interested. It wasn't a bad thing, but..."

"Yeah?"

"She recognized Rick. Seems she and her sister, and their husbands, went out last week to a play in downtown Springfield. They wanted to get a nightcap before going home, so stopped at one of the nicer bars near the theater."

Elise started to understand. "You're kidding. Last Thursday night, by chance?

"Yup. Right at the time Rick said he was at a bar."

Elise couldn't tell if she was relieved or not. "So he was telling the truth." Her eyebrows raised. "Did Anne say whether he was sitting with anyone?"

"Oh, yeah."

"And?" Elise asked, trying to tamp down the uneasy feeling growing in her stomach.

Amy took a breath and pointed at one of the pictures.

"It was Susan."

Elise felt like she was hit in the face with a brick. She could barely whisper. "Susan? Was she sure?"

"I asked her that, too. Yeah, she was sure. She doesn't know Susan, but she was adamant that Susan was the person with Rick. Anne said she noticed them because they seemed like such a 'nice couple.'"

"'A nice couple?'" Elise breathed out, then squeezed her eyes together and shook her head slowly. "So, obviously, they weren't fighting. It was just…the opposite. I—I don't get it." She tried not to think of the conversation she'd just had with Noah, when she told him how much she trusted Susan.

"I know." Amy sat in one of the patient's chairs in front of Elise's desk, shoulders slumped, hands clasped between her knees. The silence was heavy for at least half a minute, then Amy straightened her back and anger seeped into her words. "Why wouldn't she tell us about that? I thought we were friends, colleagues. I thought we trusted each other."

Elise raised her eyes, pain on her face. "I just can't believe it. Although, remember, this was before Tierneigh was attacked. So who instigated this rendezvous? Did Rick want to see Susan, or did she ask him to meet her afterward? What could either of them have known at that point?"

A smug look crossed Amy's face. "Or did it have nothing to do with Tierneigh, the lab, or whatever. Was this just a normal night out for them? Go-get-a-drink kinda thing after a long day?"

Elise couldn't control the "Yuck" that came out of her mouth, and they both giggled.

Amy said, "Maybe there's another side of Rick we haven't seen, yet."

"Maybe," Elise mumbled, staring at Rick's picture. Her eyes shot back up at Amy. "But where does that leave us, now? Rick and Susan are out, for sure. Bob Bell has an alibi, and Theo says he was in his office the whole time, on his phone. Noah said the phone records support his claim."

Amy said, "Well, playing skeptic here, if he was on hold, he could've left the room and come back later and still have been on hold."

"Yeah, might be a stretch, though…and a risk. He'd have to take the chance that someone wouldn't come on the phone, realize he wasn't there, and hang up. That would've shown on the phone records. For some reason, I can't see him running down the stairs, into Susan's office and the anechoic chamber, hitting Tierneigh, then running back up…or taking the elevator, which might've been even slower…maybe."

Amy pointed to David Nubrey's picture. "What about him? Have we really figured him out, yet?"

"No. But I think Becky kind of likes him. She gets bugged when I bring him up. She can't see why I'm concerned with him."

"Does she talk about him much?"

"That's just it…she doesn't. It's more her attitude when I bring him up. Like I'm overreacting or something."

"She's been under a lot of pressure lately with school."

"I know."

Amy stood up. "I'm going to go get some lunch. You want anything?"

Elise frowned and slowly shook her head.

Chapter Twenty-One

The afternoon progressed as usual. Elise and Amy pored over an updated research article in the work/break room on testing show dogs' hearing levels. It felt good for the moment, to think of something completely unrelated to recent events.

"I'd love to test a dog's hearing someday," said Amy. "People are so surprised to learn that we use the same kind of technology that we use to test human newborns."

"I had the opportunity once, when I first got out of school," said Elise. "I helped a friend test some puppies…English sheep dogs. I held them and cooed to them, just like human babies!"

They laughed but jumped when Lucy called out, "Leaving, Dr. Harte, Dr. MacNeal. See you at the birthday party tomorrow."

Before either could answer, they heard the side door shut and the lock click into place.

"I need to get going, too," said Amy. "You going to be all right?"

"Yeah. I just need a few more minutes to finish up some paperwork, then I'll be going."

"Okay. I'll finish locking up and turn out the front lights."

Elise headed for her office, pulled the chair out from her desk, eased slowly into it, then scooted in tight. She placed her elbows on the desk and covered her eyes with her hands. Her mind was spinning again, around her good friend's death, the attempt on her own life, the truth or possible failures at E. S. Hearing Labs and the families that could be affected…and then Susan.

She blinked her eyes open, pulled the desk phone toward her, and tapped the buttons.

"E. S. Hearing Labs…"

"Tessa? This is Dr. Harte. I was looking for Dr. Andres."

"Hi, Dr. Harte. She called out today."

"She didn't come in? Is she okay?"

"She said she had to take a personal day. Said she'll come in tomorrow to make up for it. On a Saa…turr…day." Tessa clearly did not approve of working on a weekend.

"That sounds like her," said Elise. Probably useless to try to call Susan at home, then. "If you get a chance, would you let her know I need to talk to her? I'd like to come out there tomorrow morning. It's important."

"Sure, Dr. Harte. I'll put a note on her desk and let security know you might be coming out."

"Thanks, Tessa." Elise dropped the thumb drive and paper into her purse, locked up and headed for home.

Cole sat dumbstruck at the dining room table, listening to Elise's story of her close call with a combine, not able to believe his own ears. He had been dropped off at home by his coworker after their return from Chicago. When he didn't see his wife's car in the driveway, he just thought she wasn't home, until he wanted to run to the store and saw that his truck was gone. It was only a few minutes later that Elise pulled into their driveway.

His initial reaction to her story was fear for her safety, but when he was reassured she was physically all right, his fear grew to a more serious concern.

"Cole, I'm all right," she insisted. "And Noah checked

the house and nothing else happened."

Cole circled the room, looking for his cell phone. "We need to postpone the birthday party. I'm calling Mom right now."

"Cole, no!"

Deci and Belle dove for their hiding places under the window seat.

Cole stared at his wife. "I can't have anything happening to you."

"Nothing's going to happen. I'm looking forward to the party, and so are a lot of other people. What would we do? Just sit here and lock all the doors?"

She hadn't seen him this upset in a long time…unless it was maybe over the loss of a rugby game. A half-eaten pizza sat on the table in front of them, and what she did eat, sat on her stomach like a lump. Cole didn't answer but grabbed his plate of now cold pizza and headed upstairs.

Elise gave it about fifteen minutes, then went upstairs to find him. He was in the shower and called out that he had things to do on his computer when he got out.

"Okay. I'm going downstairs to watch a movie, okay?"

"Yeah, okay."

Elise grabbed her laptop from her dresser and headed downstairs where the thumb drive and paper of circled data waited for her.

With the drama from Elise and Cole's favorite black-and-white movie, Casablanca, playing in the background, Elise searched through the circled data that she was now convinced was Susan's doing. She compared it again with the data on the thumb drive. Test subjects' personal information was hidden from her, as was the usual protocol, but what else could she derive from it?

She rubbed her middle finger in circles on her forehead

and started again, from the beginning. Susan tested real people, and how well they understood speech in differing types and levels of background noise, with and without, the new chip. She did the same tests over numerous visits to check for consistency. Sometimes an unexpected result would be considered an "outlier" and be discounted, but even that didn't make sense with the inconsistencies she was looking at now.

She focused, and soon a story formulated in her mind. Whoever did this, did it on purpose, but at the same time, didn't really know what they were doing. Someone familiar with the nuances of testing would've substituted better errors, if that made any sense. And that would leave out Tierneigh and Susan, for sure. And this might have been why Tierneigh wanted her to come out to the lab. She wanted access to the computers, to show Elise the full picture.

Elise raked both hands through her hair. She hit the button on her cell phone under Amy's name.

"Hey, what's up?" Amy slurped something just as she answered her phone.

Elise half whispered, "What are you drinking?"

"Chamomile tea."

Elise thought of the fragrant, apple-like scent. "Ooh, that sounds good. Do you have a few minutes? I hate to bother you now, but I really need to run something by you."

"No problem. Get yourself some tea. I'll wait."

Elise was in the kitchen in less than half a minute and pulled a mug and box of tea bags out of the cupboard. She tapped a button on her electronic tea kettle, completely spoiled now from this birthday present from her kids, and waited for the beep. Soon, both women sat at their respective kitchen tables, hunched over their tea and speaking in whispered tones while Deci weaved around Elise's ankles.

Elise told Amy about her "faked" data suspicions and her

theory of why Tierneigh wanted Elise to return to E. S. Hearing Labs.

Amy spoke with intensity, but still at a whispered level. "Who would do that? I mean, be so messy about it? And why? Why would anyone sabotage the data…it would only hurt E. S. Hearing Labs…and for what?"

"And is it the same person who tried to run me down with the combine? Whoever it was seemed to know about keys left in those things and all, but they're not that savvy about audiology procedures.

"Exactly. But who, Elise?"

"Don't know. There's a large enough number of people around here that have had experiences on farms. I didn't say anything to Cole about this yet. He's upset enough about last night."

"I expect so!"

Elise reflexively glanced toward the kitchen door to listen for approaching footsteps. "Listen, I really need to talk to Susan. She wasn't at the lab today, but Tessa said she's planning on coming in tomorrow morning. I'm going to run out to E. S. Labs early and try to catch her."

"You're what? What about the birthday party? You can't go out there by yourself. I'll go with you."

Elise heard a male voice in the background. Amy's voice changed to a soft, sing-song tone. "Nothing, Troy. Just talking to Elise about tomorrow."

Elise heard a mumbled response then Amy whispered, "He's gone."

"Amy, I'll go out early. You plan on going to the restaurant, okay? You cover for me, and I'll meet you there as soon as I can. One last thing. Do you think Rick would know enough about data, but maybe not enough to fake it correctly?"

"I'm not sure, anymore, about anything with him. What

if Rick's a spy for Lewelling Labs? What if he needs money for his gambling and he's doing something really under-handed just for the sake of messing things up for a while?"

Elise tried to steady her voice. "Sometimes I think I'm afraid to know. But regardless, we need to know what's going on before either more people are hurt, or we lose our business, or who knows what else."

"I agree," said Amy. "This whole thing is so awful. I hope you get some information from Susan tomorrow. Let me know when you're on your way back, okay?"

"I will."

They changed the conversation to last-minute party details, knowing full well it was an unsuccessful attempt to quell their frustrations, then hung up. It wasn't even half a minute later when Elise's phone buzzed, and her son's face lit the screen.

"Jon, you okay?"

Jon laughed. "Yeah, Mom, I'm okay. Just wanted to double-check about the morning and to give you an update on Aunt Ida. I just tried calling Dad, but he didn't answer."

Elise felt her head was one of those roulette tables that spin in circles. The flipper stopped on a wedge marked "Birthday Party."

"I think he's in the shower, honey. Did you find her? Aunt Ida?"

There was a pause. "No, Mom, I'm sorry. I tracked her pretty well until there was a problem with the ship that I'm pretty sure she was on. The problem is that schedules can change anytime, and sometimes passengers need to hop on and off more than one ship during their trip."

"This isn't sounding good."

"I know, Mom. I left messages with as many shipping lines as I could find that she might've had to change to, but I just never absolutely tracked her down. I'm just hoping she's all right."

Elise moaned. She didn't think she could take any more bad news.

Jon hemmed and hawed, then finally said, "Do you want me to call Grandma and tell her?"

Elise blew out a breath. "No, not just yet. Let me talk to your dad first, okay? We'll figure out what to do. I appreciate all your work, though. And thanks again for helping Becky with her computer."

"No prob, Mom. See you in the morning. Oh, what time is Dad picking me up again...or am I coming there?"

They spoke a few more minutes about the logistics of the morning and who was doing what, since Elise needed Cole's truck. She skirted the issue that she might be late, but then convinced herself she'd be back before anyone even missed her.

Chapter Twenty-Two

Saturday Morning

Elise stared at the ceiling, surprised that she'd slept as well as she did, but told herself it was probably out of physical and emotional exhaustion. Somewhere under her bed, Belle was closing in on one of Becky's old hairbands, her favorite toy. Elise heard her guttural mmrroww grow shorter and quicker, then a thump. She turned her head in time to see Belle triumphantly strut out the bedroom door, her catch in her mouth. If it could be that easy.

Susan. Elise grabbed her cell phone on the bedside stand and almost knocked the small brass lamp over. Six thirty. Need to go.

She showered and dressed in record time and then stood next to the dining room table, quickly arranging the decorations, gifts, sign-in book, and other paraphernalia for the birthday party. She was on her second quick cup of coffee. The first one didn't help her mood like she hoped it would. At least not yet, anyway, but she was certain that once she spoke to Susan she'd feel a ton better and be able to enjoy the rest of the day. She was sure of it.

Her daughter's face shimmied on the table, and Elise grabbed it before it made much more noise. "Morning, sweetie."

"Morning, Mom. Thought you'd be up."

Elise laughed. "Well, I didn't think you'd be up."

"Yeah, right…I get up early sometimes, and I'm excited for today. Just wanted you to know I'm going to pick up the helium balloons as soon as the party store opens and take them over to the restaurant. They should let me bring them in early, right?"

"You can try. I think it'd be okay. Could you stop by the house on your way and take what I have on the dining room table, too?"

"Okay. Actually, I think I can get Hope to come with her car, too. Aren't you going over with us? And have you looked outside yet? It looks like it's going to rain!"

Elise felt mild pounding around her temples as she got up from the table and walked to the windows. She frowned at the wind scuttling leaves in circles and ducked her head to look up through the window. A few dark clouds formed overhead.

"I think it'll be okay. I just have to run an errand. I'll be there, but it'd help me if you can get these things, in case I get held up or something…which I'm not counting on," she added. "Oh, and Amy should be meeting you there, too."

"Who's getting Grandma?"

"Your dad and Jon. Speaking of which, I'm going to give your brother a call right now."

"Okay. See you there, Mom."

Elise touched the red dot on her phone to hang up and immediately called Jon, but to no avail. Not that she really expected him to answer this early, but it was worth a try. She left him a long message with what was going on with Becky, ending with a plea to remember to pick his dad up first before going to get his grandma. She explained her car was still at the repair shop and she needed to take his dad's truck to run an errand.

Irregular footsteps thumped on the stairs, and Cole's sleepy voice mumbled, "Did you call the sheriff's station again, or did they call you?" He gave his wife a peck on the cheek as she rolled her eyes.

"It wasn't the sheriff. I was talking to Becky and just left a message for Jon. Although, I did talk to Noah last night. Didn't I tell you about that?"

Cole turned his back, let out a big noisy yawn, and headed for the kitchen mumbling, "I called him last night to find out how rugby practice went, while I was in Chicago." His voice got weaker as he walked into the kitchen. "And I thought I heard him say something like…he's closing in on someone…and he's going to get him."

Elise's head jerked up. She walked to the kitchen door. "What?"

Cole's cell phone buzzed. He raised an index finger in a "wait-a-minute" sign and shuffled toward one of the cupboards, pulled out a mug, placed it on the counter, then reached for the coffee pot. Elise's jaw tightened.

It was still dark outside, and at that point, the only light was from the overhead light from the stove, so she flicked the light on, which made Cole jump.

He scowled, but immediately changed to a cheerful, "Happy Birthday, Mom. Yeah, no problem. We're good." Cole didn't do a good job at stifling a second yawn. "Yeah…yeah…Mom. No, I'm sorry, we haven't heard from Aunt Ida…but we're going to have fun, right? There's a ton of people coming today. You just relax and enjoy the day. Jon and I will be over to get you in a few hours. Okay, love you, too."

Elise tried to hold down her frustration. She wanted more information about his conversation with Noah. "She all right?"

"Yeah." He shuffled past her and headed upstairs again.

"Cole, what did Noah mean about 'closing in on him?'"

He turned and looked down at her, one hand on the oak banister. "Huh? Oh, I dunno. Oh, wait, yeah. He was worried about you and just said something about 'closing in on him.' That's all." She heard a loud slurp as he turned and trudged slowly back upstairs.

Elise lowered her eyebrows and wondered what that meant. Her attention was pulled to a deep, rolling rumble outside. She grabbed her phone and touched the weather app. A colorful radar screen popped up and showed multiple yellow and red splotches floating across the screen, consistent with an oncoming storm. She convinced herself it wasn't too bad. According to the radar, this should clear up just before the party.

Elise pulled her lightweight jacket from the coat closet near the stairs, rested her hand on the banister, and called out, "I'm leaving now, Cole. See you at the restaurant." She didn't like misleading her husband, but she'd be out to the labs and back before he'd be at the restaurant, anyway. She mentally told Deci and Belle not to touch anything on the table, then flew out the door.

Chapter Twenty-Three

Saturday Morning

Elise steadied her eyes on the road, thinking about what Cole had just said. Noah told him they were closing in on a "him." She should've pressed him further, but she hadn't dared, given the mood he was in.

A lightness came over her, and she relaxed against the seat. Her foot lifted slightly off the gas pedal. So, Susan really didn't have anything to do with hurting Tierneigh. Of course not. Someone tampered with Susan's data, and she'd suspected that pretty much since the beginning, but of course, denied it, probably from the implausibility of it all. How could anything happen to data Susan would practically protect with her life? Elise flinched internally at that last thought but continued her line of reasoning.

Susan had asked her patients to come back for retesting. That was the right thing to do. But she found proof of the discrepancies the night before the training…then what? She went looking for Tierneigh, as a friend and colleague, but had to leave a note that Tierneigh didn't see until the next morning. But, instead of going downstairs to see Susan, Tierneigh had called Elise. Tierneigh probably couldn't find Susan, with everything that was going on, much less have the time to talk in private. That made sense. Elise brought a hand to her chest. She should've tried harder to talk to her friend.

Again, she contemplated her questions. Number one…about Susan and Rick meeting at the bar. If it was true, and they had some kind of relationship going on, then Rick would be in the clear. It would also be plausible that he'd been trying to protect Susan and their relationship, whatever that was.

Number two, did Susan know about the thumb drive? What would it mean if she did, and chose not to come clean to Elise about it? And come to think of it, what were the implications of Tierneigh giving the thumb drive to Elise, knowing Elise would take it out of the building? That was a pretty serious move, taking highly sensitive data out of the lab. She must've felt desperate.

Elise's head swirled with the implications of taking proprietary information out of a workplace like E. S. Hearing Labs.

Her mind jumped back to the "he" that Noah said he was closing in on. Theo? Bob Bell? If Rick could be cleared, could she make a case for clearing Theo and Bob, too? Maybe they were just worried about the data. It made sense that Rick would've known about it, being so close to Susan, and he might've said something to the other men. Is that what happened? She wished Susan would trust her enough to help clear this up.

Elise puckered her lips and consciously blew out a breath. She tried to focus on the scenery around her, if only for a few seconds. Most of the fields were harvested now, and she was definitely more comfortable at four-way stops, her vision clear in all directions…a lot better than before the harvest.

Whoa! She jumped, and clutched the steering wheel hard, at the sudden crack of lightning in the distance. She counted to three until she heard the thunder, then peeled each finger off the wheel, one by one, and stretched them without fully letting go. She felt moisture under her palms as she lifted her fingers.

The E. S. Hearing Labs building was visible now in the distance, and the varying hues of darkness and light, caused by the swiftly moving rain clouds over the building, mesmerized Elise. It was almost pretty, in a different sort of way. Details that had been swirling in her mind all of a sudden came to the forefront, and, as if in slow motion, formed a picture.

Her eyes widened and darted to the building's row of windows, which she could now see in the distance. She gasped. She pressed the pedal and hoped Susan was already there…because she knew now who the real killer was.

Elise's heart pounded against her chest as she pulled into the rain drenched parking lot and came to a quick stop. She grabbed her purse just as her phone buzzed, causing her to yank her hand away, as if she'd touched a hot stove. The phone buzzed again and, this time, she pulled it from her purse.

"Becky, everything okay?"

Her voice squeaked, "Mom…" then a whoosh of exasperated breath. "I'm at the house. Where are you? I don't see the rolls of crepe paper you said you had. We need them to hang up all the pictures of Grandma." She heard shuffling footsteps and more exasperated breathing.

Elise struggled to mentally switch gears and squeezed her eyes closed. "You're in the dining room now?"

"Yeah. The bag's not here. I guess I can stop at the store, but I really have to get to the Lake 'n' Bacon and get this going!"

Elise visualized her home. She walked around the dining room, the living room, the kitchen…upstairs. "Did you check the office? Maybe I forgot to bring it down."

"Hold on. I'll go look."

Her jaw clenched, and Elise scanned the parking lot while she waited. Only a couple other cars, but neither of them Susan's. Maybe she parked around the corner of the building, nearer the side door. Elise decided that made sense, because it was closer to her office. She wished she could use that door, but she needed a badge to get in.

Another shot of lightning seemed to crack right over her, immediately convincing her it'd be a lot better inside, so she threw her purse strap over her shoulder and dashed from the car, holding her hood against sudden gusts of wind and pelting rain with one hand, her cell phone pressed against her ear with the other. Those stories about cell phones and lightning weren't really true…right?

The portico helped keep some of the rain off her, but the wind still whipped around her as she let go of her hood and grabbed the metal handle, extremely grateful the door wasn't locked.

Elise slipped inside, pushed the door closed behind her, and shook herself like a dog, more to help release the tension in her body than the rain. Another cold shiver shot up her arms, but not from the rain. Being in such a large, shadowy, empty building seemed ominous…and it was the last place Tierneigh ever saw.

The usual after-hour yellow lights provided a dim glow at sporadic distances along the tops of the walls, and she wondered if any of the lab techs were in. Usually, production needed to proceed 24/7, especially during a widely advertised event like the introduction of the new chip. And there were still the usual orders of custom products, like hearing protectors and sleeping, swimming, and musicians' ear plugs.

She glanced at Tessa's empty desk and walked toward it to see if there were any signs that the receptionist might actually be in. The computer monitor was dark, and the desk cleared off, as if someone was definitely not planning on coming in until Monday. What'd she expect? She wouldn't come in if she were Tessa, either.

Elise stopped to listen, but the only sound was her own breathing, then her echoing footsteps on the linoleum floor when she walked toward the north hallway. Susan would be in her office, and they'd be able to talk, then she'd head back to Mt. Harmony and her mother-in-law's birthday party before Cole even suspected what she'd done.

Elise's head swiveled side to side, as she stepped lightly down the hallway, both arms pressing her purse close to her chest. Why did closed doors down a long, dimly lit hallway always seem so creepy? She realized then that she was tiptoeing and told herself to quit being so silly. But when she walked normally, the echo of her footsteps immediately brought her to her tiptoes again.

She stopped at Susan's office door, now minus the yellow-and-black police tape, and pushed aside that awful night's memories. She rapped lightly on the door with one knuckle.

Hearing nothing, she turned the handle and pushed it open with the back of her other hand, the cell phone still clutched in it. Becky! She forgot her own daughter!

"Hello? Becky?" No reception. Well, she couldn't worry about crepe paper now. She knew Becky would take care of it one way or another.

Elise stepped into the darkened room and closed the door behind her. The gooseneck lamp on Susan's desk was on, but Susan wasn't there. Her eyes caught a thin, vertical line of light peeking from the slightly ajar anechoic chamber door. Is there no overhead light in this place?

"Susan?" Still no answer.

Her heart constricted, and she closed her eyes for a brief second, mustering the strength to open them again, telling herself that she could do this. One more step. Her eyes adjusted better to the low light, and then she saw it...the old equipment shelf and the empty space that, yes, was still empty. The pair of headphones Elise had placed there herself on the night the EMTs took Tierneigh to the hospital were still shoved to one side of the space.

She stepped closer and lightly ran her fingers across the front edge of the empty space, letting her mind drift to that night. Susan had been in the booth with the students. They were asking questions. Susan's voice was soft and clear...all this magnificent, old test equipment...but then her mind formed a picture, and she quickly scanned the shelves but couldn't find it.

What was it that Noah said about Tierneigh's head wound? She was hit with something rounded and that brown flecks of paint were found around the—

She couldn't finish the thought.

Elise turned toward the anechoic chamber door and hissed, "Susan?"

Nothing.

Okay, time to find the security guard...or just get the heck out of there and call Susan from her car. But the sound of footsteps in the hallway caught her attention, especially when they stopped at the office door. They were a little heavier than Susan's would be, but she justified that in her mind as caused by the surrounding quiet.

"Just me, Susan—"

The door swung inward and Elise jumped. Her hand smacked hard against her chest. "David?"

Chapter Twenty-Four

Saturday Morning

The young business student took two steps into the office and stopped. He looked different. Even in the dim light, Elise could see that his hair was a mess, and his jeans and sweatshirt were rumpled.

"Dr. Harte? What are you doing here?"

A multitude of emotions ravaged Elise's stomach. She coughed, then smiled wide. "I had an appointment with Susan, but I guess I beat her. Do you have one, too? I know she'll be here any minute."

David's behavior the last couple of weeks flashed through her mind, and it unsettled her. She was confused now, and her mind played Cole's voice over in her head when he repeated what Noah said about "closing in on him." Could she be wrong? At this point, she desperately just wanted to get out of there.

He took a step toward Elise and stopped, his face searching hers. "Actually, I needed to talk to her...about something...personal."

Elise wasn't sure how to react...as if she really had a choice with the internal alarm going off in her stomach. "Is there anything I can help with?" It was a try.

"Oh, heck no...not you!"

Elise's eyes popped open at the same time his did.

He held a hand up in a stop position. "I'm sorry! I didn't mean it the way it came out."

"David, have I done something to annoy you?" She froze and clamped her mouth shut. Might not want to remind him of something he was either mad at her for or that she did to him, unknowingly. Did he find out he was a suspect on her rogues' gallery? Did he know she went into his apartment while he was out?

Elise then noticed just how stressed and tired he looked. Her eyebrows lowered, but her eyes were lasered on his face. Anything and everything to do with David flashed through her mind. From his behavior when they first met, to that strange remark about being Becky's mother, to the folder she saw him take out of Tierneigh's office…and the rudeness yesterday morning in the parking lot.

"No, Dr. Harte. No."

Anxiety got the best of her, and she blurted, "I saw you take something out of Tierneigh's office the other day. What was it?"

Even in the low light, Elise could see his face turn sickly pale. He shrank back slightly and frowned. His eyes dropped to the floor.

"I…I…"

"So you did take something…that belonged to Tierneigh." Elise was feeling a little braver now, and Susan would be there any minute…right?

But then her mind went somewhere she wished it hadn't. Was what he took from Tierneigh's office worth killing for?

Her legs went weak, and she instinctively scanned the area for either a way to get out, or for some kind of a weapon. She glanced at the office phone. It was too obvious to reach for the landline and call for help. Not with him so close.

"Oh...uh, actually, Tierneigh had something of mine...and I needed to get it."

"But you crossed the sheriff's tape. What could be so important that it couldn't wait?"

"Dr. Harte, please. I need to talk to Susan."

"You can tell Susan, but you can't tell me?"

David's face shot up. "She's not Becky's mother!"

His eyes widened, and his face paled more than Elise thought possible. She flushed in return, but relaxed slightly as her suspicions were suddenly supported. "What does my daughter have to do with this?"

They stared at each other, so intense in the moment, that neither heard another set of footsteps stop outside the office door.

Elise took a breath. "David. Do you know how to run a combine?"

"A combine? A harvester?"

"Yes."

He hesitated, then scrunched his face. "I rode in one as a kid a couple times on my uncle's farm, but no, I don't know how to actually work one."

Elise's eyes never left his face. She felt...or hoped...he was telling the truth.

He took one more step toward her just as the door flew open, and Elise watched as a brown, rectangular metal box swung toward David's head. Her eyes popped wide, her mouth opening, but just as quickly, her face crunched in horror, when she heard a thud of impact and watched David's body crumple to the floor.

Elise screamed when she saw blood oozing from the unconscious David, now in a heap in front of her. She dropped by his side, then raised her head to look at the panting rep manager, Gloria Strauber.

"I'll call for help." Elise jumped up and turned toward

the phone.

"Stop! Stop right there, Elise!"

"I'm going to call 911, Gloria." She felt dizzy and tried to brush the memory of the last time this happened out of her mind.

She ignored the rep manager and took another step toward the desk, reaching for Susan's office phone.

"I said, Stop!"

The guttural intensity in Gloria's voice was something she'd never heard come out of a human's mouth before. It confirmed to Elise, in that moment, that her suspicions were right.

She watched Gloria smirk at David on the floor, then slowly turn toward her. The hatred in her eyes made Elise's legs go numb. "Why did you have to get involved in this, Elise?"

Elise decided a white lie was totally acceptable at the moment. "I've already called Noah, Gloria...he knows."

Gloria puffed out air. "If you already told him, why are you here? By the way, you're welcome."

"I came to see Susan about something else...we're audiologists, remember?" Her eyebrows lowered. "What do you mean, 'you're welcome'?"

"I unlocked the front doors for you. I saw you drive into the parking lot from my office window. I almost didn't pay attention, 'cause I didn't recognize your truck, but saw you on the phone. I had time to go unlock the doors for you."

This confirmed Elise's thoughts as she drove to the lab. The second-floor window overlooking the parking lot, Gloria's office, the farm pictures on the wall...her access to Tierneigh...and the computers. A person who wouldn't know how to make "good" errors.

Her jaw muscles clenched. "I told you I called the police, Gloria," Elise continued the plausible lie.

"I don't think so." She took a step toward Elise and swung the tympanometer, ever so slightly, back and forth.

The old, brown tympanometer that Elise guessed was from the 1970s. It had rounded corners and definitely looked heavy enough.

Her stomach did a slow drop. She was absolutely sure now, that it was that piece of equipment she'd seen in the now-empty spot on the shelf, the night of the training. Her eyes widened as she stared at the hand holding that piece of equipment. It was covered in a mustard-colored work glove, identical to the one the fireman had held up at the Millers' farm after they found the combine that hit her.

She took a slow step backward. "Why, Gloria? Why hurt Tierneigh? She never did anything to you."

"Tierneigh found out what I was doing. What else was I to do?" Gloria's voice dropped to a mere whisper. "Everything was under control." She scrunched her face. "Then she came in early." She said the last word with a high-pitched, sarcastic tone.

A chill shot up Elise's spine. She kept her eyes glued to Gloria's. Keep her talking. She tried to remember any psych classes she took years ago, and how she could handle this, but came up blank. Whoops.

Then she remembered. The one class she'd signed up for, she ended up dropping. The teacher said they all had to do oral reports in front of the class, and she hated public speaking. Great.

Elise softened her voice and tried to do the same with her eyes. "What did Tierneigh find out, Gloria? It couldn't have been that bad."

Gloria laughed, and the tympanometer loosened slightly in her hand. "Don't you see the way they treat me around here?"

Elise took another step backward.

"I'm a manager, but do they give me an office on the third floor with the other administrators? No. They give me some dumpy little room on the second floor with those people."

Those people? "Wasn't that because you work so closely with the reps here? You have quite a staff, Gloria." Hopefully, the change in terminology would stimulate her ego and distract from the current situation.

Gloria actually relaxed and, thankfully, didn't move. "Staff...my staff...but they still don't treat me the way I should be treated."

"Who are you talking about? From what I've seen from your staff, they like you and look up to you." Elise tried to remember if Tierneigh had ever said anything about Gloria one way or the other but couldn't.

"Who do you think I'm talking about? Theo...Rick... Bob... all the management. Even Susan. She just looks down her nose at me. I've worked hard, and they are going to reap all the rewards...and I'm only going to get a pittance."

Elise took another slow step to the side now, closer to Susan's desk. Anything as a buffer. "But why Tierneigh?"

"She heard those idiots, Rick and Bob, talking in the spare office the morning of the training. I was in the stairwell and saw them. They were so stupid!"

Elise's foot bumped Susan's desk. "What did she hear, Gloria?"

"She heard Bob tell Rick about the stupid errors I put in the computer. The errors in Susan's research."

Another piece of the puzzle confirmed.

"Tierneigh didn't really know what she was looking at, or that it was me who did it, but I knew she'd figure it out, so I had no choice."

"Those numbers were pretty good, Gloria. And you even had Susan going for a while, right?"

"I just needed a little more time."

"Time…for what?"

"Didn't you find out when you went to Lewelling Labs?"

Elise flinched slightly.

"I had a good deal going with Bill out there. Of course, he didn't realize it was a little underhanded…just thought I was helping him out a little, stalling the roll-out of the chip here to give him more time to develop it at his place. But I had a few other irons in the pot, too."

Bill…the conversation Tierneigh told her sister about. It was Bill Hooper. Here she and Amy thought Gloria was on the other side of this…that she had integrity and pride in the work done at E. S. Hearing Labs.

"What about Rick, Gloria. Is he in on this with you?"

"Rick? Are you crazy? He got wind that something was going on with Bill Hooper. He and his buddy there, Bob, wanted to keep an eye on him. Rick was doing a little 'under-cover' work. I heard them talking with Theo one time down-stairs. At first, Theo thought Susan was doing something to the data…and that she brought Tierneigh in and then you. Theo didn't think anyone else was smarter than you all. Ha! It didn't last long, though. Rick decided to believe his sweetie, Susan."

Elise glanced at Susan's desk and saw the weather radio, thankful that it was still where she'd placed it the night of the training. Her hand slowly edged its way toward it.

"I still don't understand why you did this, Gloria."

"Why not? I've been treated like garbage my whole life, and I finally found a way to be treated with some respect."

It was obvious Gloria was enjoying talking to someone about her plans. Elise needed another stall tactic.

"Do you know how to run a combine, Gloria?"

Gloria stared at her, then started laughing, almost uncontrollably. Elise saw the tympanometer slip slightly in her hand, but Gloria stopped laughing, just as quickly as she started, and her fist tightened around the handle. She was starting to swing it with her arm.

"I wasn't gonna hurt you. Just scare you a little. I forgot how fun it was to drive those things. I learned during my summers at my grandparents' farm."

Elise flashed to the picture she saw on Gloria's office wall of a teenage girl with an older man and woman in front of a farmhouse. "How did you know I was at the Miller farm?"

"Your business partner told me when I called your office, that you were out looking at someone's loop system. I took a chance you got it through us and looked it up. It was too easy."

Anger overtook the numb feeling in Elise's body, and she decided to go with it. She thought of Tierneigh, and her eyes shot daggers at Gloria. "Why did you kill Tierneigh?"

"I didn't intend to." Gloria's shoulders slumped, and she almost whimpered. "It was mostly an accident. You know how clumsy you all get sometimes in those booths with all the cords and things."

Elise's hand touched the side of the weather radio. "An accident?"

"Well, let's just say it was…serendipity." Gloria smirked, and Elise felt a geyser rise in her stomach. "I followed her in here that night. Everyone thought I'd gone home, but I was waiting in the bathroom. I wanted to get into Susan's office and look around. See if I could find out what else she knew. When I got in here, Tierneigh was standing at the door to the anechoic chamber and…"

"And?" Elise glared at her.

"She told me she had something important to talk to Susan about. I knew the minute they got their heads together I was done. They were too good…knew their stuff, so it would only be a matter of time. And with Susan dating Rick, well, who do you think they were going to believe…them or me? The one they treat like dirt."

"What did you think Tierneigh was going to tell Susan?"

"That she heard me talking to Hooper on the phone that day. I told him I knew how to delay the chip's roll-out…long enough to give him time to get it going at his place. And that would've made me a lot of money." Gloria's face lit up with pride. "It was just too easy, and this chip's going to get me something way better than what that third floor could ever offer."

She laughed so hard that she didn't notice Elise grab the weather radio and throw it at her with all her might. Gloria tried to duck at the last second, and it brushed the side of her forehead and knocked her back a step, but not enough for Elise to get by and out the door. Gloria wasn't in as good of shape as Elise was, but what frightened Elise was the strength she seemed to have, based purely on her anger.

The glare on Gloria's face when she straightened up sent chills through Elise's body, and she knew right then, that the only place she'd have a chance now…was inside the anechoic chamber.

Chapter Twenty-Five

Gloria swiped a trickle of blood off her face then lunged, just as Elise tried to pull the door closed, but Gloria was too close. Elise ran into the chamber and around the speakers that circled the chair holding the KEMAR scarecrow. She felt like she couldn't breathe, and her ears rang worse than the tornado siren and the passenger train put together.

Gloria stepped into the chamber, and her eyes dropped to what she was holding in her hand. A sick smile came over her face as she stepped toward Elise.

Elise took a step backward, then glanced at Gloria's feet. She thought she saw one of the speaker cords move but had to put her full attention on the woman in front of her.

"Not again, Gloria. You can't get away with it twice."

Elise knocked one of the speakers toward Gloria, but she sidestepped it, and it fell onto the wire mesh floor. Two more steps and, again, Elise thought she saw a cord move by Gloria's ankles.

Elise shoved a second speaker toward Gloria just as she lunged, but her face contorted into a scream that fell flat against the sound-treated walls. Elise watched Gloria drop flat on the wire-meshed floor with a muffled thud, where she lay motionless, arms splayed. A speaker cord was pulled in a straight tight line just above her ankles.

Elise followed the cord to the chamber doorway, where

David lay on his stomach in a crawling position, both hands grasping the other end. His eyes were wider than Elise thought humanly possible.

She looked back at Gloria, who she now realized, had fallen on the tympanometer, and was out cold.

Elise dropped to the floor next to her as David quickly wrapped the cords around her ankles.

"I think she's out, David," she said, barely able to breathe. "We need to call the authorities."

"I think we're good, Dr. Harte." He pointed to the doorway, where Noah now stood, with a Bluestem deputy next to him.

"EMTs are on their way." Noah rushed to attend to Gloria.

The Bluestem deputy helped David up and guided him out of the chamber and over to Susan's desk chair.

Noah saw that Gloria was starting to come to and turned to Elise. "There." He pointed to the KEMAR chair in the middle of the room with one hand as he grabbed Elise's arm with the other. He pulled the scarecrow out of the chair and let it drop to the floor. "Sit. Now."

Elise obeyed.

The EMTs arrived and Chris, who had been there to take Tierneigh to the hospital, now stood in front of Elise, arms folded across his chest. He raised one eyebrow after assuring himself that she was not in any immediate distress. "Really?"

"Hi, Chris." Elise looked more embarrassed than hurt. "Sorry you had to come out again."

Chris's face softened. "Hey, I'm just glad everyone here's okay. I didn't get a chance to tell you how sorry I was about your friend."

"Thanks."

Chris picked up his bag and followed the others outside

the chamber, ready to take Gloria and David to Mt. Harmony Hospital Emergency. Noah and Elise were the last to leave.

"I hate to ask this again, but are you okay to drive? I'll be glad to take you back to Mt. Harmony…or I can call Cole."

That was like cold water on her face. "What time is it?"

Noah pointed to a wall clock in Susan's office, and all Elise could do was moan.

"I need to get to the Lake 'n' Bacon!"

"Hold on, Elise…"

She raised her eyes to his. "Hey, how'd you get out here so quickly?"

"I stopped by the Lake 'n' Bacon and saw Amy." He put a hand up to stop her from speaking. "Now don't get mad at her. She said you were out here, and something didn't feel right. I was on my way, when the Bluestem Sheriff got a 911 call from David, and they called me."

"David?" She glanced over to the empty chair where David had been.

Noah put a hand out to help Elise stand, but she shook her head. "I'm okay, really. I need to get going."

"Are you sure? No speeding, right? I'll be behind you to make sure you're okay."

Elise rushed out of the anechoic chamber and through Susan's office but bumped right into the stunned research audiologist as she stepped into the hallway.

"Elise! What's going on here?"

"It's okay. I really have to go." She took a deep breath. "Gloria's been arrested for Tierneigh's murder, and David was hit in the head with your old tympanometer, and the anechoic chamber is kind of a mess, sorry, but I'll explain it all later." She turned her back on a stunned Susan, hurried down the hall and, gratefully, out the front doors of E. S. Hearing Labs.

Elise's phone let off a series of beeps as she exited the building. She glanced at the screen and watched as a plethora of texts from Becky, Amy, Jon, and Cole ticked up, asking if she was either on her way or at the restaurant already.

She groaned and tried a slow jog toward her truck, testing the strength of her legs, which seemed okay. She slid onto the front seat of the truck and headed back to Mt. Harmony, with Noah right in the middle of the rearview mirror.

Chapter Twenty-Six

Noah followed Elise all the way back to Mt. Harmony, but it didn't help lessen the frustration she felt. As flippant as she may have been with Susan, when she rushed out of the building to get back to Mt. Harmony, she found herself fighting back tears once again. Solving a death and celebrating a life on the same day, if not within minutes of each other, was a dichotomy she wasn't familiar with, to say the least.

Elise called Amy from her truck and told her what happened. She told Amy it was okay to tell Lucy, but she didn't want anyone else to know, so as not to put a damper on the birthday festivities. Amy completely understood, and her support and concern helped bolster Elise.

She focused now on the acres of harvested cornfields, the full sun, and clear skies. The air was cool and the fields so quiet. She took slow deep breaths, and for some reason, didn't even let Beethoven in.

Noah watched Elise pull into a space in the Lake 'n' Bacon parking lot. Amy and Lucy, who must've been waiting at the front doors, jogged out to meet her. He slowed to a stop and lowered the passenger side window.

"I have to get to the station, but I'll be back. Don't want to miss the event of the year!"

Elise smiled her thanks as he drove off, then turned to the two friends she felt the closest to in the world, hugged them, then gave them a quick rundown of what happened.

After a few minutes of watching two shocked faces react to the story, she glanced at her "find location" app and said, "Cole's on his way with his Mom. We better get in there." Elise had hoped that Cole was too busy to check his app and see where she had been.

Amy grabbed Elise's arm, concern on her face. "It just hit me. I'm the one who told Gloria you were going to the Miller farm that night. I'm so sorry, Elise."

"Nothing to be sorry about, Amy. None of us knew about Gloria."

Lucy spurted, "You going to be okay?"

Elise's eyes softened, and she felt a warmth in her chest. "Oh, yeah."

If Elise had to pick one word for her first impression of the room, it would have been "joyful." Not just "content" and not "raucous," but basically "joyful." The room was a mass of red and white helium ballons and was large enough to provide one head table along the far wall. Twelve rectangle tables that could hold six people each were split on each side of a main aisle leading to the main table. All the tables were covered with white cotton tablecloths. The centerpieces consisted of red, white, and purple chrysanthemums with long, weighted, upright clips, displaying pictures of Catherine throughout different phases of her life, along with her favorite movies, favorite actors and actresses, and places she had visited.

To the left of the head table was a doorway to the kitchen with a cart stationed nearby for the birthday cake. Brass wall sconces on off-white walls provided muted lighting, except for an extra overhead light trained on the main table. The room was windowless, but the ambiance was perfect.

The "joyful" part was not just the room itself, but the

people in it. The joy of being together with friends and family was one of the first things Elise noticed when she moved to Mt. Harmony. Not that it didn't happen in big cities, but she felt there was something different here, in how people relaxed around each other and respected each other. Their smiles were genuine, and Elise could feel their happiness the first day she arrived.

Amy and Becky went off in different directions, and Elise took a moment to survey the attendees. She knew most everyone. Grady Weber and his Uncle Mike had just walked in. Oh, boy, wait until they find out what just happened at E. S. Hearing Labs!

Grady had his eyes on Marcie, who with her parents, were talking to the retired attorney and life insurance salesman from The Vibe. On the other side of the room, she saw the Jacks ladies, Helen and Anne, talking to a couple of men who played rugby with Cole and Noah. The men were mimicking a hand movement it looked like Helen was trying to demonstrate. Elise giggled and wondered if they might join the Jacks of All Trades team someday. She had a pretty hard time picturing them in powder blue sweats, though.

A momentary wave of fatigue seemed to hit her straight on, but she focused on the atmosphere in the room to buoy herself. Her eyes fell now upon a couple men from the morning gazebo group, who stood against one wall talking to Laura from The Vibe. Next to them, she recognized one of her patients, Alan, and his wife Lyla. She was surprised at first, but then realized how everyone knew everyone and, of course, some of her patients would know Catherine or the rest of the family. She watched, intent on how Alan was doing in such a noisy situation, but he was smiling, conversing easily, and seemed to be fully enjoying himself. Lyla looked up just then, smiled and winked at Elise. Elise gave her a smile and a nod back.

"Make way for the birthday girl!"

Everyone turned to see Jon standing in the doorway. He stepped aside as Catherine was escorted in on the arm of her husband.

Becky sidled up to Elise and whispered, "The red dress is perfect, don't you think?"

Elise whispered back, "This place looks great, Becky! You did a fantastic job, but I don't see the crepe paper."

"Didn't need it. Found those clips that worked great."

They watched Catherine make her way slowly through the room, acknowledging everyone and beaming from ear to ear.

Cole entered the room a few minutes later with his four siblings and their spouses. He saw Elise and came up to give her a quick kiss. "How are you, honey? You been waiting long for us?"

"Oh…no, Cole. Um, not long."

Becky looked at her. "Actually, where have you been, Mom?"

Elise pointed. "Look!"

A member of the serving crew was waving his arms to get everyone's attention, and when he did, he announced that lunch was being served at the buffet table on the left side of the room. A line of servers then paraded from the kitchen holding up large circular trays of watermelon and blueberry salad, ears of sweet corn, cornbread, potato salad, fried walleye, hamburger sliders, and a large green salad with fresh strawberries.

"Oh, that looks great!" said Elise. "Let's go…I'm starving!"

Of course, Catherine went first, with family and friends lining up behind her. Other servers brought pitchers of water and iced tea for each of the tables.

The next hour flew by. Noah made it just in time for the

lunch, which was delicious. Becky told Elise that she and Lucy were going to check on the cake, while servers shuffled through the room, clanking dishes together as they picked up the empty plates to take back to the kitchen.

Elise stood to go with the two women, but stopped when she was distracted by a figure standing in the hallway between the main restaurant and the banquet room. Her eyebrows lowered. The figure looked familiar. She gasped when none other than Theo Wrightman walked into the room.

He scanned the area, saw Elise, and made his way straight toward her. Elise decided not to wait for him to get much farther, in case this had something to do with the morning's incident, so immediately strode toward him to cut him off.

Becky watched her go, shrugged, and continued to the kitchen. Noah stood as Becky passed him, eyes lasered on Theo.

Elise tried to smile, but it was difficult. "Theo. Can I help you with something?"

"Oh, Elise…Dr. Harte. I'm not sure."

Elise felt her stomach churn. Now what? She clamped her mouth shut and waited for him to continue.

"I received this." He pulled an envelope out of his inside jacket pocket and held it against his chest. From what she could see, it looked like a private letter. He blurted out, "I was invited to the party, but I'm not sure why."

Stunned, Elise figured he must know someone, or be related to someone who wanted him to attend the birthday party, but who? She really had no choice but to invite him in.

It was then she noticed Noah walking slowly toward them. She waved him off.

"Theo, I can get one of the servers to get some lunch for you, if you'd like. I see they've already cleared off the food table."

"Oh, no, that's all right. I wasn't really sure if I was coming or not and already had a bite to eat." He slid the letter back into his jacket pocket.

"Theo, can I ask you something?"

He shrugged his shoulders. Elise took it as an "okay."

"Noah told me everything."

He nodded, still looking at her.

"But I have one question. Were you listening to Susan and me in the booth the other day?"

He looked slightly sheepish, then nodded. "I'm sorry. I was pretty upset and just didn't know who to trust around there."

The lights dimmed, and they both looked toward the front of the room.

Elise said, "I think they're getting ready to bring out Catherine's cake, so you can definitely stay for a piece of that."

Theo patted his stomach with both hands. "Not sure I need it, but sure sounds good."

"Good. Come on in and join the group. I'm going to check on the cake." Elise noticed that Noah sat back down at his table, but kept his eyes on Theo.

Cookie, wearing a pink Sweet Spot Bakery apron, stood near the cart, minus a cake at the moment, as Jon passed out sheets of paper with the lyrics to Catherine's favorite song. It was a jovial atmosphere, and some were adding to the fun by clearing their throats or warming up their vocal cords.

Jon was in his element, and he chuckled when he announced, "Will everyone please stand while we serenade the birthday girl!"

With shuffles and scrapes, the attendees stood. Jon cued the band that had set up in the back of the room, and they immediately started playing, "I've Got Tears in My Ears…"

with all chiming in.

Elise found Cole singing with his siblings and told him she was going to check on the cake. He nodded, not missing a beat, as she turned toward the kitchen door. She was surprised to see an empty space where the cart had been. She relaxed when a server opened the door, and Cookie pushed the cart out with the most perfect birthday cake for the occasion. Three graduated tiers rested on each other, covered with yellow buttercream frosting. Sugar fall leaves in colors ranging from red to yellow to orange, circled the bottom layer, then fell sporadically around the top and down the sides. Two light-wood skewers held a white banner on top of the cake that read, "Happy 80th Birthday, Catherine!" It was festive and timely, and blended with Catherine's favorite color, red, perfectly.

Cookie raised her chin as Elise approached her. "Take the cart, would you?" I left the knife in the kitchen. Be right back."

"Got it, Cookie."

Jon stepped forward, and after dramatically clearing his throat, called out, "One…two…three!" The room erupted in a somewhat off-key, but impressive, "Happy Birthday to you….."

Elise's head jerked around, but no Cookie, so she grabbed a tighter hold of the cart's handles and took a step just as someone else also grabbed the handles and gave her a hip bump.

"Let me get this, sweetie."

"What the…?" She tried to recover from being pushed off balance, as the woman put her head down and pushed the cart toward Catherine.

Catherine's eyes focused on the glow of the birthday candles, as were everyone's, until the song stopped and the server raised the lights. Catherine focused on the cake for another second or two, then slowly raised her eyes to the woman standing in front of her, eyes crossed and tongue out, head tilted to one side, staring back at her.

"Ida!!!!"

Both women screamed and fell into a massive hug, while the crowd clapped and started another round of "Happy Birthday…"

After a minute of laughing and cajoling, the two sisters pulled out of their hug, still holding onto each other, arms around each other's backs, waving to the crowd with their free hands. Jon grabbed his camera and snapped a multitude of pictures.

Elise laughed with them, which felt so good, just as Theo elbowed his way through the crowd and faced the two sisters.

His mouth was agape, and he barely sputtered out, "Ida?"

Ida's eyes fell on his. "Theo?"

Amy and Becky had walked up to Elise to help distribute the cake, but now stood as frozen as Elise was.

Elise was the first to speak. "You two know each other?" She was almost afraid to hear the answer.

Ida guffawed and Theo sputtered again. "Ida! I've been trying to find you!"

Elise's eyes couldn't get any wider or her mouth more open. Her head bounced from one to the other.

"Well, Theo, I left you the number!"

"Your number? Every time I called, someone would answer and tell me I'd reached the Shanghai Zoo."

"And who'd ya ask for?"

"Mr. Li….onne, like you told me to."

Elise slapped her hand over her mouth, then, along with Amy, Lucy, Becky, and Catherine, burst out laughing. On top of it all, they had to watch Ida walk around the table and give Theo a great big hug!

Catherine slid up behind Ida and struggled to speak. "Ida, when'd you get in? Where've you been? How long will you be here?" Then she pointed at Theo and said, "And who's that?"

Jon shouted above the crowd that cake was being served, and like kids wading through the shallow waters of Lake Harmony, the shuffling began. Amy and Lucy jumped ahead to help Cookie, as she deftly placed one slice after another on plates as fast at the women could serve them.

Head down, Theo shuffled as well, his plate now in one hand, fork in the other, to the far side of the room. Elise followed with hers.

"Theo, I had no idea you knew Aunt Ida."

Theo swallowed a large bite of cake then said, "She's your aunt? Well, isn't that something."

Elise decided not to get technical at the moment, about Ida being her aunt-in-law.

Theo swallowed, then continued. "We met overseas…in Singapore, actually. A group I met with, to do with possible investing, took me out to dinner one night, and she was sitting with a group of her own friends from some kind of steam ship or something, at a table right next to us. After dinner, I guess I started talking to her because she looked like she was a lot of fun, and she was an American. I was curious what she was doing there."

Elise smiled. "She does travel a lot. We've actually been trying to track her down for the last month or so, hoping she could make her sister's birthday party. Her showing up here was as much a surprise to us as anyone else." Then something clicked in her mind. "If she was still over there…and you were here…and you wanted to try to get hold of her, you'd have to call at all sorts of weird hours, wouldn't you?"

Theo seemed to relax, maybe because he could finally admit some of this to someone. "Yeah. That's what I was doing at E. S. Hearing Labs the night your friend was attacked, if that's what you're asking. I can't believe I didn't know what was going on down there, but I kept calling the number she gave me, and all I'd get was the Singapore Zoo!"

Elise decided the rest of that story was up to Aunt Ida to tell. She glanced in Ida's direction and saw her looking at them. Elise waved at her to come over, which Ida did, then Elise discreetly left the two together to catch up with whatever relationship it was that they had. And whatever it was, seemed to put wide smiles on their faces.

Elise stopped at Noah's table as he stood up again, glaring at Theo. She told him what Theo told her, especially about why he was at his desk the night Tierneigh was attacked.

"And you believe him?"

Elise let out a long breath. "I'm not sure anyone could make up something like that, Noah."

He nodded. "Think you're right." He looked at his watch. "I need to get going. You going to be alright?"

"Yes. About as best I can be, under circumstances like this." Then she remembered something. "Noah, Cole said you made a comment last night about 'closing in on him.' Who were you talking about? Was it David?"

Noah scrutinized her face for a couple seconds, then his eyebrows raised as it came to him, and he laughed.

"What's so funny?"

"I was talking about 'The Hawk.'"

"The Hawk?"

"Yeah, the rugby guy that plays winger on one of the teams up north. He's real cagey and always gets by us, but our team's got his number now. Can't wait 'til we play his team again, 'cause he's going to be surprised!"

Elise blew out a breath as her eyes slid to her husband.

Noah squinted. "You okay?"

"Oh, yeah."

Sounds of the party breaking up caught their attention, and Elise saw Marcie and her parents get up to leave.

"Oh, my gosh," said Elise. "I need to get everyone over to the Miller farm for their Pumpkin Fair, now!"

"You're kidding."

"No, I'm not." She waved down Cole, Becky, and Jon.

"So let me know what hospital you're in after you have your breakdown, okay?"

Elise couldn't help but laugh. "Just bring me a nice, large, pumpkin spice latte and I'll be fine."

Chapter Twenty-Seven

══ I ══

Monday Morning

Elise grabbed a large pumpkin spice latte from The Vibe and got to the office early. It was the beginning of a new week, and she wasn't quite sure how she was going to feel. She needed some time to herself.

She sat at her desk and thought about the last couple of weeks. Gloria was in custody and not talking, but with the information from Elise, David, and now Bill Hooper, they'll be able to bring a strong case against her.

She thought of David. He told her, in a brief conversation later at the Miller's Pumpkin Fair, that he was embarrassed by something he did as a teenager, that involved very loud music. It affected his hearing, and he didn't want her, or Becky, to think badly of him. Tierneigh and Susan knew about it, and that was the information in the file he took from Tierneigh's office. Becky visited him in the hospital when she found out what happened and burst with awe that David had "saved her mother's life." Elise smiled at the thought. Looked like the crush was going both ways.

A brief conversation with Susan the day after the party revealed her reluctance to tell Elise about her relationship with Rick. She admitted she still wasn't sure about it herself, but workplace relationships weren't a good idea, and she was taking it slow. She apologized to Elise about keeping it from her and worrying her so much. And no, Rick didn't say anything to her about Tierneigh overhearing him and Bob the morning of the training, or about that red-circled paper they had. Susan admitted she was petrified when she couldn't find it.

Elise swung her desk chair around to face the bookshelf behind her and placed the now framed picture of the three friends—Elise, Amy, and Tierneigh—right in the front, where she could draw on its strength whenever she needed.

She swiveled back to her desk and computer, clicked on the day's schedule, and paused. Through tears, she read the name of her first patient. Evan Brown. Tierneigh's dad.

Elise closed her eyes and pressed her fingertips against her eyelids, no longer taking anything for granted. Her family, her business, her friends…herself. She saw Tierneigh's smiling face in her mind and whispered out loud, "I'll take care of him," then couldn't help but smile herself, as a soft warmth enveloped her.

A click from the office's side door opening caught her attention, and two voices sang out, "Morn…ing!"

She took a deep breath, stood up and answered, "Happy Monday, you two."

THE END

Organizations for Further Information

American Academy of Audiology (AAA)
https://www.audiology.org
Ph: 800-AAA-2336
TTY: (703) 790-8466
Email: infoAud@audiology.org

American Speech-Language Hearing Association (ASHA)
https://www.asha.org
Ph: 800-638-8255
TTY: 301-296-8580
Email through website: "Contact the ASHA National Office" page

Academy of Doctors of Audiology (ADA)
https://www.audiologist.org
Ph: (866) 493-5544
Email/other platforms: Through website

Hearing Loss Association of America (HLAA)
https://www.hearingloss.org
Ph: 301-657-2248
Email through website: "Contact Us"

Marion Downs Center
https://mariondowns.org/
4280 Hale Parkway
Denver, Colorado
(303) 322-1871
Email through website: "Contact Us"

About the Author

C. T. Merritt, Doctor of Audiology, was born in Long Island, New York, grew up in San Francisco, raised a family with her husband in Sacramento, and lived in the beautiful state of Washington. They moved to Springfield, Illinois, for a temporary assignment and eventually decided to stay, thoroughly enjoying the four seasons, especially the fall with its harvesting activities.

Dr. Merritt worked in the field of audiology for over thirty years, in varying capacities and venues, including on the board of the California Academy of Audiology in its beginning stages and later as president, and on the Ethics Committee of the American Academy of Audiology.

Since reading her first Agatha Christie book and Carolyn Keene's Nancy Drew mysteries, she wanted to be a librarian and writer, in that order. She didn't make librarian status, but did write her first in a series, *Death by Decibels, A Dr. Elise Harte Mystery*. Dr. Merritt is a member of Sisters in Crime and the Authors Guild and can be found online at www.ctmerritt.com.